"From the day I was saved, I have longed to have a dream where I walked and talked with Jesus. I would fall to sleep at night thinking about it, praying God would allow such a dream to happen, then thirty years later it did! But it did not happen as I had hoped in a dream. It happened when I read *Quest for the Nail Prints*, and through the characters of the book I walked and talked with Jesus in the days before His crucifixion. I still long for my 'dream,' but for now I look forward to Don's sequel!"

—Bill Nielsen, Managing Editor, B & H

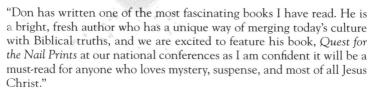

"Don has written one of the most fascinating books I have read. He is a bright, fresh author who has a unique way of merging today's culture with Biblical truths, and we are excited to feature his book, *Quest for the Nail Prints* at our national conferences as I am confident it will be a must-read for anyone who loves mystery, suspense, and most of all Jesus Christ."

—Dr. Joe Pettigrew, author, In the Zone

"I felt as if I was one of the disciples experiencing first hand the last week of Christ's ministry on earth. I realized the need for me to get back into the scriptures to learn for myself the fulfillment of God's promise. I have been in church and Sunday school all my life, but never felt as involved in the New Testament story as I did in this book."

—Dennis R. Roaten, Disciples of Christ

"What a masterful job you did in creating a situation I have dreamed about before myself. Seeing Jesus has always been my first option if I could travel back in time. I'm not sure how I would handle it. I pray that this book will put you right up there with the bestsellers of all time. Your book is the second best book I have ever read, with the Bible being first."

—Phil Reasons, Thompson's and Formbys, Ret.

"Reading *Quest for the Nail Prints* was more than just reading a book. To me, it was a personal experience and journey. Through the eyes of the ones traveling back into time and meeting Jesus face to face before His death, it was as if I were the one actually doing it. Don Furr paints

a mental picture so real and vivid that I felt I was the one meeting Jesus, getting to know His chosen disciples, watching Him heal the sick and teach to the crowds, and watching Him agonize over what He knew He had to do. Jesus was so real to me in this book. I actually saw His humanness in not wanting to go to the cross, but going out of obedience and genuine love for His children. The characters came to life for me. It was interesting to see the disciples depicted as they were, and their interaction to their Master. This was more than just a book—it was a true experience of something extraordinary."

—April J. Stockdale, Promise Land Bookstore

"Don, you have done a remarkable job of bridging that very long journey between the head and the heart. To stand and witness the crushing pain that he endured for me, illuminates, with brilliance, the path he paved for my broken soul to be healed. I will carry this journey in my heart. Thank you for allowing me to get my own feet dirty by guiding me on a personal walk with him."

—Scott Fitzgerald, Facilitator, Discovery

"Reviting! If you want to see if Jesus Christ is real, read this book. Don captures the realism of how a First Century or Twenty-First Cenury person might have a dynamic relationship with the living Christ. You won't want to put this read down, it will keep you up at night!"

—Reverend Joseph Capebianco
Pastor, First Baptist Church, Lakeland, TN

"Author Don Furr has truly given us a masterpiece. The words I read brought feelings of pain, hurt, joy and laughter so vivid until I felt I knew Jesus much more personally. If anyone has a loved one or friend who does not know Jesus as their Savior, please get this book for them and let the drawing of the Holy Spirit work through this book to lead them to Christ. You will not be dissaointed."

—Peggy Jean Ramming, recording artist and internet evangelist

A fictitious account of an actual event . . .

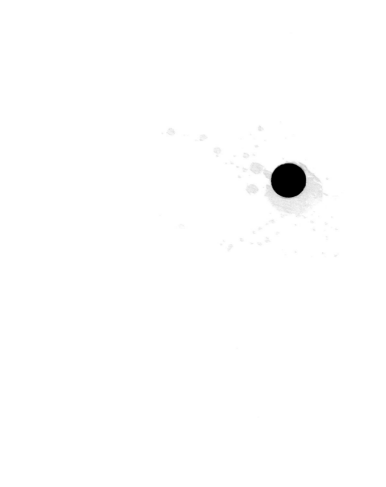

QUEST
FOR THE
NAIL PRINTS

A *novel by*

Don Furr

Charlotte, Tennessee 37036

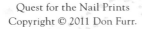

Published by Sheaf House Publishers, LLC.
Requests for information should be addressed to:

Editorial Director
Sheaf House Publishers, LLC
3641 Hwy 47 N.
Charlotte, TN 37036
jmshoup@sheafhouse.com
www.sheafhouse.com

Library of Congress Control Number: 2010938344

ISBN: 978-1-936438-02-0

Scripture in this book taken from:
The Holy Bible, New International Version®, NIV®
Copyright © 1973, 1978, 1984 Biblica, Inc.™

Cover design: Chris Morey, Ciras Imaging (www.MyCiras.com) and
Demetria Hazelgrove, Exhibit A, Inc. (www.exhibitainc.com)

Interior design by Donnis Sealey, Digital Couture (www.digitalcouture.org)

11 12 13 14 15 16 17 18 19 20—10 9 8 7 6 5 4 3 2 1

Manufactured in the United States of America

To Karen.
I am a better man because of you.

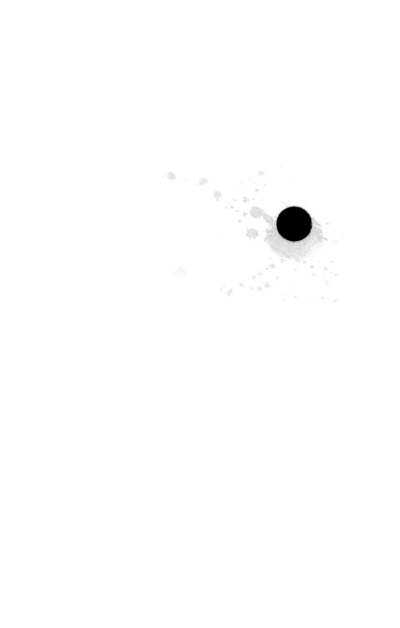

Why the Hole?

The idea of the nail hole surfaced during the first draft. From the very start, I knew the part the nails would play. From there, the process simply took its natural course. The idea quickly flourished into the nail prints marking every page, much in the same way I picture the nails touching every page of our lives. It only seemed natural that they should touch every page of the story.

Quest for the Nail Prints has been a dream come true for me! I have lived it, dreamed about it, I've even carried my laptop all over the world while writing it. From my home here in Tennessee to the icy waters of Alaska. From Mount Haleakala on Maui to Paris to London to Spain and Amsterdam. From the mountains of Romania to the dusty roads of Jerusalem—twice even!

This story has bits and pieces of all of those places intertwined within its pages, and yet, it's as if the story has only begun. In my heart I guess I'll never be finished with it, not completely, but for the sake of the reader, there is a final chapter. I hope you enjoy the journey as much as I have.

Why Not Dream?

Beyond the realm of what some would call "the box" for lack of a better term, a theory stirs deep within my soul, an insatiable desire floating unconstrained somewhere between the boundaries of truth and my imagination.

The concept of time travel.

And though logic seemingly wars against it, I wrestle in vain with a creative spirit that vies for a chance to speak out.

I want to see my mom again. I want to watch her milk a cow as a child, to learn to drive a model T in her uncle's pasture, to watch her dance the jitterbug. I want to be there when she beats tuberculosisand makes eyes at my dad for the first time.

And more.

I want to revisit my childhood home, my grade school, the teachers who were so dear to me, my first puppy love. I want to watch as my wife plays as a child, to marvel at her youth and innocence. And I want to be with my younger brothers when we were all little boys, to pull them close and tell them how much I love them without wondering how it will look to the other kids on the block. Are those times gone forever? I hope not, but if by chance they are, why not dream?

And even more.

I want to see things that I can only imagine. I want to stand in the grass at Dealey Plaza in Dallas, Texas, on that crisp November day in 1963 and find the truth. I want to walk with my brother in the sweltering jungles of Vietnam and watch as

he is poured into the mold of a man. These things are important to me.

And much more.

I want to walk with Jesus. I want to talk with Him as He peers into my eyes and tells me the secrets of why. I want to touch His face and callused hands, knowing full well that my only response could be nothing more than a trembling smile as He brushes away my tears and peers into my soul. I want to hold Him close and never let go. And I want to touch the scars and thank Him for what He did for me.

A lesson in futility? I hardly think so.

Events in time, at the very least, can be witnessed again if for no other reason than the absolute certainty that light can be predictably and precisely measured. And with that light the past travels in perfect unison. This is a certainty and in and of itself suggests that it has not vanished at all. For it exists as surely as the distance between my head and heart are fused by my soul. And yet it is locked away deep within the mystery we know only as the mind of God.

—Don Furr
March 2011

"Time is not at all what it seems. It does not flow in only one direction, and the future exists simultaneously with the past."

—Albert Einstein

ONE

Flight nurse Ellen Barnes yanked the page from the fax machine and raced down the narrow corridor that led to the doctors' quarters. For courtesy's sake, she rapped once on the door, then burst into the dark room.

"Elizabeth," she barked. "Pile-up on I-40 at the twenty-five mile marker. RCC says they have a thirteen-year-old male, critical—"

Stretched across the bed, the young resident stirred. It took a moment for her to identify Ellen's voice.

"Doctor Stewart!" she snapped, flipping on the light to illuminate the dark room.

Dr. Elizabeth Stewart sat up. "A thirteen-year-old?"

The flight nurse focused on the report. "Well, so far we've got a DOA, two non-critical, and the boy's being extricated right now. They say they'll have him out by the time we get there."

The clock said 1:55 a.m. Elizabeth had been asleep a mere forty minutes. She swung her legs over the side of the bed and struggled to focus.

1

The only sound was the rain assaulting the single window of the cramped, unadorned room. This was her second twenty-four-hour shift this week at Memphis Hospital Wing, an air medivac unit serving the Elvis Presley Memorial Trauma Unit, the only level-one trauma unit for two hundred miles in any direction.

Obviously Medivac services had gotten a call and patched through to the "red phone" that set the medical team's life in motion. Hospital Wing's policy was that no flights could depart with ceilings below or forecasted below 500 feet. If administration made the decision to make a flight, and then couldn't make it to the scene because of weather or, even worse, they picked up the patient and couldn't make it back to the trauma unit, a critical patient would have little chance of survival. The conditions on this night were marginal at best.

From its berth in the nearby hangar, the piercing whine of the jet engine rattled the walls as the chopper blades spooled up to full rpm. Elizabeth stood up, pulled her shirt on over her head, and dropped her crucifix inside. She double knotted her scrubs and reached for the door. Her heart skipped a beat. She tripped the light, and she and Ellen sprinted down the cinder-block hallway and into the hangar.

The smell of jet fuel was intoxicating, sending adrenaline coursing through Elizabeth's veins. She and Ellen grabbed their headsets and mounted the maroon and gray A-Star.

Elizabeth was a good fit for the disaster business, with a stint in Desert Storm and two years at the MED under her belt. Ellen was also a seasoned medical pro, serving three plus years in the ER and with LeBonheur's Pedi-flight. They made a tough team who never cracked, no matter how intense the pressure.

"You two buckled in back there?" the pilot buzzed in.

"We're in. Let's roll!"

Elizabeth was sorry to see that Al Burnett was their pilot. *Nothing but a hotshot chopper jockey,* she thought. Worst of all, Burnett was a good old boy who still didn't take women seriously. He was always pulling more "G's" than necessary on takeoffs and showing off with other stupid stunts.

"Med Com, Wing Six is airborne," Burnett chirped into his headset.

He canted the helicopter into the pitch-black sky. Clearing the stretch of power lines that draped the north end of the tarmac, the chopper with its weary crew climbed out over the hazy city.

"You're not gonna hurl, are ya, Doc?" Burnett asked. His mouth formed an obnoxious grin.

Elizabeth shot him an icy glare.

"Well, whatever you do, Doc, don't think about greasy pork chops."

Ellen shook her head. It was clear his adolescent humor irked her as much as it did Elizabeth. Of course, she also was prone to take Elizabeth's side. In this day and age girls had to stick together, especially in this business.

Elizabeth hated to admit it, but Hotshot reminded her of her twin brother, Tom, and the days when they were both smart-aleck adolescents with no intentions of growing up. The two of them had the benefit of good looks: identical features, coal black hair, and chocolate-brown eyes. Also inherently intelligent, Elizabeth had made the most of her blessings.

Tom was a different story. Although he was by far the more personable of the two, sadly, he had spent most of his life looking through the bottom of a bottle. And now . . . well, now things were even worse. Tom's condition was deteriorating.

"Ahh!" Ellen screamed as the helicopter swerved side to side, slamming her into Elizabeth.

"Hang on," Burnett yelled.

† † †

From a thousand feet in the air and looking east toward the horizon, the westbound traffic on I-40 looked much like the final scene of the movie *Field of Dreams*. Headlights from hundreds of cars and trucks stretched as far as the eye could see, seemingly all the way to Nashville, some two hundred miles to the east. Even the two lanes on the eastbound side had slowed to a crawl while the rubberneckers satisfied their morbid curiosity.

The Tennessee Highway Patrol had already marked a

landing zone with flares and positioned a trooper to guide them in. Blue lights from a half dozen state trooper cars reflecting off the wet Plexiglas danced vertically up the windshield, and the tall grass rippled violently beneath them as the struts contacted the ground and spread their stance.

Elizabeth flung open the door, and she and Ellen dashed toward the ambulance gurney, pure adrenaline pulsing through their veins. The scene was horrific. The twisted mass of metal, broken glass, and smoldering rubber instantly reminded Elizabeth of the decimation she'd witnessed in Kuwait. It was a memory often recalled, but rarely by choice.

"Vitals?" Ellen asked the EMT.

"B.P. sixty over forty, pulse one hundred, respiration weak. Fractured right tibia . . . ah . . . right femur. Severe internal trauma, as far as we can tell. I've got him on a line of straight saline."

Glancing at his watch, the EMT added, "He's thirty-five minutes into golden hour, and he's comatose."

Golden hour. The first hour after a traumatic accident and the most critical time for the victim. This young patient only had twenty-five minutes left to have the maximum chance of survival.

"We've gotta get this kid airborne now!" Elizabeth's voice was frantic.

Ellen readied the ship while Elizabeth and the paramedic wheeled the critical patient toward the helicopter, their gurney crunching over gravel and shards of broken glass. A highway patrolman hurried alongside, holding the IV and shielding the boy's face from the pelting rain. He shoved his Stetson down hard as they neared the chopper.

Hurriedly they loaded the gurney, and the highway patrolman slid the door shut behind them with a clap.

Catapulting into the rainy night sky, the helicopter with its crew and critical cargo disappeared into the blackness forty minutes into the golden hour.

Two minutes later lightening was flashing from every conceivable direction, and they were dropping violently within the bowels of a storm, yawing as much as thirty degrees to either side. The motion slammed Elizabeth and Ellen about the cabin like a pair of rag dolls. Everything that was loose clanked and clattered across the floor. Only the victim, who was strapped tightly to the stretcher secured to the floor, remained stable.

A minute into the wild ride, Ellen nudged Elizabeth and yelled over the unearthly din. "I'm getting sick. Can you take over?"

Elizabeth took the BVM bag, never missing a beat, while Ellen hurried to find something to throw up in. She turned her back to Elizabeth and gave up dinner.

"Memphis Approach, Wing Six is inbound to the trauma unit. Four souls aboard."

Souls. Why does Burnett always use that term?

"Wing Six stand by . . . Ah, we have an amendment

to your route. Advise when ready to copy."

Burnett pulled a pen from his sleeve. "Wing six, go ahead."

A *change of course*, Elizabeth thought. *Not good.*

Ellen wiped away a thin stream of blood that trickled from the corner of the boy's lacerated lip and took the bag from Elizabeth, who settled back into her seat and pulled out a tattered pocket Testament. She placed her hand on the boy's chest and began a silent prayer.

"Doctor!" Ellen shouted. "We're flat line!"

"Prep him for defib. He'll never make it, not without damage," Elizabeth added.

Ellen pulled the contacts from the Life Pack defibrillator while Elizabeth ripped open the boy's shirt. She squeezed the last of the contents from the tube onto the contact pad and spread the gel.

"Clear!"

Ellen confirmed.

The shock jolted the boy's body. His eyes winced— then nothing.

"Do it again! Set two hundred and clear!"

Ellen confirmed. Again, no response.

"Memphis Approach, Wing Six out of one thousand for point five. We have an in-flight emergency. Patient has arrested. Request direct trauma unit."

Now the rain was deafening. It pounded the aircraft violently as Elizabeth braced herself against the door, her hands, slick with sweat, slipping off the cool, metal door handle. She glanced at Ellen, whose face paled with terror as an opaque sheet of water wrapped its glossy fingers around the windshield and streamed past the windows on both sides.

Every flash of the strobes reflecting off the clouds froze their movements. Elizabeth blinked hard and wiped the fog from her window. She saw nothing but a dark canopy of dense blackness on all sides.

Then suddenly an aura of light appeared through the cloud layer below. A few seconds more and they were free from the maelstrom.

"We're out!" Burnett buzzed.

The helicopter clattered in and pulled into a hover as Burnett quickly brought the rotor blades to flat pitch. They hit hard on the wet asphalt.

Two large male nurses in surgical greens ran to the chopper as Ellen swung out the portable stretcher, and Elizabeth pulled the release pin. "Go, go, go!"

While Ellen stayed behind with the ship to head back to base, the team and their critical cargo raced toward the E.R., down painted brick hallways littered with people who had been shot, stabbed, beaten—the typical after-midnight crowd at the MED. Tragic as they were, these people were only a blur. Elizabeth glanced at the clock by the elevator. It read 2:43 a.m.—a little less than an hour since Ellen had first awakened her.

Seconds later the gurney punched through the stainless steel doors into Shock Trauma One. It was already vibrant with activity.

Team leader Dr. Vincent Busak pried open one of the boy's eyes. "We've got to open this boy up!" he barked. He donned his glasses and snapped on his gloves.

Elizabeth stood by the table but mentally shrank into the background, staring fixedly. This situation was not unlike so many she had been in before. Patients came and

went, died and survived; yet this one seemed . . . strangely personal. What was it about this boy that seemed to touch her soul? She really didn't know.

Father, I lift this boy up to you. He's so young, he doesn't deserve this. Please Jesus, please help him.

Self-consciously brushing away tears, she looked at the child and saw, for the first time, a most beautiful pair of hazel eyes return her gaze. A lopsided grin etched the boy's swollen face, and his lips quivered to speak.

Elizabeth gasped and the room fell silent. Tendrils of hope pervaded her senses as she reached for his hand. And then, as with so many others, the boy's eyes rolled back and half closed. She turned to Dr. Busak and read the conclusion in his eyes.

"I'm sorry, Doctor. So much time had passed . . . "

Elizabeth's throat tightened to a knot. A stony silence permeated the room while one team member somberly unhooked the monitor and pulled a sheet over the boy's face.

She clenched her eyes shut. Golden hour had passed.

"Time of death . . . 2:51 a.m.," Busak said, glancing at

the clock on the back wall. "Do we have a name?"

"It just came in," a nurse said, her voice flat. "Rogers—Brandon R." She signed off the paperwork and hung the report on the foot of the bed.

Elizabeth heaved a deep breath and reflected on the past hour. Was there anything she would have done differently? Anything she *could* have done that might have

made a difference?

Lost in thought, she glanced down and noticed her pocket testament on the floor. She picked it up, tempted to run her fingers across the blood stains on the gold-leaf edges. She thought about another man whose blood had stained those same pages and wondered why He hadn't heard her plea.

Two·

In a musty, nondescript office on the fourth floor of
Georgetown University's Mitchell Hall, Professor Leonardo
Van Eaton perused the morning edition of the *Washington
Post*. A stogie lay smoldering in an overfull ashtray on his
cluttered desk, a scarred French-country reproduction that
hardly befitted his position.

He flipped the page, stirring the thin layer of smoke
that wafted toward the ceiling. The only light in the room
came from a banker's lamp perched atop a pile of weeks-old
newspapers and a sliver of sunlight that managed to slip
past the dusty blinds on the room's only window. He looked
at the mounds of test papers that balanced precariously on
one corner of his desk like unsteady chimneys and cringed.
One more detail to hamper preparations.

Van Eaton had endured several tedious nights of
study, preparing for a speech he was scheduled to deliver
to a board of his peers. This would be his sixth consecutive
year to address the International Council of Religious
Educators, but his first visit to the Jama Masjid in New

11

Delhi. His reading had taken him well into the morning hours the two previous nights, but he still was far from ready. And now that the conference was just three days away, he was feeling a bit pressed, to say the least.

The professor carried two hundred forty pounds wearily on his five-and-a-half-foot tall frame. When his doctor had pointed out that this was a far from acceptable combination on the weight-height chart, Van Eaton had merely shrugged. What did he have to live for anyway?

His long, thinning hair, now more gray than black and badly in need of a trim, affirmed the fact that his personal appearance had become less of a concern as the years quietly slipped by. His rounded face and grandpa-like features gave the impression that he was a man of mild demeanor, but this was hardly the case. He was brash, a man of casual ruthlessness hardened by the thorny hand that life had dealt him—and he was a master at spreading the grief.

Physical maladies that accompanied his age had initially inflected a sobering amount of fear into him. Cancer specifically was a major concern. His father and uncle both had succumbed to colon cancer, while his mother had been stricken with ovarian cancer when he was in his freshman year at college.

After so many seemingly indiscriminate deaths, Van Eaton had grown weary of the disease. Family members wasted away, and with each death went a little of his own spirit. He could only think of it clinically now, of the words, but not the emotion. In fact, while he still feared pain, he did not hold any dread of the outcome.

A graduate of Georgetown University, the professor had attained his masters in political science and gone on to earn his doctorate in religious history. During his undergraduate years in the mid 1960's, while Lyndon Johnson was president, Van Eaton secured a position as liaison to Benjamin Rosenberg, Israeli minister of foreign affairs, a long-time constituent of Levi Eshkol, the reigning prime minister of Israel. Van Eaton was drawn to Rosenberg from the get-go. He found the man fascinating, a virtual cornucopia of Jewish history. Integral dealings with the religious caucus of Israel proved to be invaluable, as his studies often dealt directly with issues concerning the nation of Israel. Having a friend the likes of Rosenberg had proved vital in keeping Van Eaton focused on his studies.

The trill of the first period bell jolted the professor to the present. Rising with effort, he tweaked his hearing aid and tripped the light. The chafed heels of his wingtips left scuff marks on the polished tile floor as he shuffled to his first class.

An angular, sullen girl propped forebodingly against his desk, her eyes pinpointing him as he walked through the door. Her arms were folded tightly across her chest, clutching a stack of papers.

Van Eaton knew what was coming. The girl was "born again" as she put it. She wouldn't have been born the first time if he'd had a say.

"How could you, Professor?" she spat. Her hair bristled as she spoke.

Van Eaton coughed and continued toward his desk. He sat down and superficially straightened his paperwork.

She threw her papers down in front of him. "Are you against all Christians or just the ones who stand up to you? You knew I needed that grade."

Van Eaton peered over steepled fingers and met her gaze. He looked at the large red D he had circled at the top of the page. He slid his eyes back to her.

"All evidence to the contrary, young lady, I'm not against Christians at all. But I do have a problem with certain individuals who are so busy proselytizing and who are so clouded in their thinking that they can't consider other avenues of thought."

"Other avenues of thought?" She glared through emerald green contacts that momentarily distracted him.

"You are intelligent enough to know that Christianity is not the only plausible idea out there. There happen to be many other wonderful ideas that make a good deal of sense—provided you have the good sense to listen."

A deafening silence filled the room.

"What was it you said?" He took the papers from her hand and thumbed through several pages. "Yes, here I have it marked for you. You said, 'He is the only way'—*He* being Jesus I can only assume—'that anyone will gain favor with God.'"

"Yes, so—"

"Well, you write as if I were the brunt of your argument, as if you are trying to convince me."

Her eyes brightened and a tentative smile swept her face. "Maybe you are." Her reply seemed to mock him.

The professor smirked. "You're the pupil, and while I do have my own views on the Almighty, I don't make it my goal in life to sway others into believing my way. I simply present the facts."

"But—"

"I am a professor of religious studies, not some slick talkin' Elmer Gantry trying to pry another dollar from somebody's back pocket. In this class, my opinions are not important, nor are yours."

By now the class was seated, and all eyes were fixed on the pair. The air was so saturated with tension that a pin drop would have resounded like a sledgehammer. A moment passed, then the young student gathered her composure and walked toward the back of the classroom.

"Sad," he mumbled.

She instantly stopped and turned. "Yes. It is sad when a person has the knowledge of so many opinions of God and yet doesn't have the courage to confess his own."

† † †

An endless sea of weary-eyed commuters inched their way along the DC Beltway as Van Eaton made his exit. He turned onto the street where he had lived for more than thirty years, pulled his Dodge into the drive of his East Fairfax home, and turned the key to the off position. He sat motionless in the silence, enjoying the warmth of the sun as he reflected on the day's events. He had had many run-ins with students, but this girl touched a part of him that he had thought was untouchable.

To put it mildly, he didn't like to have his ideals questioned. His bedrock principle had always been listen, learn, and keep your opinions to yourself. But this student had to intrude. Who was she to question his objectivity?

While children played noisily next door, the professor gathered his belongings, got out, and locked the car door. He plucked the newspaper from the driveway and noticed the kids had moved to the opposite end of the yard. Good.

Entering his disheveled kitchen, he rinsed a dirty glass and poured a drink. Then he went out the sliding patio door and landed on a lounger next to the pool. It was still covered for winter. He squirreled away his reading glasses and soaked up the spring sun.

This house was a special place that he and his wife, Carolyn, had found on a Sunday drive in the late 1960's. At that time the street had been lined on both sides with hundred-year-old oaks, neatly manicured lawns, and amiable neighbors.

The neighborhood had changed little since then. Van Eaton was glad. This was his solace and the only place he could escape the hassles of life. He put his head back, closed his eyes and reminisced about his Carolyn.

† † †

Van leaned over the pew and punched his friend, Brent. "Who is that?"

"Carolyn Cochran. She's with an ad agency in East Hampton," Brent said. "She's high-class, man. Too much

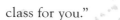

class for you."

"You might be right," Van admitted.

He tried to follow her with his eyes while she found a seat with her friends. It wasn't easy. She was a petite girl, barely 5'3" in her heels.

"But then again . . ."

The music started and the choir filed in, in flowing robes and with hymnals in hand, while the members found their seats. Home for spring break during his second trimester at Georgetown University, Van was visiting Yorkshire Baptist Church at the request of Brent Perkins, one of his college roommates, while Van's father was out of town.

Van didn't hear a word of the sermon that day. He couldn't even tell you who was speaking. He only knew that he had seen an angel, and her name was Carolyn Cochran.

"Is she dating anybody?"

"Shh!"

Nobody here at church," said Brent.

Van arched an eyebrow.

After the service, he nonchalantly moved into the

aisle and waited to intercept her, but somehow she had already made it past him.

"I lost her."

"Who?"

"Carolyn—the little angel. I lost her in the crowd."

"That's okay man. She'll be back tonight."

Van smiled. *Well, I just got religion.*

That night the services were filled with the same fire and brimstone Van had been raised on, but the last thing on his mind was walking the aisle. He found a seat directly behind Carolyn.

Occasionally he would catch a glimpse of her profile when she chatted with the girl next to her, but she was oblivious to his stares. He kept hoping she would glance back at him and he'd be bold in returning the gaze, but she never did. Finally the service ended.

He bravely tapped her on the shoulder. "Excuse me, but I wanted to introduce myself. I'm Van . . . um, Leon Van Eaton."

She gave her friend a questioning look, but took his hand. Hers was warm and soft as she delicately touched his.

"Hello—Van is it?" she asked. "I'm Carolyn Cochran."

"Van is good." He leaned against the back of the pew. "What do you do?" he asked, as though he knew nothing about her.

"Why? Are you in the market for . . . something? He looked embarrassed and she laughed. "Just kidding, but you do seem to get right to the point. I'm a market scheduler for Eagle Outdoor."

Van reddened but tried to stay on track. "The Billboard Company I see all over town?"

"That's it. What about you?"

"I'm a student at Georgetown."

"On spring break?"

"Yeah, I'm out all week."

While they stood talking, the crowd dwindled to only

a handful—though neither noticed, and for good reason. It was more than obvious there was chemistry between them.

"How do you know Brent?" she asked.

"Oh, we're roommates."

Suddenly Brent stuck his head in the back door of the sanctuary. "Hey! A bunch of us are going to Krystal. You two want to go?"

Van glanced at Carolyn and smiled. "Sure, how about you—Carolyn is it?" *I'm so smooth.*

"I can't. I've got to fly to Minneapolis in the morning."

He glanced at his watch. "Oh, come on," he insisted. "Just for a little while."

Carolyn smiled.

The next four hours passed like minutes as Van and Carolyn spent the entire evening gabbing away. Every word led to another story until she finally noticed the time.

"I've got to go! It's eleven-thirty!"

"What time is your flight?"

"Nine o'clock."

She dug through her purse for her keys. Van stretched and noticed that everyone else had already gone.

They crossed the empty parking lot, and when they got to Carolyn's car Van took a deep breath and asked the question he had mulled over for the last hour. "Would you mind if I took you to the airport in the morning?" He felt uncharacteristically shy.

Carolyn smiled. "Oh, I couldn't ask you to do that."

"I really wouldn't mind. I don't have anything else to

do. Oh. That sounded great.

"Oh yeah, spring break." She paused for a moment, looking into the night sky as if seeking guidance. "Yes . . . I'd like that."

The night was now quiet and cool as the moon hung low in the black Virginia sky. It was a good feeling, and both savored it. He wanted to kiss her but did not.

Early the next morning Van pulled up in front of Carolyn's apartment. He found her door cracked open and looked in, saw her kneeling on her suitcase, trying to snap it shut.

"Do all women try to take everything they own with them when they go out of town?"

"Oh, hey, come on in. You're bad."

"You really shouldn't leave your door open like that."

"I know," she said. "But I saw you drive up."

Kneeling beside her, he put all his weight on the opposite side of the suitcase and squeezed it shut. He snapped the latches, hoping they would hold.

And then it happened. There was a glance, a quivering smile, then he took her face in his hands and guided her lips to his. Carolyn melted, though she kept her head and resisted enough to let him know that she had been raised right.

And with one innocent kiss it was more than apparent, at least from Van's viewpoint, that there was definitely something there. Carolyn had sensed it too, he knew, though she never would have let on.

The two stood, still holding hands.

"I just have to turn off the lights and I'll be ready," she said.

She hurried to the back of the apartment, leaned into the bathroom and glanced into the mirror. She was glowing. *What was this college boy doing to her?* She hadn't felt this way since Tommy Turbin had written her a love letter in the ninth grade.

He twisted his heavy body in the lounge chair. She had been everything he'd ever wanted. He never seemed to tire of thinking about the girl he fell in love with so long ago.

Losing her more than two years prior still weighed heavily on his heart. His days had become stark and meaningless. They seemed to run together now more than ever before. Days became weeks, weeks became months, cool springs gave way to hot and humid summers, and the multi-colored hues of autumns became stark and blustery winters as life went on. Had he not immersed himself in his work, he might very well have considered orchestrating his own untimely demise.

In the warmth of the afternoon sun, Van Eaton stared at the pin oak he and his young bride had planted that first year. He could still see Carolyn's beautiful green eyes twinkling as they looked over their "baby" oak. Now it stood naked against a pale blue sky, its bare branches

shivering in the cool breeze.

It was nearly forty-eight hours before his flight was scheduled to depart for New Delhi. He put his head back, squeezed his eyes shut, and drifted off into a dreamless sleep.

THREE

Elizabeth sat alone in the MED's cafeteria, staring at the white-faced clock that hung over the doorway. It was twenty minutes past one, nearly twelve sleepless hours since the death of her young DUI victim.

Her thoughts ran in circles. She rubbed her eyes and saw the lifeless, ashen face of Brandon Rogers. The image vanished when a heavy hand landed on her shoulder.

"Hey, you going incognito or something?"

The voice belonged to Ray Roaten, the MED's chief of staff for the trauma units.

"Yeah . . . or something."

Ray pulled a plastic chair from the next table and sat down. "I heard you had a rough night. Would you like to talk about it?"

"What makes you say that? Death is a part of the job, isn't it?"

Ray waited.

Elizabeth gulped her lukewarm coffee. Her eyes strayed. "People get hurt. They come to me for help and sometimes they die. It's that simple." Tears welled in her eyes.

"Well . . . it's a lot of things, but I wouldn't say it was simple."

"Look, Ray, I'm the last person you need to worry about around here. There are a lot people who are on the edge, but I'm not one of them, okay?"

"So what happened?"

"I thought you already knew."

"All I heard is that you lost a teenager last night, but I don't know any of the details."

"You want details? Fine, here are the details. We made a scene flight, made a pick-up and the boy didn't make it. That's it." Tears spilled from her bloodshot eyes as she spoke. "We just couldn't save him."

"Liz, I know it's hard to see people die. But you save a lot, too."

"Maybe that's it. Maybe I'm just sick of seeing people die." She cradled her chin in her palm. "Does it ever stop?"

Ray wagged his head and scanned the room. "No."

Elizabeth dabbed her cheek and stuffed the tissue in her coffee cup. "Thanks, Ray. I feel much better now."

Roaten clutched her shoulder and smiled. "Deal with it any way you want, but the important thing is deal with it. Don't let it get in your head."

"Yeah. It's just the way it happened. I think I'm crying because I'm more angry than anything else. That drunk might spend a couple of days in jail, but he'll be out before that kid is cold in the ground, and his family will have to live with it forever."

"So does the guy that killed him."

"Don't kid yourself. I was there when they brought him in last night, and all he was interested in was how much Lortab he could get his hands on."

Roaten drummed his fingers on the table. "You need

a break. You need to put this stuff behind you—"

"Well, some of us don't have the luxury of taking off."

Ray took the jab and flipped open his cell phone. He punched in a number and waited. "We might have a solution to that problem."

Elizabeth glanced up and smirked. "Sounds like a setup to me."

"Mabel, I think I've got just the person." There was a pause. "Yeah." Ray hit the end button.

"Call it what you want, Liz, but it'll get you out of this place for a couple of weeks."

Elizabeth straightened in her seat. "So what's the skinny?"

Roaten leaned toward her and propped his elbows on the table. He glanced around the cafeteria.

This must be top secret, Elizabeth thought. But that was just Ray.

"We've received funding through a grant from the IRC to send a representative to help jump start the new trauma unit at Rashaman Medical Center in Jerusalem."

"Israel?"

"Yep. You would take on the role of advisor and do some hands-on training in trauma techniques and the like—"

"You want me to go to Israel? I thought you wanted me to get away from things?"

"Call it gaining a new perspective."

"I don't know—"

"What's to know? As far as I'm concerned, you're perfect for the job. You're single, you're one of my best residents—and frankly, you need to get away more than anybody I know."

"Excuse me, but there's a war going on over there, and I had my fill of that kind of duty in Kuwait."

"It's not as bad as the news paints it, and you know it. I've been there twice in the last seven years, and it was always fine. Besides, you'll live in the staff quarters on site. I've seen the facility; it's like Fort Knox."

Elizabeth straightened up in her chair. "Okay, so I need a passport."

"HR can have it here in two days."

"Well, what haven't you thought of?"

"It's really a great opportunity, you know."

Elizabeth smiled thinly.

"Most residents would jump on the chance to have this listed on their records. It would be a nice feather in your cap—and on your résumé."

Elizabeth knew that Ray was right. If nothing else, she would be getting a paid vacation. Not that she had ever wanted to go to Israel, but it would definitely be a change.

"So when do I leave?"

Ray shrugged. "Is Friday too soon?"

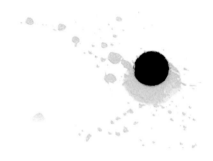

FOUR

Reverend Paul Ryann sprinted out the kitchen door of his east Memphis home and jumped in on the passenger side of his wife's Camry. Laura was already buckled in. He checked his watch as she pulled out of the driveway. It was five-thirty.

"You got everything?" Laura asked. Her eyes never strayed from the road.

"Uh, yeah, I think so."

"Tickets?"

"Yeah."

"Passport?"

"Uh, huh. The only thing I'm missing is you," Paul said with a wink.

She reached for his hand.

Paul's dream was finally coming true. He was going to the Holy Land, booked on Delta flight 1260 from Memphis to Cincinnati, which departed at 6:55 a.m. It would be the first leg of a ten-hour flight to Tel Aviv. And though it was a wedding anniversary present from his parents, he would be taking the trip alone. Laura had a prior obligation to teach an adult education course at the local community college and felt bound to honor it. And the truth was that she was afraid.

For Laura, visiting the Holy Land didn't have the same allure as it did to Paul. Not that she wasn't interested by any means. It was just that she wasn't gung-ho on traveling to

another country, and especially to such a place as Israel. There had been so many suicide bombings and terrorist acts over the past few years that the thought of going there scared her to death. And really, she didn't want Paul to go either, but this trip had been his lifelong dream.

It would also be during Palm Sunday, which was reason enough not to go, at least from her point of view.

Laura merged onto the 240-loop as Paul pulled his tickets and passport from his briefcase and slid them into the breast pocket of his sports coat. He turned to his wife and held her image for a few seconds.

Laura was a portrait of beauty. Her auburn hair glistened in the morning sun, shimmering hues of brown and red when she brushed a stray lock from her brow. Her slender nose was a perfect match for her silky lips and wide-set cerulean eyes. They were eyes that could melt an angry heart or just as easily back down a rattlesnake.

Her beauty was literally to the point that Paul had become overly protective of her, and rightly so. Not that he was worried so much about Laura, but it was like a pastor friend had once told him, "Women flee temptation, while men slowly crawl away, hoping to be overtaken."

Paul was no slouch either. His large frame supported his 220 pounds adequately, and though he had thickened somewhat in the middle, he carried it well. His hair was thick, though not as much as in his younger days, and he had grayed slightly at the temples. He walked with a slight limp from an old baseball injury, and he stooped slightly

because of his height. When he entered a room, he exuded an air of confidence, and though he had all the finesse of an eligible bachelor, he was not for sale. Laura kept him on a short leash, but in her heart, she really knew there was no need. Paul lived by principle rather than personality, and the walls of his world were bound by his faith.

As the morning sun slipped into the low-lying overcast, a misty rain coated the windshield. Paul stared blankly at the passing landscape while the rain trailed delicately off the windshield and formed tiny streams that streaked across the side window.

His stepfather, Robert Kidd, had been diagnosed with stage-four prostate cancer only a month prior, and his condition was rapidly worsening. Paul was worried—not solely about the cancer, though the prognosis was grave— but also because his dad had some unfinished business. Paul had never really been able to get a definitive answer from him as to his relationship with Christ. And the whole matter was forcing Paul to have second thoughts about the trip. Then there was yesterday.

† † †

Dr. Greg Lawrence tapped lightly on Robert's door and stuck his head inside. His gray-bearded smile was warm and reassuring as he motioned to Paul and his mother. The three stepped into the hallway.

Dr. Lawrence believed that Robert's cancer had

originated in his prostate, though it had quickly spread to his kidneys. And though subsequent tests had indicated the possibility of a transplant, Lawrence wasn't hopeful. The cancer had been so aggressive that it was attacking the surrounding organs as well.

Then there was his age. He was seventy-two, and despite the fact that he seemed to be adjusting well to dialysis, he was showing signs of dementia. This would only be the first of many symptoms, Lawrence explained. Nausea, the loss of bladder control, insomnia—the list went on and on.

Then there was the uncertainty of how the body would react to the dialysis itself. Dr. Lawrence had shared that in most cases the body would initially reject the dialysis, much like it would a transplanted organ. So far, though, Robert's immune system hadn't done so.

Lawrence had also brought in Dr. Nancy Harts, an oncologist from St. Jude. Harts was a real piece of work. She spoke candidly to Paul and his mother, telling them that a transplant would only be a temporary fix even if he were a candidate. She went on to explain that the cancer was so advanced that even chemotherapy would do little to stop the spread of the disease. Her frankness struck Paul as being rather brutal, and even though she maintained a soothing voice throughout the conversation, her message conveyed a painful hopelessness.

"We're not in the miracle business, Reverend Ryann," she said. "I believe that's your profession." Her words

dripped sarcasm.

After the meeting, Paul walked to his car, got in, and sat for a moment in the stillness. He replayed the meeting with Dr. Harts over and over until his cell phone broke the silence.

"Hello," he said. "Paul Ryann."

"Paul?" It was Laura.

"Hey, honey."

"Do you know a man named William Jackson?"

"I don't think so, why?"

"He just called and asked if you could meet with him this morning. He said it was very important that he see you today."

"William Jackson—*Bill* Jackson—from the ball team?"

"No, he sounded like an older man."

"Did he say what it was about?"

"No, but it seemed rather urgent."

"Did he leave a number?"

"No, he was calling from a pay phone. He just left an address and asked that you meet him at nine this morning."

It was eight-thirty.

"Okay, what's the address?"

"It's 488 West Warner," she said.

"West Warner?" *Oh man, that's way over on the west side of town, off Jackson Avenue.* He scribbled down the number. *A pastor's job is to answer needs.*

† † †

It was twenty minutes after nine when Paul pulled off the 240 loop. Snaking through a barrage of maintenance barricades, he pulled onto Jackson Avenue. Every house seemed to be the same: decrepit and moldy, run down, most in desperate need of repair, and some only a bulldozer could fix.

"We're not in Kansas anymore, Toto," he mumbled. He cautiously locked the doors and wondered if anyone heard the locks click.

When he turned onto West Warner, a different picture emerged. The houses, mostly brick, were well kept and not unlike many of the seasoned neighborhoods that were patched throughout midtown Memphis. Sculpted hedges adorned newly mowed lawns, and the tang of freshly cut onions wafted through the air vents. He began to feel a little more at ease with his surroundings. The feeling quickly vanished, however.

He pulled to the curb and slipped the car into park, then peered at the charred remains of an old church. He turned off the car and took it all in. Only two of the brick walls that formed the perimeter of the building still stood, and the roof lay in what must have been the sanctuary. A large, dingy, white steeple, deformed and melted to a mountain of bricks, lay next to two charred double doors still attached to their frame. Above the header, the words, COME INTO HIS PRESENCE WITH THANKSGIVING

were still legible.

Paul hoped the man he was supposed to meet wasn't looking for a handout for his church. Paul's own congregation had done well to keep their heads above water during the lean summer months.

He got out of the car and walked toward the remains. The morning sun dried the early morning dew, and steam rose from the rubble as if the fire had just been extinguished. And though the fire had long since been put out, the stench was still very prevalent.

Paul turned and pushed the remote on his keychain, and his lights flashed twice. Then he stepped over a single strand of yellow caution tape that flapped aimlessly in the breeze. As far as he could tell, the only item left intact was the sign on the lawn.

WEST WARNER M. B. CHURCH
488 West Warner Street
Rev. William Jackson, Pastor

As he neared the doorway, a restless feeling suddenly

stole over him. He couldn't quite explain it, but he somehow knew this place. He was certain of it, but he'd never been here before—or had he?

"Some kind of mess, ain't it?"

Paul turned to face the elderly black man walking toward him. "Yes. It sure is."

"William Jackson." The man extended his hand, and

Paul shook it heavily.

"Paul Ryann. It's a pleasure."

Jackson appeared to be in his mid seventies, though he may have been older. Patches of silver-gray hair stuck out from under his hat, and his blissful smile revealed a mouthful of perfect teeth. He wore black trousers supported by black suspenders over a white shirt buttoned to the top and a gray cardigan sweater. Paul would have known he was the pastor by his looks and demeanor alone.

His skin was a deep, shiny black like polished shoe leather glistening in the sunlight, and his face shone with a magnificent glow that gave Paul an overwhelming sense of security.

"What happened?" Paul asked, though he'd already figured it was pretty much the same story as usual.

Crack heads broke into buildings, stole anything that wasn't nailed down, then demolished the contents for sport, and set it on fire. Fires averaged one a month in the worst parts of town.

"Arson." Jackson turned and walked toward the building. "Well, at least, they think so. Police don't have any suspects, of course. It's probably gonna be difficult to find who did it. I'd imagine only God knows for sure."

Paul followed him around the back of the ruined building. "Was anyone hurt?"

"Yes, we lost one member, but . . . "

Paul caught his eye. "But what?"

"Well, I just think he was ready to go. And now I

imagine he wouldn't have it any other way."

The older man stopped and looked into the charred shell of the old church. "You know, young man, years ago I had an old dog. His name was Happy." Jackson pulled a handkerchief from his pocket and mopped his brow. "He was as spoiled as a brand new grandbaby. Why, we couldn't sit down at the supper table without that old dog right at our feet, just beggin' for a handout. Now he had his own dog food, mind you. We kept him a bowl out on the porch. But one day one of my boys sneaked him something' right off his plate. And I tell you the truth, from that day on—"

"He was ruined," Paul said.

The old pastor shook his head and flashed a reassuring smile. "That's right. And you know, son, that's how God is. He doesn't say a whole lot about heaven 'cause if he did, I'm afraid we'd all be ruined."

Paul smiled as he considered all the levels of meaning. He also knew that this man wasn't looking for a handout. He truly had a heart for Christ, there was no doubt.

"And how is your father?" Jackson asked.

Paul was caught off guard by his question. "How did

you know about my father?"

"Your wife told me this morning on the phone."

Of course. "He's . . . well, he's not good."

"Cancer?"

"Yes, sir." Paul kicked a burned timber and scuffed his shoe on the grass.

"I see. And does he know the Lord?"

Paul's gaze fell to the ground. "I—I don't know. He always says he's all right with God, but I can't help but think he's just trying to make me feel better."

The elder pastor stopped and stared directly at Paul.

"Well, son, why don't you let God try for a while?"

"What do you mean?"

"You know man couldn't save the children of Israel, and man couldn't feed five thousand people with two fish and a couple of loaves of bread. But God, he did, and, brother, he can."

Paul felt a strange sensation as Jackson spoke, as if the man knew more than he was letting on. But how could he possibly have known anything about him? They had just met.

"Maybe your situation is something that only God can handle."

"You may be right. But I can't stop trying just like that." Paul snapped his fingers for emphasis. "To tell you the truth, I've considered canceling something that I've been waiting all my life to do simply because I'm afraid he might not make it till I get back."

"You're going to Israel, are you not?"

Again Paul wondered how Jackson knew. Surely Laura hadn't talked to this man about all of his problems.

"Yes, I am."

Jackson's eyes brightened. "May I tell you something, son?"

Paul nodded, guardedly.

"Go on your trip. You might even say it's been planned."

Paul drew back. "What do you mean?"

Jackson smiled and returned Paul's gaze with eyes like polished porcelain. "Long before even you knew, *He* knew."

Paul pulled away from Jackson. "Who knew? What are you talking about?"

Jackson stopped and peered through the only intact window that remained in the church's walls. Barely taking his eyes off the pastor, Paul looked in too. The roof lay scattered over what was left of the charred pews. The piano, now nothing more than a pile of splintered wood, steel, and strings lay in a tangled mess.

"Please listen to me. I do appreciate your predicament, but there's something you must know." Jackson took Paul by the arm and led him away from the building. "The only reason I called you this morning was to do my best to convince you to go on your trip. I don't know all the specifics, but I am certain that God will reveal them to you in His time. Do you understand what I'm saying to you?"

A chill crept slowly up every single vertebra in Paul's

back. He had heard of events like this before, but this was the first time he had ever experienced one.

"I—I think so." Paul gazed directly into Reverend Jackson's eyes. "If God has told you to tell me to go, I certainly have no choice in the matter."

His words suddenly haunted him. He felt as if he had just signed onto something bigger and deeper than he could

comprehend.

Jackson nodded and smiled. He reached for Paul, and Paul, to his own surprise, accepted the embrace.

"Excuse me. Who's there?" The voice came from the front of the church.

"We're back here," Paul answered.

Reverend Jackson nodded toward the sound. "That'll be Barbara. Now if you will excuse me, pastor, I have other duties to attend to. It's been a pleasure meeting you."

The two men shook hands, and Jackson hurried around the corner of the building and out of sight.

Paul stood silently, allowing everything he had just heard to sink in. The message that Pastor Jackson had delivered numbed his brain. His hands were moist with perspiration, and he suddenly felt dizzy. He made his way back to his car, where a young black woman met him.

"Excuse me. I'm Barbara Arnett, the church trustee. Are you from the insurance company?"

"No, ma'am. I'm Paul Ryann, pastor over at Park View Baptist." The two shook hands. "I just stopped by to meet with Pastor Jackson for a few minutes."

The young woman's face went blank. "I'm sorry . . . Did you say you were meeting Reverend Jackson?"

"Yes, that's right. I was just talking to him."

"Sir, I don't mean to doubt your word, but that simply can't be. Our pastor died in the fire."

FiVE

The ride to Memphis International from Elizabeth's Germantown apartment took about twenty-five minutes, a relatively long time considering it was only eight miles. It was raining, and the south loop was bumper to bumper with sleepy-eyed commuters wielding cellular phones and mugs of hot coffee. Elizabeth could see some of them actually texting while they drove.

If they could see what I see at the MED, they wouldn't do that stupid stuff.

Germantown was one of the more affluent neighborhoods of the Memphis metro area, and most of the local realtors steered their clients in that direction. But Elizabeth's tastes were hardly extravagant. And while she occasionally mused over Beemers and Prada pumps, the whole keeping up with the Joneses thing was never more than a fleeting thought. Besides, she thought of everything as temporary now that she and Brad were sort of involved.

Brad Drake was a great friend. In fact, nobody but a true friend would have agreed to keep her English sheepdog during this trip. Winston was a tremendous pal, but he was a handful. She only hoped Winston's neurotic behavior wouldn't be the undoing of her relationship with Brad. She figured that if he survived this, she would give serious consideration to moving to the next step in their relationship. Well, maybe. She was still pretty gun-shy after her first marriage to an actor, a dark time in her life she

referred to as *Star Wars*.

Oh, well, time will tell!

Arriving at the terminal, she opened the door and realized that the tail of her coat had been pinned in the jamb. She swore. Not altogether out of character, but she did hope the cabbie hadn't heard her. She retrieved her bags and solemnly tipped him.

In the car ahead, a man reached to kiss the driver. Elizabeth straightened her coat and listened to their goodbyes.

"This trip will be good for us, honey, I know it will," Paul said. "I love you."

"I know, too. You'll bring back stories and pictures, and we'll build our memories of it that way. I wish I could be with you, sweetheart, but it's good I can be with your dad."

Laura was trying hard to give him a cheerful sendoff, but there was sadness in her eyes. "You'd better go. You'll miss your flight."

He turned and extended the handle on his bag with a click. He stepped up on the curb as she pulled away.

Lord God, watch over her while I'm gone. I don't know why this trip has come at this particular time, especially now with dad so sick, but I know you're in it. I know you are.

He turned and walked to the curbside check-in and handed the attendant his ticket.

† † †

Professor Van Eaton sat in a corner table in the airport coffee shop, cradling a hot café mocha while he considered his itinerary for the day. Catching an early flight out of Dulles, he had arrived at Memphis ahead of schedule, which gave him plenty of time before he had to make his connecting flight to Cincinnati. From there, it would be eight hours to Tel Aviv and another three and a half to New Delhi. He slipped the schedule back into his pocket, hoping he could get some sleep once they were in the air.

At the gate, he found that most of the passengers had already boarded the plane. He shambled to the counter.

"Ticket, sir?" the attendant said. Her breath was heavy with peppermint.

Van Eaton slid his briefcase on the counter and searched through every pocket. The ticket was in the last one.

"Now what've I done with my glasses?"

"I believe they're on your head, sir."

Van Eaton snorted and gathered his carry-ons. He

followed the jetway down to the plane and handed the flight attendant his boarding pass.

"Ah . . . 28D, on the left, three quarters of the way down," she said.

Van Eaton grinned as though there was a secret between them. He got to his seat and buckled in.

As the last passenger searched for her seat, Van

Eaton watched, hoping that it wouldn't be next to him. She stopped one row ahead.

"Sorry folks, I've got the middle seat."

A man in the aisle seat stood, while the woman placed her coat in the overhead bin. As she did so, a prescription bottle slipped from the coat's pocket, landing in the professor's lap. Van Eaton glanced at the label before handing it back to the woman. It was Mepergan.

"Thank you," Elizabeth said.

She slid the bottle into her purse and slipped into her seat. The window passenger smiled and extended his hand.

"Paul Ryann."

"Elizabeth Stewart."

With a painted-on smile, the flight attendant recited the required emergency procedures while the plane rocked and gingerly backed away from the gate, its brakes whining in protest. Elizabeth fastened her lap belt and settled in for the hour-long hop to Cincinnati.

The slightly noxious smell of jet fuel whistled through the air vents. It reminded Elizabeth of the ride through hell she had taken just three nights before. She hoped this trip would help erase the images.

Rashaman Medical Center. She pulled her itinerary from her valise and took a closer look. *Okay, I arrive in Tel Aviv Saturday afternoon, and—what?* She sat up straight in her seat. "I'm gonna kill Ray."

"I'm sorry, what?" Her seatmate glanced at her.

"Oh, I was just thinking out loud." She paused, but felt an urgency to explain. "I just noticed I've got three days before I have to be where I'm going. Three days with no itinerary."

† † †

Paul pressed the recline button on his armrest. *Three days to relax!* He couldn't remember having three straight days to himself his entire ministry—at least until now.

For Paul, God's call had come somewhat later in life than for most. At that time, baseball encompassed every fiber of his being. The Shreveport Indians specifically, then a farm club to the Houston Astros had traded two players from a neighboring club for his talent. It could only be described as a dream come true. Had it not been for his conversion to Christ, and soon after, surrender to the ministry, he probably would still be in baseball.

It was also during this time that he met Laura, a pre-med student at *UT Med,* a Memphis affiliate of the University of Tennessee at Knoxville. From the moment his eyes met hers, his world had been forever changed.

It all began with a series against the Redbirds, the St. Louis Cardinals franchise that had moved to Memphis that year. Paul had been scheduled to pitch the third of a four-game series and had just finished warming up in the bullpen. He propped against a chain link fence and pulled his cap over his face as visions of an angel flitted through

the halls of his mind.

The night before, a couple of rookies had talked him into carousing down on Beale Street. Bad idea. It was the first in a string of mistakes that eventually landed the two ballplayers in jail and left Paul to find his way back to the hotel alone.

Wandering down nameless streets and dark alleyways littered mostly with drunks and an occasional lady of the evening, he wound up at the entrance of an elaborate old church. His eyes followed the long stone stairway up to two massive wooden doors at its summit. Fluted casework and hand-carved finials adorned the entrance on both sides, and stained glass windows glistened from within. The building actually seemed out of place with its surroundings and had an alluring charm that drew him closer.

Suddenly the doors swung open and a drove of teenagers poured from its foyer. "Only five minutes!" a voice yelled from inside. "We are locking up for good after this."

"What's going on?"

One of the young women turned and gazed into

Paul's dimly lit face. "I'm sorry, what?"

It was at that very moment that time stopped and nothing else mattered. Paul stood gazing at her like a deer caught in the headlights.

"Sorry for yelling. Did you need something?"

Paul was speechless.

Finally he furrowed his brow and took a deep breath.

"W-what's—" His voice cracked like an adolescent's. He cleared his throat and tried again. "What's going on?"

"This is a lock-in," she said. "Our church has one for the youth a couple of times a year." There was a lengthy pause. "Are you a member here?"

"No, I'm not from around here." He slowly regained his senses. "What's a lock-in?"

"Oh, it's kind of a big slumber party where we have all kinds of neat things to do."

"Like . . . ?"

"Well, games. Sometimes we split up into teams and do things. We have Bible studies, skits, you know—fun stuff."

Now Paul was beginning to feel like himself. "And what about you? Are you a . . .youth?"

She crossed her arms and glanced away. "Well, what do you think?"

Dear lord, what do I say now? "I sort'a hoped you might be closer to my age." His heart was on the verge of pounding out of his chest.

"And how old is that?"

Suddenly the chapel bells rang, and a voice from the top of the stairs called out, "Let's go young people, it's time to get started. Laura, I need your help up here."

Laura . . . hmm.

"I have to go," she said. "It was nice meeting you." She turned and started back up the stairs along with the other young people.

"I—I play for Shreveport! We're playing at McCarver Stadium tomorrow night," he yelled.

She turned and grinned, then disappeared through the doors. He wondered if she had heard him over the chapel bells.

The ominous crack of a bat had jolted Paul back to the present. A foul ball ripped past the third-base dugout and streaked toward the handful of players that had congregated at the fence. Half dazed, Paul jumped to his feet and lunged for the ball. The ninety-mile-an-hour projectile found its way solidly into his open glove with such momentum that it spun him around—placing him face-to-face with the one fan he wanted to see: Laura.

She did hear me!

Laura gazed straight into his eyes. "Nice catch."

Though he couldn't hear a word over the crowd, he read her lips, and, oh, what beautiful lips they were.

"I can't believe you came!" A smile swept over his face.

He turned to throw the ball back into play, then he stopped and turned back to Laura. "How 'bout a souvenir, young lady?"

He pulled out a pen and wrote June 9, 1978.

Six

The 737 banked sharply toward its final destination as the smog-laden city of Cincinnati appeared just off the left wingtip. Descending onto the final approach, the hydraulics whined and the air rushed louder as the flaps extended and slowed the aircraft to landing speed. In their customary fashion, the fight attendants reminded the passengers to raise their tray tables and bring seatbacks to their upright and locked position as they prepared to land.

Flights on Fridays generally bulged with weary-eyed commuters on their way home from a long business week. This flight was no exception. To Paul it seemed to be jam-packed with mind-numbed travelers who were stuck on a hamster wheel and didn't know how to get off. And then again, maybe that was just the way he perceived them.

By all rights, God had blessed Paul with a pastor's heart. He had a real love for people, and there were few times during his ministry that he hadn't felt a real burden for the lost. But there were times when he felt less than adequate to share his faith, and on occasion he chose to keep to himself. This had been one of those times.

† † †

As Elizabeth stepped off the plane ahead of Paul, the flight attendant touched her arm. "Excuse me. Your coat."

"I just can't seem to lose that old thing, can I?"

"I'm afraid you're going need it. They're calling for snow today," the flight attendant said.

"Hopefully I won't be here long enough for that."

"Are you connecting?"

"I'm going on to Tel Aviv."

"Oh—it's warmer there?"

"The Weather Channel said they were going to be in the 80's for the rest of the week."

Tel Aviv. Guess I'll get a second chance to talk to her after all, Paul thought, overhearing their dialogue.

† † †

Gathering his carry-ons, the Professor unbuckled his seatbelt and stepped into the aisle. He slid his tie snugly to his throat and watched as the flight attendants scoured the plane for anything that was left behind. One attendant plucked a magazine from the seat and glanced at the cover.

"Hipp'-o-crates," she mispronounced.

Van Eaton glanced at the cover. "Hip-oc'-ra-tees. It was that young woman's with the coat."

"Oh, I bet she wanted it, too," she said.

"Did I hear her say that she was going on to Tel Aviv?"

"I think so."

"Well, that's my connecting flight as well. I'll see that she gets it."

Van Eaton took the magazine. When he got into the concourse, he visually scrolled through the endless maze of numbers that filled the monitors and located the flight.

† † †

"Well, hello again," Paul said as Elizabeth reached the gate.

"You're going to Israel too?"

"Yes, I am." A tremor of excitement filled his voice. He pulled his tickets from his coat pocket and placed them along with his passport on the counter.

"Are you from Memphis?"

"We've been there almost twenty years," Paul said. "I'm from Shreveport originally. And you?"

"You're all set, sir," the gate attendant said. "It's open seating and they'll be boarding momentarily. The flight's only about half full."

Elizabeth turned again to Paul. "I've lived there all my life."

"Ladies and gentlemen, flight 714 to Tel Aviv with continuing service to New Delhi is now ready for boarding," the gate attendant's voice echoed shrilly over the address system.

From behind them in line, Van Eaton motioned to Elizabeth with the magazine. "The flight attendant asked me to give this to you. I believe you left it on the plane from Memphis."

"Thank you. I'd forget my head if it wasn't screwed on."

The professor moved past them to his seat. He pulled a blanket and pillow from the overhead bin and sat down.

Even though they had been told it was open seating, Paul took his assigned seat on the aisle directly across from the professor. He saw that Elizabeth took a window seat in the row ahead of him.

As the last of the passengers boarded the aircraft, Paul noticed that the entire row where Elizabeth sat was empty. He slipped into the aisle and leaned over the seat. "Mind if I take the aisle seat?"

"Not at all. I'd enjoy the company."

Paul smiled and gathered his bag.

† † †

Elizabeth pulled a report from her valise and lowered her tray table. Learning just three days earlier that she was going to Jerusalem had offered her little time to prepare for the trip, and she intended to do that now. But then her thoughts drifted inexorably to what had happened the day before. She had managed to make a quick trip to Dallas to see her brother before she left for Tel Aviv. Visiting

Tom had become a regular event over the past year, and occasionally she dropped in without notice.

When she pushed open the door to her brother's room, to her surprise she found Tom sitting up in bed, a Gideon Bible resting on his lap. He looked haggard, as if he had been reading most of the night.

When he saw Elizabeth's face, he immediately reached

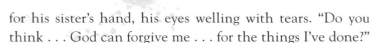

for his sister's hand, his eyes welling with tears. "Do you think . . . God can forgive me . . . for the things I've done?"

She was suddenly inundated with compassion. She sat on her brother's bed and held his hand tightly while they both wept. She then had the marvelous opportunity of leading her brother to Christ.

For the next three hours the two siblings shared their hearts, reminiscing over the past and talking about the promise of a new future. It was as if they were kids again, but without rivalry or adolescent envy, only genuine concern for each other.

As the hours passed and their time grew short, Elizabeth was in no hurry to leave. Love Field was only fifteen minutes away, and she now relished every minute with her brother. Pulling Tom's frail body to hers, she hugged him and silently thanked God that their kinship now went beyond mere fraternal blood.

"They're starting me on a new drug next week," he said. "Maybe this will be the one."

Elizabeth smiled and brushed back her tears. "Maybe so."

†   †   †

"What do you do, Paul?"

Paul sat up in his chair. He had wondered how long it would be before he was asked the *question*. Once people learned he was a minister, conversation sometimes had a

strange way of going down a religious path—or no path at all, for that matter.

"I'm a pastor."

Elizabeth closed her magazine and focused on him. "Oh. What church?"

"Park View Baptist Church, in Cordova. Have you heard of it?"

"Park View or Cordova?"

"Either."

"Cordova, yes. Park View, no. I'm sorry."

"That's all right. We're small, but we're growing," he added. "Do you attend church?"

"Yes, I do," Elizabeth replied. "I teach a Sunday school class of middle school girls at Grace Church in Germantown."

"You're a brave soul!"

"Yeah, a lot of people say that, but I just love that age. They're old enough to ask intelligent questions and even get into some interesting conversations, but for the most part, they haven't cultivated that smart mouth yet. You know? They're still . . . innocent, I guess."

"I wish I had a hundred just like you."

Elizabeth shrugged.

"So do you like a big church or a small church?" Paul stirred a second package of creamer into his coffee.

"Oh, a smaller church I guess."

Paul used to feel the same way, but over the years his ideals had shifted, especially since he had taken over his current pastorate. Emerging from rural roots where small churches were commonplace, he began to figure it was common sense that a growing flock meant success.

Wasn't that the whole point of bringing the Word to people?

He equated a successful church with a large congregation, and since his was not large or growing, he felt like somewhat of a failure. What made things equally difficult was that his church seemed to be filled with people who were content with being small.

"What about programs, facilities, and activities that larger churches offer to their people?" Paul asked gingerly. "Do you think that people should have the opportunity to enjoy those kinds of things?"

"I guess so. But there is still something about a small congregation where everybody knows everybody else, don't you think?"

Paul suddenly felt as if he was defending a deep, dark secret. He had had this mindset for such a long time that it was difficult to think about it any other way. Had his own ambitions seeped in and somehow replaced God's? He wasn't sure, but he was going to find out.

"It's kind of like McDonald's," Elizabeth said. "The

stores don't get any bigger for the most part—they just build more stores in other communities.

Paul had to chuckle at the analogy, though he admitted it made perfect sense.

Elizabeth slumped back into her chair and peered out the window. A blanket of milk-white clouds stretched to the horizon in every direction as far as the eye could see. They had been in the air almost three hours.

The low drone of the engines could almost lull a person to sleep, but Paul was hardly a candidate. The young doctor had a point, and her remarks had made sense.

† † †

Van Eaton gave up on his speech for a bit, discreetly increased the volume on his hearing aid, and eavesdropped on the conversation. Elizabeth and Paul's discussion pricked the festering wounds of his past life, and the infection ran thick.

Big church, small church. If you ask me, they're all just crutches.

Stepping back over forty years was as easy as closing his eyes. And though memory lane was long and wide, its potholes were filled with pain.

It was the little things that took him there most often. The pungent scent of Pine Sol, an old song on the radio, Chanel No. 5. Any number of things would whisk him back to a place he didn't want to be.

† † †

Though highly educated and a learned scholar of all major religions of the world, Van was not a religious man himself. Not by a long shot. He only chose religious history as a minor his freshman year at the request of his mother who was footing the tuition that year. It became her obsession when the soft-spoken mother of three was diagnosed with ovarian cancer. Van would do anything to help ease her pain, so he pursued the path he knew she would want.

Over the next few months he watched his mother fight a valiant battle and lose. Though her physical body withered, her faith intensified as each painful day ushered in the next. And though she didn't understand why, she never blamed God for her situation, as she put it. She only accepted the fact and put her house into order for what she knew would inevitably come.

Van, on the other hand, hardened toward God with every day she suffered. When she passed away, he never forgave her or the God she served. Only when Carolyn came into his life was he able to abide churchgoers. She was faithful to her beliefs, but she never pressed the issue with him. She believed he would eventually come around, but when she died, that hope died with her. He could muster only feelings of anger toward God, and that certainly wasn't taking him any closer to church.

† † †

Now the words to his speech were much slower in coming. His thoughts became more lethargic as he pushed himself to continue, and he soon realized that it was pointless—at least for now. He unbuckled his seat belt and stepped into the aisle, gently straightening and arching his back.

Standing quietly, he noticed that most of the center section of the plane was unoccupied, other than the two people in front of him. And although he considered moving to another seat to finish his work, a peculiar urgency persuaded him to stay.

"It's just that I've been in a lot of churches that I thought were too big," Elizabeth was saying. "You know the type: two and three services on Sundays and the nurseries overflowing. And they had to beg for volunteers to work in those nurseries. What's the rule—twenty percent do eighty percent of the work?"

"Boy, that's the truth." Paul said.

Elizabeth unfastened her seat belt. "I need to step out."

Paul stood. She stepped into the aisle and stumbled into the professor.

"Excuse me." She straightened her blouse.

Van Eaton nodded, but made no comment.

As she disappeared toward the back of the plane, two flight attendants worked their way forward, handing plastic-wrapped baskets to those who were awake. Van Eaton took a basket and requested hot tea. For a moment he cuddled the cup of hot water between liver-spotted hands, then dipped a tea bag into the steaming liquid.

✝   ✝   ✝

Paul stared out of the small window. The clouds below had formed a thin, broken layer as veins of navy blue ocean lay in the midst of the vast, chalky abyss. Suddenly he was in another place.

Since his conversion and later surrender into the ministry, Paul had dedicated himself to be all that God wanted him to be, though often he found himself struggling over just whose will he really followed. He had initially entered seminary with all the intentions of making the world a better place. But now, nearly twenty years later, he wasn't exactly sure what his goals were. He still had a burden for the lost, but his own life was none too calm. Most of all, his stepfather consumed his thoughts.

Robert had been the only father Paul had ever really known. His natural father had left his mother for his secretary when Paul was only five. And although the courts had awarded joint custody of him and his two sisters, his father left the state never to return, nor did he pay a dime in child support.

His stepfather was the exact opposite.

Robert Kidd was everything Paul's own father had never been. He not only loved Paul's mother deeply, but

61

he cared for the children as if they were his own flesh and blood. They never felt any less. He was kind and gentle, slow to anger but quick to show his love, and always seemed to be in tune to their needs. He was not afraid of hard work and proved it time and again.

Many nights he wouldn't make it home until after Paul and his sisters were in bed and was often gone again before they awoke. Yet they always knew he had been there. He would leave the girls a flower or some little something on their pillows and would write Paul notes, letting him know that he was the man of the house while Robert was gone. Paul never forgot how good that made him feel.

Though he heard that his natural father had died of a heart attack a few years earlier, he felt no real remorse. It took him a while, but eventually he was able to feel empathy for the man he never knew. Had his father even once tried to contact Paul or his sisters, things might have been different, but he never did. Paul never knew why.

As the thoughts of his father quietly faded, Paul glanced up and noticed the disheveled academic standing in the aisle.

"Weren't we on the same flight earlier?"

"Mmm, hum." Van Eaton leaned heavily aside as Elizabeth passed and returned to her seat.

"You were on the Memphis flight," Elizabeth said.

"That was my second leg." Van Eaton sighed.

"Oh? Where did you start out?"

"Dulles. At five this morning."

"Elizabeth Stewart." She extended her hand.

Van Eaton hesitantly pulled his hand from his pocket. "Leon Van Eaton."

"And this is Reverend Paul . . . " There was an awkward pause.

"Ryann," Paul added, and they shook hands. "I forget the names of my own church members half the time," he told

Elizabeth. "Don't worry about it."

"You're a physician," Van Eaton's bushy eyebrows rose with his words.

"Does it show?" Elizabeth asked.

"Well, actually . . . the magazine."

"Oh, yes. So what takes you to Israel?" she asked.

"Nothing," Van Eaton said with a cool aloofness. "I'm going on to New Delhi."

"Oh? What's in New Delhi? Or am I being too nosey?"

The professor unbuttoned his collar and loosened his tie. "No, not at all. I . . . ah, I'm scheduled to speak."

"What do you do?"

Now the professor seemed bothered. "I'm on staff at Georgetown University. I'm currently working—with little success, I must admit—on a speech that I'm scheduled to deliver in New Delhi on Tuesday. And you?"

"I'm headed to the new trauma unit at Rashaman Medical Center in Jerusalem," Elizabeth answered. She offered more information than she normally would have, but for some reason, it just seemed like the right thing to do.

Van Eaton nodded.

"I pastor a church in northeast Memphis," Paul volunteered. The professor again nodded. "What do you do at Georgetown?"

Van Eaton massaged his neck. "I'm a professor of religious and cultural history."

"Really? I'd love to hear more."

Van Eaton settled against the arm of his seat. "For

instance?" Now he was becoming more cantankerous than courteous.

"Oh . . . I don't know," Paul said. "What led you into that field?"

"My mother."

Paul laughed. Van Eaton didn't.

"I'm sorry . . . I thought you were kidding."

"No."

Paul's words suddenly tasted like ashes in his mouth.

Elizabeth broke the awkward silence that followed. "So you are a professor of religious history?"

Van Eaton nodded.

"Well, that sounds interesting. Do you favor one in particular? Religion, I mean."

Van Eaton circled the question for a moment. "With regard to religion, I am merely a spectator," he said somberly. "I would find it difficult to take sides and remain objective in my teaching."

"So you're saying you don't take sides," Paul prodded.

Van Eaton nervously fingered a razor nick on his chin. "I'm saying that, as a professor of religious studies, I impart my knowledge to my students—objective knowledge and nothing more." He smirked as though his logic was flawless.

Paul settled back into his seat and gazed up at the overhead bin. *This guy is a real piece of work.* "But you do have an opinion." He couldn't imagine what was making him push this guy so hard.

Van Eaton rolled his eyes overtly. It was one of several

demeaning mannerisms he'd cultivated over the years.

Paul chose his words carefully. "I can sympathize with your objective stand on religion with regard to your position, Professor. But I was referring to your subjective belief." His eyes sparkled with hope.

Van Eaton crossed his arms and widened his stance. "Reverend, I have long since believed that my students have the right to unbiased teaching."

Paul turned even farther in his seat. "But I'm talking about *your* belief, Professor. Gut level, deep down belief."

"Belief evolves from whatever we perceive as truth." Van Eaton acted bothered, though in fact he loved the banter.

"Okay, so let me get this straight," Paul said. "You said that belief evolves from what we perceive as truth?"

"Yes."

"Then would it be safe to assume that what you or I may perceive as truth might possibly not be truth at all, which also suggests the possibility of having faith in the wrong thing?"

"Faith?" The professor chuckled under his breath. "Are we talking about faith now?"

Paul leaned forward and propped against the arm of his chair. "Faith is as much a part of life as is eating or even breathing. It's at the very core of any belief."

"The professor smiled. "There are two caveats here. There is belief, which I think we both can agree is based on perception, and there is faith, which is neither intellectual nor logical. It is simply an easy way of explaining what you

don't understand."

Paul's smile eroded. "Well, you're partially right. Faith is neither intellectual nor logical, but it's what God requires from all of us—to totally trust in Him—through faith. And I'll go even farther than that to say that is impossible to please God without it."

"So let me ask you a question then, *Reverend*." If I were to take sides as you suggest, how would I be able to remain impartial? Or be objective?"

Paul processed the question while praying a silent prayer. "Does God not say that He would rather that we were hot or cold, and not lukewarm?"

"Your paraphrase is hardly applicable."

"Sure it is," Paul insisted. "What makes you think it doesn't apply here? You say that you cannot take sides, and yet God says we must."

Van Eaton stiffened. "That's your opinion, Reverend. But from where I stand, I see nothing of the sort."

Paul thought further. "Well what do you think makes an effective teacher?"

"I believe—"

"Ahh!" Paul interrupted. He became aware that Elizabeth was looking from one to the other as they spoke as though watching a tennis match.

"All right," Van Eaton conceded. "It is my opinion that an effective teacher should know everything that he can know about the subject he teaches, that he must be credible and without opinion in what he communicates.

Objective."

"So you're saying that a person can teach what he doesn't believe?" *Gotcha!* Paul thought.

"Are we to teach our own beliefs?" Van Eaton asked. "Or are we to teach the unbiased truth?"

"Isn't that what teaching is—teaching what we hold to be true, or what we *believe* to be true?"

Van Eaton paused and considered the question. Though he believed what Paul was saying had some validity, he wasn't about to agree with him. It just wasn't in him.

"I don't want to force my revolutionary convictions down anyone's throat," he said.

"I'm not saying—"

Van Eaton held up his hand to stave off Paul's protest.

"Let me finish. I know what you're doing, and I suppose you're trying to do what you think is right, or what you *believe* is right. The only thing is, I'm not interested in what *you* believe. I'm only interested in the facts. That's all—just facts."

As the conversation lulled, two flight attendants maneuvered their stainless steel cart down the narrow aisle. Paul took a soda. The professor ordered whiskey.

Again Paul stoked the fire. "I want to ask you a question, if I may."

Van Eaton opened the tiny bottle and poured it over the ice in his glass. He nodded.

"What if I were, say, a drowning man," Paul said staring at the luggage bin overhead, "and you had a life preserver. Would you throw it to me?"

"Again, I know where this is going."

"Well?"

"I dare say I would," Van Eaton answered, sipping his spirits in a mocking way.

"Or if I had a horrible disease that you had the cure for, and all you had to do was give it to me, would you?"

"Hmm, let's see . . . "

Paul let out a sigh and looked away.

Van Eaton smiled. "Yes, of course I would."

"Then can I do any less?" Paul asked pointedly.

Elizabeth grinned sheepishly.

Suddenly, Paul recalled the words of the old black pastor. A few short days ago William Jackson had seemingly appeared out of nowhere to offer him the strangest bit of advice. And now he had a feeling that all of this was somehow connected.

"You asked earlier how, if you were to take sides, you would be able to remain impartial."

Van Eaton nodded.

"Well, my answer is simple. You can't. A man can't

remain impartial on the subject of Christ. In Matthew 12:30, Jesus said point blank, if you're not with me, you're against me."

Van Eaton sipped his drink casually as Paul continued.

"We all ultimately must choose which path we will take. To not answer God's call is to say no to Him," he said in a soft, but steady voice. "This isn't just about teaching a  curriculum. This is about eternity. Your eternity."

Paul took a deep breath and slowly exhaled, amazed at the words he had just delivered. They seemed to come from nowhere. And yet, he knew.

"I don't need a lesson in Christian apologetics," Van Eaton countered. "You're talking about something you simply can't prove."

"Oh?"

Van Eaton slurped his drink and irritatingly crunched the ice. "You can no more prove that Jesus was the Son of God than you can prove that there is life on other planets. That's the problem with you—with Christians in general. You're all the same. You think you've got something that no one else has."

Paul stared sympathetically at the professor. And though Van Eaton's words were benign to him, he wondered how many students the man had infected over the years with his blatant disregard for Christ.

"You know, I can't see the air that slips beneath the wings and keeps this airplane aloft either. But I know it's there just the same."

Van Eaton thought for a moment. "Yes, that's true, but it's tangible. We can feel the wind as it blows, and we can see its results after a storm."

Paul patted the armrest beside him and breathed deeply. "You see this seat?" He ran his fingers over the cushion. "I can tell you that it will support you and even that it will be comfortable, but you and I both know that the only way you'll really know for sure is for you to try it. And it's the same way with Christ. It's something you just have to try for yourself. I can't explain it any better than that."

The professor grabbed his briefcase. "You assume too much, sir!" he snapped. "I have tried it, and I have no intention of carrying this conversation any further." He struggled into the aisle and started toward the back of the plane.

"Professor—"

Van Eaton waved him off. "We're done here, Reverend," he said coldly. He found a seat several rows back and sat down.

"Please call me Paul."

Paul sat in silence and mentally replayed his words. He wondered if there was anything he possibly could have said that would have made a difference. And though he wasn't exactly sure, he believed that God must have had a purpose in what had just happened. Most of all, he had to remember that it was simply his job to plant the seeds no matter how stony the soil, but the harvest was God's.

The monitors lining the ceiling blinked and sprang to life.

"It looks like a movie is about to start." Elizabeth smiled and patted Paul's arm.

The two donned their headsets and tuned in.

† † †

As the aircraft began its final descent into Israeli air space, Paul peered out the window. The plane was surrounded by the shimmering blue-green waters of the Mediterranean.

It was now early Saturday afternoon in Tel Aviv, and the sun was still high in the sky. He realized they had somehow missed a day—and a night's sleep. The dream Paul had carried for most of his adult life had finally arrived.

SEVEN

Tel Aviv. The airport buzzed with activity. Commuters whisked in and out of gates, moving in droves, many babbling in what was clearly not English.

At least the signs are in English.

Elizabeth stiffened at the presence of automatic weapons dangling from the shoulders of Israeli soldiers. The scene brought back too many memories of the time she had spent in Kuwait. Her senses sharpened as she felt a heightened uneasiness.

No, there really isn't even a semblance of absolute security anymore.

Paul seemed oblivious, focused solely on getting to the city.

When the line bottlenecked at the escalator, the professor shambled over. "Well, ladies and gentlemen, I hope that your stay will be a pleasant one," he said with a cool deference.

Elizabeth smiled and extended her hand, amazed that he even spoke at all. And though it was fairly obvious how he felt about Van Eaton, Paul seemed to be determined to keep things friendly. He shook the man's hand heavily.

"So you're on to New Delhi."

Van Eaton tugged at his cuffs and exposed a coffee stain on his sleeve. "Ah yes, and you're off to confirm your beliefs," he said dryly.

Paul didn't take the bait. He simply waited without comment while the professor gathered his things and walked away.

Elizabeth stepped onto the escalator, with Paul behind her.

"I'm sorry," she said.

"Oh, he's a troubled man," Paul said. "He needs our prayers."

The escalator emptied into a stale, smoke-tinted room that resembled more of a pool hall than a baggage claim. Unlike the United States, Tel Aviv allowed public smoking, and people were definitely exercising their right to do so.

"Where are you staying, Paul?"

Paul reached inside his coat pocket. "Ah . . . the Hotel Cavalier. On Sultan Suleiman. And you?"

"I'm on Sultan Suleiman too, at the Meridian. That must be hotel row."

Pulling their bags from the conveyor, they located the exit and headed to customs.

"Passport, please." The guard's face was stoic, his gaze probing.

Elizabeth slid her credentials across the counter, and Paul did the same. The guard studied their photos and focused on their names.

"Traveling together?" His manner was curt.

Paul exchanged glances with Elizabeth. "Well, not exactly. We met on the plane."

The guard offered a slight nod as if he knew the rest

of the story. Paul appeared to be ruffled by the implication.

"No, we're not traveling together," he said coolly.

The guard stamped both passports and slid them back without comment.

They both passed through the glass double doors that led to the street and walked to the curb.

"I'm sorry about that," Paul said.

"It's okay. People are going to think what they want to think."

"You're right." Paul extended his hand. "Well, it's been quite a trip."

Elizabeth took his hand and smiled. "We could share a cab if you want."

"I don't know . . . Do you think the customs agent would approve?"

They both laughed out loud, but Elizabeth could tell the thought did worry Paul a little.

† † †

The cab driver said the ride to the old city would take about thirty minutes, but Elizabeth soon realized it should have taken much longer. Puffing furiously on an unfiltered cigarette and gripping a soda between his legs, the caffeine-stoked cabbie bullied his way into traffic. Elizabeth scrambled to fasten her seatbelt, and Paul followed her lead.

She caught short glimpses of the scenery on the way to Jerusalem. The quasi-modern architecture of Ben Gurion Airport quickly vanished into ancient motifs and barren landscapes. Gazing out over the wide expanse of desert and mountains that formed the horizon, they might very well have been on a highway in Arizona or New Mexico had it not been for the signs that read Beer Sheba or Bethlehem. And, of course, one didn't usually see herds of camels and Bedouin shepherds in the states.

Suddenly the driver motioned to the next exit. "Excuse me, excuse me—you want go Bethlehem first?" His broken English slipped through brown-streaked teeth.

Paul glanced at Elizabeth. "What?"

"Bethlehem! Bethlehem! One hundred forty shekels. You want go there first?" He pointed to the exit.

"I just want a bed and an air-conditioned room," Elizabeth said.

Paul agreed reluctantly.

† † †

Arriving at the entrance of Elizabeth's hotel, Paul could see the Hotel Cavalier at the end of the street. He opened the door and exited, holding the door for Elizabeth. He paid the driver in U.S. dollars and slipped the unfamiliar change into his pocket. They gathered their belongings and stepped up on the curb as the cab sped away.

"Holy smoke. I feel lucky to be alive!" Elizabeth pulled her luggage onto the concrete walk. "Well—it's been quite a trip."

"Yes, it has." Paul scanned the street. "You think you'd like to have dinner later?"

Elizabeth smiled. "Sure. Besides, I owe you half the cab fare, however much that is." They both laughed. "Can you give me a few hours to settle in and give me a call here at the hotel?"

"I can do that," Paul said.

"I'll see you then." Elizabeth turned and disappeared through the hotel's leaded glass doors.

Paul mingled with a glut of commuters and tourists as he hurried down the street toward the Hotel Cavalier. He ascended the marble staircase and stepped inside, admiring the ornate lobby, its walls clad with swirls of pearl and five-hundred-year-old tapestries. In the center of the room an elegant crystal chandelier dangled poetically from the high ceiling, and sconce lighting accented fluted marble columns along both sides of the room. He stood in the midst of the lavish surroundings and silently thanked God for his parents, who had paid for this trip, knowing they didn't really have the money.

His heart welled with emotion as he thought of his father—and of Laura.

† † †

"Would you try again operator?" The patois Paul heard was barely discernible. "She's probably asleep," he explained.

After several rings, someone picked up the receiver, fumbled, and dropped it. After a moment, a groggy but familiar voice came on the line.

"Hellllo."

"Elizabeth?"

"Haaay . . . " she said slowly. "What time is it?"

"It's 7:30," Paul replied.

"In the morning?"

"Night." He laughed.

"Oh, my . . . I was dead to the world."

"I'm sorry I woke you."

"No. I'm used to it."

"Well, I'm wired. Are you hungry?"

"Sure." He could hear the bed rustle. "Can you give me thirty minutes?"

"No problem."

"Where should I meet you?"

"There's a nice restaurant here in my hotel."

"You're kidding. I'm definitely staying in the wrong place!"

† † †

Crossing polished marble floors, Elizabeth walked to the restaurant entrance and found Paul already seated. Tall red candles in hurricane lamps occupied the center of mahogany tables adorned with linen napkins, stiff and ornately shaped, and fine china and sterling silver.

"This is nice," she said.

Paul stood and held her chair. When she was seated,

he resumed his seat and slid a tour brochure across the table.

"I picked up a couple of these in the lobby. I didn't know exactly what your plans were, but if you're interested—"

Elizabeth's face brightened. She thumbed through one brochure. "Here's one that goes to the old city. Bethlehem, then over to Jordan—oh, but it's a three-day tour. I don't have that much time."

"How about this one? Morning Star Tours." Paul turned the brochure toward Elizabeth. The front page pictured a late-model tour bus with the Temple Mount in the background and inlaid photos of the Mount of Olives and the Holy Sepulcher. "This one starts at the Wailing Wall—through the old city—the Via Dolorosa, Calvary. What do you think?"

"I'll follow your lead. Like I said, I don't have to be anywhere until Tuesday."

Paul looked over the schedules. "Here's one that leaves at nine in the morning."

"Nine's good. No reservations required," she read.

"Their buses run every hour, and they stop here at the Cavalier."

"That'll work," Paul said. "So what looks good? I'm starving."

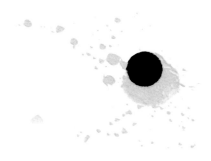

Eight

The lobby of the Hotel Cavalier bustled with activity as Elizabeth scanned the dusty magazine rack, looking for something—anything—to read that wasn't in Arabic. She pulled a month-old copy of *Time* magazine from the rack and found a seat next to the tour booth. It had been manned the night before. It was now empty.

Flipping through the pages, she stopped at an article on the Shroud of Turin.

> The Holy Shroud is a twelve-foot length of hemp cloth claimed to be the burial garment used to wrap the body of Christ after his crucifixion. Housed in a small church in an obscure hamlet near the northern border of Italy, the Shroud of Turin has spent the last century under close scrutiny of the scientific community.
>
> The curators of the Church of Turin believe unequivocally that the garment is authentic, but scientific testing of sample pieces using carbon dating claims otherwise; testing concluded that the material dates back as early as the eleventh century, though church officials vehemently argue the point. They claim to have documented proof that the shroud has survived

two fires—one in the fourteenth and the other in the seventeenth century. They hold to the idea that smoke from those fires meshed with the fibers, thus altering its chemical composition. The majority of the scientific community agrees that the exposure of heat and smoke with fibers of ancient hemp will, in fact, change its chemical composition, but go on to state that while it is possible, it is not probable.

Elizabeth was fascinated at the possibility that such a garment could actually exist and even contain traces of the blood of Christ. While she pondered the possibilities, a hand fell heavily on her shoulder.

"Good morning."

"Good morning to you."

"Did you sleep well?"

"Hardly a wink," Paul said. "I'm still on Memphis time."

"Well, it's one in the morning at home."

"You're kidding. I couldn't sleep if I wanted to. You look good."

Elizabeth smiled. She wore pleated khakis, a white button-down shirt and Sperry Topsiders with no socks.

"What—this old stuff? I only wear it when I don't care how I look."

"A movie buff too? Oh, we're going to get along just fine."

Elizabeth grabbed her Nikon D90 and backpack. She slung both over her shoulder.

Paul was also dressed casually and carried a camcorder

and a nylon case. He stopped long enough to make sure that the lens cover was off and the unit was on.

† † †

At first glance, the city was not unlike any other city, Paul thought. One might witness this sort of scene in any sizeable city in the world, and yet there was an altogether different allure. Even in the midst of masses it was there, whispering on the breeze that wafted through the streets, pervading the senses like a strong perfume. Even the birds of the air sang its praise.

Jerusalem! Jerusalem!

Her crumbling walls loomed against powder-blue skies, ancient edifices poised majestically as constant reminders of a heritage that had spanned more than six thousand years—and would, perhaps, six thousand more.

Paul stepped off the curb, camera in hand, and panned the scene. Working his way up and down the streets on both sides, he captured the old city wall that stretched for hundreds of yards in both directions before curving out of sight.

As he took in the drama, the reality of it, he brushed the tears from his eyes and drew a long, deep breath. He sighed as he exhaled. He was finally here! Everything was so perfect, so spiritually elegant, exactly the way he had pictured it would be.

He closed his eyes and breathed again. The air was

distinct, filled with smells of freshly baked breads, pastries, and automobile exhaust—though mostly the latter—and an occasional wisp of ripened fruit from the vendors who peddled goods on the curb.

For the most part the masses were dressed in blacks and grays. Hijabs and thobes shrouded Muslim women from head to toe as they mingled with tourists in cargo

shorts and Polo shirts. Even with temperatures already in the eighties and expected to reach the nineties by mid-afternoon, this was how they dressed—while their men wore shorts and shirtsleeves.

"I can't imagine having to wear all that," Elizabeth said. "I'd burn up. When I was in Kuwait—" She stopped. *Do I really want to bring up that subject here?*

"What were you saying?" Paul asked.

"Oh, just that I'm so hot natured I'd be miserable in all those layers."

Paul watched two women cross the street and step onto the curb. "You know, I read somewhere that the women, for the most part, are opposed to it."

"But none of them will say so publicly," a surly voice came from behind.

Elizabeth and Paul turned to greet the familiar face. Professor Van Eaton cupped his hands to his face and lit his cigar. Dark circles hung like pockets under his eyes.

"Professor, what are you doing here? I figured you would be in New Delhi by now," Paul said, actually wishing he were.

"Inasmuch as I wanted to be, the airline had other ideas." Van slipped his hand into his pocket and glanced at his feet. "After you left, I waited at the gate for about an hour. Then another hour passed, and finally they told us that they were having a series of problems with the aircraft and that it wouldn't be ready until late this afternoon at the earliest."

Elizabeth shook her head. "You're kidding."

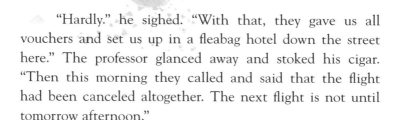

"Hardly." he sighed. "With that, they gave us all vouchers and set us up in a fleabag hotel down the street here." The professor glanced away and stoked his cigar. "Then this morning they called and said that the flight had been canceled altogether. The next flight is not until tomorrow afternoon."

"I'm sorry, Professor," Elizabeth said.

Paul feigned grief.

"Anyway, I thought . . . " Van paused.

"What?"

"Well, I thought if you two wouldn't mind, I might tag along with you today."

Elizabeth looked at Paul. "How did you know we would be here?"

Van Eaton scratched his head and looked at them strangely. "I don't know. I just did."

Elizabeth shrugged. "It's okay with me. I'm just along for the ride anyway."

Paul glared without thinking. *It seems rather odd considering our earlier conversations, but—*

A mimute later a tour bus pulled to the curb. Giving

in to the inevitable, Paul ushered the other two on board. Before they could grab seats, the bus took off in a cloud of blue smoke.

The elderly driver picked his way through the congested streets and toward the first of the sights. He flipped on his microphone and began his lengthy oration in a heavy Israeli accent.

"In just a few minutes, you will see the first of the more prominent sights of the city of old Jerusalem, the original walls of the Temple Mount. This wall is referred to as the Wailing Wall and will be just ahead on your right. It is only one of two left standing and was actually built on top of Solomon's Temple walls—"

He swerved slightly to avoid a cyclist, then continued. "The walls of Solomon's Temple are actually below the Temple Mount walls, hidden below ground level for many centuries. Just recently though, the city of Jerusalem has opened a series of tunnels that run adjacent to the Temple walls."

He paused and took a swig from a plastic water bottle he pulled from under his seat. "These are called the Rabbinical Tunnels. He wiped his mouth on his sleeve. "Following the tunnels to the end will ultimately lead to the Via Dolorosa, which to Christians is the final road that Christ walked on his journey to the cross."

The Via Dolorosa. Paul's mind reeled at the thought. Elizabeth too seemed intrigued, though less so than Paul, and Van Eaton even less than that.

Pulling a flyer from a clipboard on the dash, the driver read, "There will also be a reenactment today of the triumphal entry of Christ into Jerusalem. For, as most of you know, Christendom traditionally refers to today as Palm Sunday."

The bus slowed and pulled to a stop. "We are at the entrance to the walled city, the Dung Gate," the driver announced. "You will have approximately thirty minutes to visit the Wall, but should you decide to stay longer, another bus will be along shortly."

The three unlikely sojourners gathered their belongings and stepped onto the sidewalk.

The Dung Gate was a strikingly picturesque stone archway. Spanning perhaps ten feet across and the same dimension in height, the massive portal featured a second archway inset in the stone, which rose another three feet. It was bordered with fluted sandstone that resembled teeth.

The three passed through the portal to a series of metal detectors, all of which were under camera surveillance and each manned by two armed guards. Paul and Van Eaton seemed oblivious to the guns, but not Elizabeth.

And Ray believes it's perfectly safe here, she thought. *They don't carry guns in safe places.*

How odd it seemed to pass from ancient to modern in only a few steps, but that was the way it seemed to be. Three-thousand-year-old stone walls littered with rusted street signs and crumpled McDonald's sacks. Comparing the growth of McDonald's with the growth of churches, she had to stifle a laugh.

Crossing the cobblestone plaza that encompassed as much as ten acres all told, they mixed with waves of tourists from every ethnic and social background, cameras bumping off their chests as they made their way toward the Wall. A single strand of iron chain laced together a row of waist-high metal poles that were spaced equally apart. The chain dangled freely between each pole and formed a perimeter between the

plaza and the Wailing Wall itself. As they drew closer, they found that the wall was also divided into two sections—one for men and a lower level on the far right for women.

The wall, consisting of sandstone blocks in a variety of sizes, stretched three hundred feet from left to right and was perhaps half as tall. Sprigs of green foliage clung tightly to crevices in the upper wall, and paper notes containing prayers were shoved into many more crevices at the base. People of all ages gathered there, mostly Orthodox men who stood chanting and reciting their prayers, many of them rocking and swaying as they quietly delivered their messages to God.

"Look at that." Paul pointed to a TV camera mounted on a pole directly across the plaza. "It seems so out of place here, doesn't it?"

"I read somewhere that that it is a live camera hookup to the Internet and that it's updated every thirty seconds," Elizabeth said. She focused and snapped a shot.

"You're right, young lady," Van Eaton chimed in. "We pulled it up several times this last semester. I had forgotten it was there."

† † †

Paul moved closer to the wall, filming with every step. The sight was captivating, and although he had witnessed it many times before in magazines and on *CNN*, being there was altogether different. The scenery, the city, the whole setting was even more impressive than he had imagined it

would be. Witnessing firsthand the place where Jesus had walked had a way of deepening his faith all the more. If he had a thousand more lives to live, Paul thought, he would live them all for Christ. Of this he was certain.

Joining the throngs of tourists and locals who trooped up the long stone stairway, the trio entered the section known as the Arab Quarter. Clay pottery and hand -woven rugs of every size and shape artistically adorned stone-hewn storefronts that lined both sides of the streets. Shops offering everything from leather goods to raw meat to an endless variety of gold and silver jewelry, costume and otherwise, filled wooden display cartons and jammed shelves to the hilt.

Even with the flagrant intrusion of commercialism, it was intoxicating, and Paul drank it all in, driven by a strange wanderlust that encompassed his very being. He squinted through the viewfinder of his camera as if it were a looking glass to a time long since passed. He focused on the old as well as the new, relics of the past mingled with the junk of the present—and sometimes the two were indistinguishable—though it was really a moot point. He was there and that was all that really mattered.

Father, thank you for letting me see all of this, to walk the streets where your son walked—where he lived and breathed, and where he died. Tears welled as he prayed. *Thank you Lord.*

Van Eaton followed but paid little attention to the sights, and for good reason. Old memories were running thick and invading his thoughts.

How Rosenberg would have loved to show me his city.

Serving over four years and under two administrations as host to Benjamin Rosenberg, Israeli minister of foreign affairs, Van had witnessed firsthand the defeat of Egyptian forces in the historic six-day war. He even once met the one-eyed Israeli patriot, Moshe Dayan. During this time the Nixon administration moved into the White House, vowing peace with honor and promising to be out of Vietnam before the end of Nixon's term.

Then, in a shocking development, Prime Minister Eshkol had died suddenly and was quickly replaced by Golda Meir, who brought in her own faculty and foreign affairs staff. Rosenberg soon returned to Israel. Van was devastated. Rosenberg had become his closest friend and, more important, his mentor.

They had parted in Washington in early spring. The warm days had coaxed the cherry trees into showing their colors. Even a few patches of green could be seen in the fields around the Washington Monument, but the nights were unseasonably cold.

Under the cloak of night, an entourage of Mossad agents and Jewish dignitaries departed for Dulles Airport. Turning onto Pennsylvania Avenue, the procession passed the White House one last time. Van gazed through the window, past Rosenberg's distinct silhouette. A single

tear dripped from the corner of his mentor's eye and was immediately absorbed into the fabric of his trousers. Van smiled and touched him on the arm. Rosenberg acknowledged his touch, but continued to look away.

The crisp air glazed the darkened windows as they turned past the Federal Reserve and the Capitol building. Rosenberg wiped away the fog with his sleeve and took one last look.

Arriving at Dulles Airport, the first of the three limousines stopped just past the double egress doors marked Customs—Foreign Ministry. The first vehicle unloaded, and the other two followed suit. Not recognizing any of the people who exited the first limo, Van assumed it was a decoy.

The second vehicle, holding the foreign affairs minister, now unloaded. Two hefty bodyguards took charge of the sidewalk and opened the vehicle door, their eyes scanning the vicinity for any movement. After a moment one man made a motion, and Rosenberg opened the door and stepped out of the limo along with Van. His cheeks flushed cherry red.

"Well, here we are, my friend." Rosenberg tightened his lips and breathed deeply through his nostrils. "I shall miss the chill of Washington."

Van smiled and breathed a warm cloud. He knew his friend hated the cold and was only trying to make conversation. They stood awkwardly, exchanging glances, as neither man really knew exactly what to say. Finally

Rosenberg broke the silence.

"And I shall miss you, son," he said with a broken voice. Van embraced his friend. "This is not the end, my friend," Rosenberg insisted. "You must come to see me—in Israel."

Van nodded but felt it would never happen. Unfortunately, his fears had held true. Just two months later Rosenberg had died suddenly of a brain aneurysm, and Van was not even notified until two weeks after the funeral. Another piece of his spirit had been snuffed out.

It was more than twenty years since he and Carolyn had come to visit Rosenberg's family. Visiting the grave of his old mentor had put closure to his death, but Van still remembered how difficult it had been to let go and how his precious Carolyn had been the fire that had forged the healing process. And now she too was gone.

Goodbye, my friend! He moved along slowly, stung by the unexpected depth of the pain.

† † †

Paul inched his way farther up the street, missing nothing:

the storefronts that lined the narrow streets, the merchants that peddled their goods on every corner, and the children who played as if nothing so important had ever taken place there. And yet this was where it all happened.

Jesus may have stood in this very spot!

Suddenly Paul stood still. "Did you hear that?"

"What?"

He glanced at Van Eaton. "I thought I heard someone scream for help. It sounded like it came from back there." He pointed down a blind alley.

They each stood on high alert, waiting to see if they could hear anything else, though it was almost impossible considering the goings-on in the street.

Undaunted, Paul started down the dirty alleyway— and even it was picturesque. The ancient stone walls that lined the narrow corridor appeared to lean inward, almost touching at their peaks as they stood against a perfect blue sky. Rusty iron fire escapes that crumbled at their supports lined both sides of the corridor, forming a gridwork overhead that doubled as makeshift clotheslines. That these people were poor was more than apparent, if for no other reason than the clothes that were draped across the rusty rails.

Intrigued by the somber beauty, Paul all but forgot that he was supposed to be following a cry for help. At the end of the alley, a narrower alley crossed it, running to the right and to the left. He guided the viewfinder around the corner and stopped. His heart suddenly hammered in his chest.

At the far end of the alley two men in military greens

appeared to be having their way with a young woman. Crouched between the two men, she stared at the ground and held perfectly still. Even from that distance, he could tell that whatever was going on was without her consent.

As he watched, one guard stood on her left side holding an automatic weapon, while the second man undressed from the waist down. The woman glanced up and saw Paul at the

corner with his camera.

Suddenly, she screamed. "Ezrah! Ezrah! Help me pleeze!"

Whirling around, both men realized that they had been caught on tape. Instinctively, the soldier holding the Uzi slammed its butt into the woman's head. She dropped to the ground like a rag doll, thick, red blood gushing from the wound.

The other soldier swung around and squeezed off a burst from his Uzi, riddling the stone walls up and down and spraying bullets all around Paul.

When the smoke cleared, Paul was halfway down the alley screaming at Elizabeth and the professor. "Get out of here!"

He caught a glimpse of Van Eaton, who took one look at Paul, then immediately threw himself into the crowd. Beside the professor, Elizabeth hesitated for an instant, then did the same.

Stumbling headlong into a string of trashcans at the mouth of the alley, Paul lost sight of them. Jumping to his feet, he flung the strap of his camera over his shoulder and filtered into the crowd.

Frantically he shouldered his way through the melee, trying to catch a glimpse of Elizabeth and the professor. His fear fed his strength, and he pushed farther. Glancing back, he saw a soldier round the corner and quickly shoulder his weapon.

Paul punched his way along, leaping up with every other step in an effort to see over the crowd. He caught a glimpse of the professor and quickly caught up with him. The two darted

between two storefronts. Midway down, they stopped to catch their breath.

Van Eaton thrust his hand into his pocket and pulled out a small inhaler. As he breathed in the healing mist, Elizabeth came up behind them.

"What . . . was the shooting all about?" She bent over, grabbed both knees and heaved. "And why . . . are they . . . after us?"

Paul looked back over his shoulder. "It looked like . . . they were . . . trying to force a young woman . . . to have sex with them." He drew a deep breath. "They saw me taping them. Dear God, that poor girl. I think they killed her."

"Are you sure? I'm a doctor; I should help!"

Paul grabbed her arm. "Are you crazy? This isn't Memphis now. You can't just hail an ambulance. They were shooting at me!"

"Yeah, well, I've been shot at before," she said under her breath.

Van Eaton sucked in a breath. "One of them just ran past up there." Cringing, he pointed in the direction they had taken.

Elizabeth scanned their surroundings. "We're not gonna

get out this way. We're boxed in."

Paul suddenly noticed a narrow break between two of the buildings. Behind them a stone stairway led into the darkness. He wedged through and motioned to Van Eaton and Elizabeth to follow.

Elizabeth slipped through easily, but she and Paul had to exert considerable force to drag the professor through the opening, ignoring his groans of protest.

Paul started down the stairs. "Down here!"

"But where does it go?" Van Eaton still struggled to catch his breath.

"We don't have any other choice! They're coming!"

Winding down the murky stairway, Paul led the way into the shadows. At the bottom of the chasm a massive wooden door blocked their way.

Paul quickly pulled on the rusty handle. Locked. He pulled again with all his might, but this time the handle broke off in his hand and he slammed back against the wall.

Squeezing his eyes shut, he prayed frantically. There was nothing more anyone could do.

Suddenly the door cracked open about an inch, its uneven bottom wedging against the floor. A hand curled around the frame and forced the door open farther.

Fearfully the three waited for their executioner—or savior.

A moment more, and the door opened enough to reveal a figure standing in the shadows. The dim light exposed a man who was darkskinned and bearded. His eyes sparkled in the darkness, and he seemed not at all surprised that they were there. He motioned to them, and they rushed inside without hesitation.

"If you will follow the tunnel," he said, pointing into the darkness, "it will lead you to safety. Keep taking the passages to the right, and you will find yourselves outside in a minute or so."

The man's voice had such a calming tone that he was easily trusted, though trust had become secondary to necessity. Behind them, the sound of feet shuffling down the stairway suddenly echoed off the stone walls.

"You must hurry," the stranger insisted.

Immediately Paul sprinted down the corridor, the other two hot on his heels. Melting into the darkness, he glanced over his shoulder one last time, but saw no one—and there was no time to think about it.

Cold shadows eventually gave way to stark sunlight, and they found themselves standing in the middle of an empty street lined on both sides by crumbling stone buildings with boarded-up windows and doors. Dry-rotted power lines crisscrossed overhead and formed a tangled web that gave a strange definition to the otherwise sterile skyline. Embedded on a limestone-block wall directly across the street, a faded marble sign read: *Via Dolorosa*.

Farther down the street Paul noticed a lone soldier propped against a metal-framed door with no glass. A wisp of smoke trailed from the man's mouth as he glanced in their direction. He continued reading his newspaper.

With a calm but hurried cadence, Paul led his companions down the street in the opposite direction. When they reached the corner, he glanced back in time to see a figure emerge from the tunnel. A soldier.

The man motioned to his friend, who took a last drag from his cigarette and thumped it into a shrub. The two

met in the street.

A moment later, the soldier turned and pointed toward them. Paul shoved Elizabeth and Van Eaton around the corner ahead of him, and they took off at a run.

Sprinting down the narrow street that stair-stepped down every ten feet or so, the three frantically yanked on every door they came to. They were all locked. They fumbled their way farther, terrified that at any second the soldiers would be upon them.

Then Paul pushed and a door flung open, the key still in the lock. Grabbing the key, he rushed inside with Elizabeth and the professor shoving in behind him. He thrust the key into the backside of the lock and turned against the cylinder. It broke off, but not before the bolt slid into the jamb. They were safe, at least for the moment.

Paul pressed his face against the door and took several deep breaths. The cold metal felt good against his sweating brow. He shook nervously and squinted through the shadows.

The room had no windows and only the door through which they had entered. Beneath it a thin sliver of light filtered, providing faint illumination. Gradually his eyes adjusted to the darkness, and he strained to make out their surroundings.

As far as he could tell, the room was about twenty feet square. The ceiling was high, more than ten feet over their heads, he guessed, and when he took a step, the floor sounded as if it were made of wood.

Together they moved cautiously deeper into the darkness, their footsteps echoing off the walls. Suddenly, the door rattled and a voice jabbered from the other side.

They all froze. "They're right outside the door," Elizabeth whispered.

"Shh!" Van Eaton ordered. "I'm trying to hear what they're saying!"

The voice continued.

"They're wondering if we're in here, and . . . he says the door is locked, but he can break it down. But . . . they're not coming in."

The voices trailed off, and they all let out their breaths in relief.

For a moment there was stillness, then suddenly there was a crack, and the section of floor where they were standing dropped nearly a foot. They all stood frozen, fearing to move. Then before there was time to blink, the floor beneath their feet collapsed with a horrendous crash.

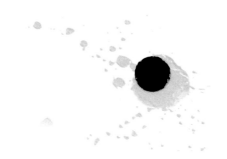

Nine

(11 Nisan, 33 A.D.)

An eerie stillness blanketed the dark abyss, much like a cold winter morning after a deep, wet snow. Gradually the choking dust began to settle, and a trickle of light found its way to the bottom of the chasm.

Elizabeth rubbed her eyes and tried to focus. "Professor . . . Paul?" she whispered, too frightened to raise her voice.

"My arm . . . " Van Eaton moaned. He dragged his fingers over the jagged bone that had punched through the skin. "It—it's broken." His speech slurred.

"Hold on. I can help you," Elizabeth said. "I've just got to free myself. Paul, are you okay?" Silence followed. "Paul!"

"Yeah . . . how about you?"

"I'm okay."

Elizabeth staggered to her feet and stood, perched on an unsettled mound of timbers. She steadied herself against the outer wall, which appeared to be made up of hundreds of smooth stones that formed a cylindrical pit. In the dim light she surmised that they were at least ten feet down, and to make matters worse, she could hear water trickling under her feet.

"Be careful. There are nails sticking out all over these boards!" She cautiously picked her way toward Van Eaton.

"Keep coming . . . I can see you. Is that water I hear?"

"I think so."

He touched his ear. "My hearing aid . . . "

"It must have dropped under the boards."

The professor lay across several large beams, with one leg dangling down between them. When Elizabeth reached him, she was surprised to find him as calm as he was, considering his gaping wound. Empathy swelled in her heart when she discovered the jagged bones protruding through his forearm and a steady stream of blood surging from the wound. She had to act quickly or he could slip into shock at any moment.

Pulling off her belt, she threaded it under Van Eaton's arm and slipped it back through the buckle. Blindly she swept her hand over the timbers around him until she found an eight-inch nail. She pulled it from a rotted beam, placed it through the leather strap, and twisted it tight.

"Ohh!"

"I'm sorry, but I'm gonna have to set this arm."

"I . . . I was afraid you were going to say that."

Elizabeth gently clasped the broken limb with her left hand and gained a firm grip with the other. She could hardly make out the professor's face.

"You ready?"

"Just do it!"

She pulled back the flap of skin and exposed the jagged bone. It had severed the radial artery, which was the cause of all the blood. She wedged her knee under the professor's armpit and gently grasped his wrist. Then she took a deep breath and stretched the bones apart. Van Eaton screamed, but Elizabeth stayed focused. Taking the butt of her right hand, she forced the fracture back into place.

Fortunately, the professor hadn't heard the crackling bones or felt the pain: He had passed out.

From across the room, Paul dealt with his own set of problems. He was wedged tightly between two timbers at the waist, and a third, larger beam had fallen perpendicular across the two, pinning him against the wall with one arm twisted behind his back.

With only one arm free, he reached blindly and found a nail in a beam above his head. Clinging to it, he tried to pull himself loose, but the harder he tugged, the more the timber around the nail crumbled. Suddenly it let go, and Paul slid deeper into the hole. To make matters worse, one foot landed in water.

"Uh oh." Urgency filled his voice.

Elizabeth checked Van Eaton's vitals as best she could. His breathing was shallow, and his pulse was weak but stable.

She loosened the tourniquet a half turn. The bleeding had stopped.

Good.

She ran her hands down the professor's free leg to his foot, removed his shoe, and pulled his sock off. After jamming his shoe back on, she wound the sock twice around the break and tied it off. Gradually she loosened the tourniquet. Still no sign of bleeding.

"We've got to get him out of here. Can you make it over here, Paul?"

"I . . . I'm trying . . . to get out. Hold on."

With all his strength, Paul thrust the nail he was holding into the beam over his head. It buried deep in the soft wood. Then he pulled delicately against the nail. It wiggled, but held and appeared strong enough to support his weight.

"I . . . think I've got it."

He pulled gingerly at first. But when the nail held, he exerted more force unil he pulled himself free. He worked his way over to the other two.

"He's lost a lot of blood and he's in shock."

"Yeah, and I've got some more good news. I think this place is filling up with water."

"I know."

The timbers creaked and squealed as the water noticeably rose in the room. Paul knew he and Elizabeth could tread water if need be, but Van Eaton was unconscious and trapped under several large beams.

"I figured that as the water rose, these timbers would float," said Elizabeth.

"Some of 'em are, but I don't think they're moving much."

"Well, he's wedged in, but I can't feel anything trapping him on this side. Can you reach down on your side and see what's got him stuck?"

Paul slid in beside Van Eaton and sank down into the black water, canting his head to the side to keep his face above the surface. "It feels like his leg . . . ah . . . right at the knee . . . is between two beams. I don't think . . . I can move 'em."

"We've got to do something or he'll drown."

And it's my fault. "I'm sorry I got us into this."

"Forget it," she said. "Here, hold his head up."

Paul cradled the professor's head and lifted it as far as his body would allow—which, at this point, was only a few inches above the water. He shifted to get a better grip, but Van's head slipped from his fingers and slid beneath the water. Bubbles gushed from the professor's mouth and nose as his head came to rest below the surface. Paul instantly thrust him up out of the water.

"Keep his head up!" Elizabeth shouted.

Now the situation was beyond critical.

"The water's rising at least an inch every couple of minutes," Paul said. "Given that the top of the pit looks to be about ten feet up, we've got about two hours or so to tread water."

"But what about the professor? We've got maybe five or six minutes before . . . " Silence followed her words.

Paul squinted through the darkness. "How long is that piece of wood floating beside you?"

Elizabeth ran her left hand the length of the board. "Maybe four feet."

"See if you can stick it down between the two beams here."

She maneuvered the end of the post between the two

beams and levered it back and forth.

"Careful—the water's splashing over his face every time you do that."

"It's not budging!"

"Here, hold him up for a second." Paul drew a couple of deep breaths and disappeared under the water, shivering as he groped blindly through the pitch-black waters.

If I can just get hold of something to push against, I think I can get him loose!

He wormed his hand between the professor's thigh and the beam and positioned his shoulder against it. Planting both feet against the outer wall, he pushed. Nothing.

He broke the surface and gasped a breath. *Dear God help me—I can't do this alone!*

He sucked in another breath and dropped below the surface, positioned himself, and pushed with all his strength. The beam suddenly moved, but not enough. With the last ounce of air in his lungs, he pressed again and the beam finally shifted. Van Eaton was free.

Paul broke the surface. "Thank you, Lord, thank you!" he gasped.

†   †   †

Standing waist-deep in the dark waters, they clutched their unconscious friend and contemplated their fate.

"We can just wait for the water to rise and float us out of here," Paul said.

"Yeah," Elizabeth agreed, but the timbre of her voice gave her away. "Not that it matters, but . . . I can't swim."

Paul combed his fingers through his hair. "You can float, can't you?"

"Yeah, but what about him?"

"Well, we've got a little while before the water is high enough to be a real threat. Maybe as it rises some of this stuff will come apart, and we'll be able to float up with it."

Suddenly Elizabeth lost her footing and wedged against another nail. "These nails are everywhere!"

"What did you say?"

"These beams are full of nails."

"Wait a minute. Can you hold him a minute?"

"What are you thinking?"

"I've got an idea." Paul drew a deep breath and dropped under the water. A moment later, he surfaced. "This is what." He clutched an eight-inch nail he'd pulled from a rotted beam.

He took the point of the nail and followed a groove between the stones until he found a void. The nail slid in smoothly. He clasped it with both hands and pulled himself halfway out of the water.

"I think this could work."

"I see what you're doing. There's one here at my feet too."

Paul took a deep breath, went back under the water, and after a few moments came up with two more nails.

He maneuvered back to the wall, where he steadied himself with the nail that was already there. He drove a

second spike in with the butt of his hand. With two nails now in place, he pulled himself completely out of the water. Waterlogged, he felt as if his weight had doubled.

"This isn't going to be easy."

He dropped back into the water and scoured for more nails. After a few minutes, both he and Elizabeth were able to find enough to do the job. Paul slipped them into his back pocket and again started up the wall, systematically placing each nail close enough to reach the next.

He inched his way higher and higher up the wall while Elizabeth looked on.

"You've got to hurry! The water's up to my neck!"

"I'm almost th-th-there." Paul shivered. Finally, he pulled himself carefully over the edge of the splintered floorboards. They creaked and sagged under his weight, and he quickly moved back to where they felt solid. "I'm out!"

"Thank God! Now we've got the professor," Elizabeth said. "Look around and see if you can find anything up there that we could use to pull him up."

Van Eaton moaned.

"Is he coming out of it?"

"Yeah, I think so."

Paul moved across the floor, feeling his way. On the opposite wall, he found a length of fabric draped between two hooks. He ripped it in half lengthways and tied the ends together, forming a cloth tether. Edging over to the hole, he knelt and dropped one end down to Elizabeth.

She looped it under the professor's armpits and tied a knot at his chest. "Can you hear me?"

Van Eaton opened his eyes and nodded.

"Can you pull yourself up with your good arm?"

"I . . . I think so."

Elizabeth took the hand of his uninjured arm and placed it on the first nail, then she positioned her shoulder in the small of the professor's back.

"Okay, Professor—here we go."

Elizabeth crouched and pushed while Van Eaton pulled against the nail, his broken arm dangling like a prosthetic limb at his side. Paul took up the slack, slowly lifting him out of the water. The fabric tightened around Van's chest, and he groaned.

"I'm sorry."

Van Eaton squinted up through the shadows at Paul, recalling the heated discussion they'd had on the plane. Twice in two days he'd had to defend his beliefs—or the lack thereof—and it had bothered him more than he'd let on. It was one thing for his students to engage him in the classroom; it was quite another to be accosted by a total stranger.

Oddly, Paul didn't seem like a stranger at all, and hadn't even when they first met. It was a bizarre feeling—the sense that you knew someone you had never encountered before.

Funny how fast animosity can disappear in a life-

threatening situation, Van reflected now. It was obvious Paul lived what he preached.

As Paul pulled from above and Elizabeth pushed from below, Van Eaton methodically made his way up the wall until he was within Paul's reach.

"Take my hand, Professor."

Van Eaton awkwardly extended his hand, and Paul heaved him over the edge and pulled him to where the boards were solid. He gently inspected the professor's wound while Elizabeth climbed to the top.

"Like rock climbing at the Y," she said, scrambling over the edge of the broken boards to join them.

Paul huffed, mentally giving her more credit than he'd first thought. The climb had nearly killed him.

The professor leaned up, and the three huddled on the dark, dusty floor taking slow, hard breaths and trying not to think of what might lie ahead.

TEN

(11 Nisan)

Elizabeth crouched and peered through the stale darkness, trying to catch a glimpse of the backpack she'd been holding just before the fall.

"I know I set it down right over here just before—there it is." She pulled her North Face bag from the rubble and rummaged through its contents, finally retrieving a smaller, more rigid bag the size of a small shaving kit and a bottle of water. She unzipped the leather pouch and poured out its contents: a roll of gauze, a handful of alcohol wipes, and the most important item of all. Mepergan.

"Are you allergic to any medication?"

Van Eaton shook his head.

"Well, take a couple of these. It'll take the edge off." Elizabeth handed him two tablets and snapped the lid shut. "Hang on to these."

Van Eaton dropped the pills in his mouth and took the bottle from Elizabeth. He swallowed hard.

"I think . . . I'm going to be sick."

"Just try to hold on, Professor, the medication should

111

take effect pretty quick, and there's something in there for your stomach too."

Elizabeth wound his swollen arm with gauze and tied it off. "We're going to have to get you to a hospital and get a proper set on that arm."

Van Eaton glanced toward the door. "What about our friends outside?"

She shrugged. "I don't know. I just know this arm needs attention."

"There it is." Paul plucked his camcorder from the floor and pressed the power button. It was dead.

"Don't you think you've caused enough trouble with that thing?" Van Eaton's tone was heavy.

"Look," Paul whispered. "I didn't do anything wrong, you know."

"Yeah, well, you might want to tell that to our friends outside."

"Maybe they wouldn't listen. But their superiors might."

"I don't know, Paul, we're Americans and a long way from home," Elizabeth reminded him. "What makes you think they'd believe us anyway?"

"Because I have the tape."

"I can't argue with that, but we've got to get out of here in one piece first."

Paul considered their dilemma. At last he headed toward the door. Sunbeams pierced its cracks and illuminated the dust that hung in the air like smoke.

He pressed his face to the roughhewn frame and peered into the street. It was empty. Then suddenly the light that pierced the door flickered and reappeared. Again it happened—and again.

Paul drew a deep breath and squinted through the crack. "Something's going on," he whispered. But I can't tell what."

He looked as far up the street as the door would allow and watched while people poured into the street. The air was suddenly electric. People gathered on rooftops and in every conceivable nook along the way. Paul tried to see who or what was coming, but it was no use. The crowd now swelled to the walls on both sides of the street and blocked his view.

"What's going on?" Elizabeth demanded.

"It must be that reenactment. Remember the tour guide?"

"That's right—it's Palm Sunday."

"Any sign of those soldiers?" Van asked.

"I can't see a thing, but even if they are out there, we'd stand a better chance out in the open than if they found us in here. There's wall-to-wall people out there."

"Well, you want to try it?" Elizabeth said.

"I don't see why not. What have we got to lose?"

Elizabeth helped the professor to his feet. "Whoa . . . I'm a little woozy."

"I'll bet. That was a hundred milligrams of Mepergan." She draped her backpack over one shoulder and pulled Van's good arm around the other. "Tell me if I hurt you."

"Thank you for the pills. I—I don't know what I would have done without them."

Elizabeth glanced at Paul. "Why don't you step out there and take a quick look around first?"

Paul nodded and pulled hard against the handle, but it didn't budge. Then he remembered the lock.

"There's no lock on this door." Paul glanced around the room and hesitated. "This isn't the door I locked—the one we came through." He raked his hand across the rough wooden slats. "It was metal."

"It doesn't matter. Let's just get out of here."

With both hands, Paul pried the door open, scraping it against the stone floor as he pulled. Two men stood in the doorway, facing the street.

"Excuse me, Paul said, his voice guarded. "Can we get out?"

The two men studied Paul and his companions with blank stares, then looked down at their wet clothing dripping pools at their feet.

When Paul repeated the question, Van Eaton grabbed him by the shirtsleeve. "How did you do that?"

"Do what?"

Van Eaton wiped his face. "You just spoke the most fluent, colloquial Aramaic I ever heard."

Paul exchanged glances with Elizabeth.

"I'm telling you—you spoke perfect Aramaic!"

"It must be the Mepergan," Elizabeth mumbled.

They both shouldered Van Eaton and wrangled their way through the door. Snaking through the thickest part of the crowd, they pushed through a sea of faces, hoping none of them would catch a glimpse of a black beret or an Uzi.

When they reached the far side of the street, Elizabeth propped Van Eaton against a tent post and stepped back into the street with Paul. "I'll keep an eye on him. Why don't you take a look around?"

Paul craned his neck and massaged his chin. "Okay. I'll be back."

Van Eaton stroked his arm and gazed up at Elizabeth. It was clear that uncertainty flooded his soul as he attempted to speak.

"C-can you hear the voices?" he asked. "Can you understand what they are saying?"

Elizabeth welled with empathy for the professor. *He's hallucinating.*

"Can you hear the voices?"

"No, Professor, I'm sorry, but I don't."

"That's what I'm talking about—say that again."

"Say what again?"

"Anything—just say anything."

"Calm down. Everything is going to be okay."

Van Eaton gaped at her. A tremor in his voice, he said, "Look, I am a professor of religious history. I speak four languages fluently, and I distinctly hear two languages when you speak!"

The professor's words begged a reply, but Elizabeth said nothing.

"I can hear English and Hebrew—or Aramaic—with every word you speak! Do you understand me?"

"Understand what?"

"See?"

"See what?"

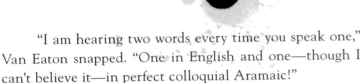

"I am hearing two words every time you speak one," Van Eaton snapped. "One in English and one—though I can't believe it—in perfect colloquial Aramaic!"

This guy's Looney Tunes, Elizabeth thought.

† † †

Paul threaded his way deeper into the now-exuberant crowd. The people waved palm branches and garments in the air and scattered them on the ground in front of a lone rider on a donkey, who was still some distance away. Paul was amazed at the realism and painstaking detail that all the participants had taken to make the whole play seem so real, even down to removing any modern items from along the street.

Beaming, he shouted to Elizabeth over the crowd. "Can you believe this!" He waved his arm at the montage of players who cleared the way for the Messiah. "This is the very ground where it all actually happened! This is unbelievable!"

Elizabeth glanced at Van Eaton, who appeared to be in a daze. "We still need to get him to a hospital. His arm is not life threatening, but I'm afraid he may be having an allergic reaction to the medication, and that's nothing to play around with."

"I'm allergic to nothing!" Van Eaton scoffed. "I distinctly hear two voices every time both of you speak! Is that so hard for you to understand? Surely, if I can hear two voices at once you can understand one, can you not?"

"What about the other people here? Are they speaking

in two languages?"

Van Eaton furrowed his brow. "You just said the words *two languages* in two languages. I'm really having a problem with this."

Elizabeth was speechless. She couldn't help but discount what the professor was saying, considering his state of mind.

"I've seen this too many times to give any validity to it," she told Paul, her back turned to the professor. "This isn't rocket science. He's obviously hallucinating."

Paul took the measure of the professor's words. If being a counselor in the ministry had taught him anything at all, it was to listen and consider every word a person said. He was convinced that the professor believed implicitly that what he was experiencing was real, and even though it was far fetched to say the least, Paul felt deep in his soul that somehow the professor could be telling the truth.

"Professor, what is the second language you hear?" he asked.

"It's Aramaic—or at least a form of it, a language

that was spoken here centuries ago." Van Eaton massaged his arm. "Do you think I'm making this up?"

"No, I'm just trying to understand it. What about the other people? What languages are they speaking?"

"Just one language. It's Aramaic, there is no question."

What the professor was saying made no sense. Paul could hear the people around them talking and shouting, and they were definitely doing so in English.

As they considered the drama, the actor who played Jesus drew near to them. Slowly and confidently he moved through the throngs until he was within a few yards of where they stood. Even with all the commotion, he paused and flashed a compassionate smile.

Paul couldn't look away. The man was amazingly steadfast and resolute. His face was leathered and coarse, and yet it beamed! He was beautiful. He was homely. He was fascinating to behold, and although he was an actor, he seemed perfect for the part, down to the frayed sandals tied around his dusty ankles.

He was clothed in an ankle-length tan tunic under a darker outer garment bound around the waist with a wide leather belt. He was dressed virtually like every other person in the crowd, and yet he was somehow different.

This man is as much like Christ as any man could ever be, Paul thought.

The crowd, the authenticity of the setting, and the special attention to detail all made for an unforgettably realistic performance. And yet, there was something more, something that was strangely familiar about this man.

"That was the man," Van said, his voice raised above the din of the crowd.

Paul turned his eyes to the professor. "What?"

"In the tunnel! That was the man who led us through!"

Paul's eyes flitted to Elizabeth, who nodded. He was

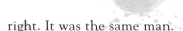

right. It was the same man.

While the procession drifted farther down the crowded street, the man they'd hailed as Messiah stopped and gazed back into the crowd. He took the arm of one close to him and motioned in the direction of Paul and his companions.

The man came to meet them in the street. "The Master wants you to join us." He gazed curiously at their clothing as he spoke.

"Now?" Paul asked.

"No. We'll go to the outskirts of the city tonight. Then after that, He'll let us know." He smiled. "He always does."

Elizabeth stepped closer to Paul. "Who?"

"Why, Jesus of Nazareth!" the man said with a spirited tone.

The air was suddenly thick with consequences not yet defined. Paul harbored the illusory hope that the man somehow spoke the truth.

"I must hurry back," he said, moving away. "But please join us." His voice faded as he melted into the crowd.

Suddenly Paul's mind was ablaze with the inconceivable notion that what was happening was actually real. While they stood staring in the direction the procession had taken, the throngs of people who had gathered seemingly from nowhere only moments before were now disbanding almost as quickly, leaving trampled palm branches and a few articles of clothing lying in the street. Dirty-faced children quickly gathered the remnants and scurried off in every direction.

"What is going on here?" Elizabeth asked. "And why did he call him Jesus—just as if He were?"

Van Eaton rolled his eyes and ambled back to the edge of the street.

"Let him go," Paul said. "We'll deal with him in a minute."

"Not to change the subject, but did you notice all of these tents and this . . . this whole market thing when we ran through here earlier?" She motioned to the tents that lined the street on both sides.

Paul looked around. "To tell you the truth, I don't remember any of this. But I thought it was just me."

He studied their surroundings more closely, recalling the foot race that brought them to the well room, but everything seemed different.

"We ran down this street, right?" Elizabeth glanced in both directions.

"That's right, and then we rounded the corner . . . " Paul's voice trailed off as cold fingers kneaded his spine. He stared at Elizabeth. "Where are we?" The obvious question now seemed anything but.

Elizabeth absorbed the question but gave no immediate answer. "I don't know," she said slowly after a moment, "but we seem to be drawing a few stares. We probably ought to get out of the street."

† † †

Elizabeth crossed the street to Van Eaton, who steadied himself against a pole that supported a frayed awning flapping lazily in the desert air. The professor rubbed his arm and focused on her.

"What are we going to do?"

She shrugged. "I don't know. This whole thing is weird."

He dabbed the sweat from his brow with his sleeve. "What are you saying?"

"It's just that . . . everything looks different. Just look around."

He directed a superficial glance around him. It was clear he also sensed that something was amiss, but that appeared to be as far as it went.

Paul walked out into the street. "Where are all the power lines?" he asked, as if questioning his own sanity. "I know they were there."

Suddenly the color drained from his face. "Ah . . . I know this sounds crazy, but, do you think it's possible . . . I mean . . . could it be possible?" He stared at Elizabeth as if looking right through her.

She moved closer to him. "What?"

Paul's brain scrambled to make sense. "I know we are in Jerusalem," he said flatly.

"And?"

"And, I know this sounds crazy, but have we somehow—I can't believe I'm saying this. Have we somehow traveled back in time . . . to the time of Christ?" A look of marvel swept over his face.

Elizabeth's skin prickled.

"And you said *I* was hallucinating!" Van Eaton mocked.

"Hold on, Professor, let's think about this." Elizabeth surveyed their surroundings and considered Paul's theory. "Why are there no wires or poles? They were obviously there when we ran down the street earlier. And all of these tents. I don't remember any of this before—"

Suddenly, a strange voice interrupted. They all turned to see a wormy looking man standing under the awning. He was dressed in a long tunic like the people in the crowd, with a turban wound around his head. His eyes bulged as he took them in from head to toe.

"Who are you?" His voice was heavy with suspicion and threat. "I have never seen such strange clothing—"

"We just arrived from Rome," Paul cut him off hurriedly. "It's the latest fashion there."

Elizabeth glanced at him, eyebrows raised. He

returned her look, giving his head a slight warning shake.

Still obviously on guard, the man began to straighten his wares. "Do you see something that interests you?" His voice was nasal and obnoxious.

"Ah, I'm sorry. We were just leaving." Paul turned to go.

"Wait, my friends." The man's tone was now more receptive. "Your speech suggests that you are educated. Please come closer. I have many fine goods that should interest you."

Elizabeth stayed behind Paul as he went to look over the merchant's seedy collection of clothing.

Van Eaton backed away, looking alarmed. *How could they have even understood what the man had said? He was speaking Aramaic!* And an even greater oddity was the language they returned. It was their voice—and it was in two very distinct languages!

"Do you see anything you like?" the merchant repeated. He grinned lopsidedly and exposed a mouthful of decaying teeth. "What about this fine headdress?" His attention centered on Elizabeth.

She took the length of blue cotton cloth he offered and slipped it over her head, letting it drape over her shoulders and down her back. She cocked her head to one side as if looking into a mirror.

"How do I look?"

"You look like you belong here," Paul said.

"What did you say?"

"You look like you belong here. You know, a local."
Immediately his eyes widened with wonder as he caught on.

Rummaging through the stacks of garments, he found several linen tunics that would work. He pulled one from the stack and held it up against his shoulders. *One size fits all,* he thought.

"See if you can find something you can wear," he whispered to Elizabeth.

"What?"

"Well, if we're truly when and where we think we are, we have to dress the part, don't we?"

"I guess so," Elizabeth conceded.

From the stack Paul pulled a smaller, more colorful cotton tunic decorated with intricate needlework. He handed it to her.

"Try this one."

She held it up to her shoulders. It was a little long, but it would do.

While they sifted through the wares, Van Eaton made his way over to where they stood. In his hand were two more pills.

"Do you have some water?" His breathing was now more labored.

"Right here, my friend."

The merchant lifted a wooden pail from under the table and plucked the ladle from the murky water. He handed it to the professor who stuffed the pills in his mouth and washed them down.

"Professor, we need to talk," Elizabeth said. "We've decided to buy some clothes."

"For what?"

"We want to try to find the man they called Jesus of Nazareth," Paul said.

Van Eaton huffed and shook is head.

"I know, I know—it sounds crazy. But do you have a better suggestion?"

Van Eaton stroked his arm and glanced at them both. "I just know my arm is killing me and I need some attention here."

"Look around you, Professor," Elizabeth demanded. "Do you see *anything* around here that looks like it did when we came through here earlier?

"Well what do you want me to do about it?"

"Just trust us," Paul said. "I can't help but believe this could all be happening for a reason—and I think we need to follow the people in the procession."

"Then what?" Van Eaton asked.

"I don't know. Just come with us," Paul pleaded. "We don't have all of the answers. We just feel like we need to find the man they called Jesus and see if we can figure out what's going on."

Van Eaton heaved a sigh. "Well, I guess I don't have much of a choice do I?" He kicked the dust as he spoke.

Paul pulled a third tunic from the pile, along with some heavier garments the merchant called mantles, headdresses, and a couple of wide leather belts. He drew Van Eaton along with him to the back of the tent to change.

Elizabeth dug through the clothing and selected a mantle and a matching wool belt she felt coordinated nicely with the blue head scarf. When the men rejoined her, looking properly authentic and carrying their damp clothing rolled in a bundle, she went to the back and replaced her clothing as quickly as possible.

She rolled up her clothes as the men had, deciding, at least for now, to keep her shoes. Satisfied with her appearance, she followed the men into the street, feeling a little less conspicuous—or at least as much as three Caucasians could be.

"And my payment?" the merchant called after them indignantly.

Elizabeth glared at Paul. "I didn't think about that," she whispered, "but if we're right in our thinking, our money won't be any good either."

She returned to the tent, placed her backpack on the table, and peeled open the Velcro flap. The merchant watched curiously.

"I know I had my money here somewhere." As she rummaged through the contents, a pair of prescription Ray-Bans slid out onto the table. She picked them up and without thinking slid them on.

Gasping, the merchant stepped back. "May . . . I . . . see them?" he asked, staring curiously at Elizabeth's face.

Behind her she could hear Paul's snort of laughter.

"Sure, but they're prescript—" She stopped, pulled the glasses from her ears, and handed them to the merchant, who awkwardly put them on.

His eyes widened with excitement. He stepped from behind the table and hurried into the street, dancing like a wild man, before racing back to her.

He leaned close to Elizabeth and breathed the nastiest breath she'd ever smelled. "How much?" he asked eagerly.

"I . . . I don't know," she answered.

"Just name your price!"

Suddenly she had an idea. "How about the headdresses and the clothing?"

"Yes, take them," he answered.

"Maybe three of these bedrolls?"

"You mean the sleep mats? That's fine—yes."

Noticing several goatskin bags, she plucked one from the pile and pulled the wooden plug. It contained a pungent, full-bodied wine. "And this one along with the two empties?"

The man's smile eroded. "You drive a hard bargain, my friend, especially for a woman. That wine is very special—from my sister's wedding nearly three years ago." Then his smile returned. "We have a bargain, then." He extended his hand to put an end to the trade which he felt still weighed heavily in his favor.

† † †

The threesome rolled their belongings into their sleep mats. Fumbling with his good arm, Van Eaton rolled up his soggy wallet and inhaler between the rough layers of hemp cloth. He worked his wristwatch up his arm and glanced at the face. It read April 5. He hid it under his sleeve.

Elizabeth removed her watch as well and carefully

shook it out. The face had been smashed in the fall, and the crystal was full of water, but she wanted to keep it. It had been a gift from Brad.

Now situated, the unlikely trio started down the dusty road in hopes of finding the man who had been hailed the Messiah. Three lone threads in a tapestry without a clue as to the magnificent pattern God was weaving.

ELEVEN

(11 Nisan)

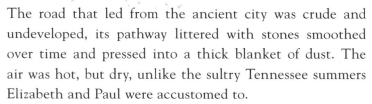

The road that led from the ancient city was crude and undeveloped, its pathway littered with stones smoothed over time and pressed into a thick blanket of dust. The air was hot, but dry, unlike the sultry Tennessee summers Elizabeth and Paul were accustomed to.

Following the roadway southward, the trio stirred the powdery soil with every step, occasionally rousing small dust devils that whirled and vanished with the desert breeze. On either side of the beaten path, an occasional wisp of green pushed through the rocky soil, with a scrub bush or two here and there. But as a whole, there was little foliage, and there were certainly no shade trees close by.

The desert sun scorched everything within its blistering grasp. Even the clothing they wore didn't shield them from the burning rays that penetrated the coarse fabric. Squinting at the road ahead of them, Elizabeth wished she had her Ray-Bans back.

"You know, if this is truly happening the way we think it is, how is it that we understood the merchant back there in the city?" she asked. "Or for that matter, how did he understand us?"

Paul stared vacantly into the distance. "I don't know. This is all so surreal. Maybe the whole two-language thing with the professor is part of it." He nodded back to Van Eaton. "What do you think about him?"

"Well," Elizabeth whispered, "he's got problems that's for sure."

"That's a given."

"No, I'm not talking about his arm. There's something else going on there." She stepped up the pace, keeping out of earshot from Van Eaton.

"What do you mean?" Paul asked.

"It's just that: what we're doing—or what we're trying to do," she explained. "The Professor seems to have a real problem with us trying to find . . . trying to find Jesus." Her gaze fell to the ground. "That sounds so weird."

"Tell me about it."

"Anyway, it's almost like he's against it. I guess we just need to give him a little more time."

"You know, as bizarre as it sounds, it's almost as if the soldiers and the whole thing with the well was supposed to happen." Paul massaged his temples as he spoke.

"I know. I feel the same way. I guess all things really do work together for good—"

A smile inched across Paul's face. "To them that love the Lord."

The professor lumbered along like a disgruntled bear, cradling his arm and occasionally tugging at his tunic as he walked. The desert sun had begun to take its toll, and Paul could see that Elizabeth wanted to rest as much as he did. They stopped and waited for the professor to catch up.

Paul looked toward the city and noticed the skyline, how it was all so very different from what he'd seen the day before. His eyes followed the crisp contours of the massive walls painted against the wide expanse of desert and how they formed a jagged edge against the late afternoon sky. This was certainly not the view they'd witnessed from the taxicab the day before. It now held more of a rustic charm—a sort of mysterious ambience, pure and undefiled by the modernisms of man.

His thoughts were numbed as he considered all the events that had taken place since the early morning. The tour, the apparent murder, the fall into the well, and seeing the one they called Jesus. He squeezed his eyes shut and prayed, though he didn't know exactly what to say. But most of all, he hoped that when he opened his eyes, he wouldn't find it all just a dream.

"This isn't easy, you know?" Van Eaton snapped. He clutched his arm and sighed.

Paul draped his arm around the professor and turned him toward the city. "Look at it, Professor. It's certainly not the sight we saw yesterday—is it?"

Van Eaton coughed and spit on the ground. "I saw nothing. I was in the airport until ten o'clock last night. I told you that."

Paul recoiled.

A slender pole with a large clay pot fastened to one end and a large stone strapped to the other balanced precariously over the open cistern near the edge of the road. Van Eaton watched as Elizabeth removed the plugs from the wineskins and dipped them into the cool water. She then took the

wine from the third skin and mixed it with the other two. Replacing the plugs, she shook the bags.

"What are you doing?" Paul asked.

"This will purify the water, somewhat at least," she said. "This water seems to be okay, but the stuff the professor drank back in the city looked awful."

"It was awful." Van Eaton instinctively reached to adjust the volume on his hearing aid, then remembered it was long gone. "Could I . . . ah." He gestured for the wineskin, his bushy eyebrows rising as he spoke.

"Just a little. You've had two hundred milligrams of Mepergan in less than four hours," she warned.

Van Eaton took the pouch and pressed it to his lips. He swirled the wine in his mouth, savoring the taste. With a gulp he swallowed. It was exquisite. He turned the pouch up again.

"Whoa, Professor, I said a little." She took the pouch and replaced the plug.

Van Eaton arched his back and peered through open fingers at the sun. He nudged Elizabeth as two women approached, both delicately balancing large clay pots on their heads.

Taking care not to make eye contact with the men, the two women positioned their jars in front of the counter-weighted beam and lowered the container into the pool. Then they both hung on the end of the pole and swung the jar to the edge of the cistern in a clearly common routine.

Paul laid his belongings on the ground and offered to help. The women seemed surprised that they had even been spoken to at all.

"Thank you, sir, but we have wrestled with the *shaduf* before."

Again, their words mystified the professor. There were still two, very distinct languages—though the words were less discernible.

He watched while Paul filled the pot and returned the pole to its original position. The older woman gracefully lifted her jar to her shoulder, then to her head. Paul helped the younger woman with hers.

"We are looking for a group that traveled this road earlier today, led by a man on a donkey," Paul said.

The woman's olive-toned face brightened immediately and she smiled, exposing a slight gap between her two front teeth, "You mean Jesus of Nazareth?" she asked eagerly. " Yes, they are just over the next rise."

Paul made eye contact with Elizabeth and smiled. *Jesus.*

"He healed my sister only a few days ago." She motioned toward the older woman who seemed impatient.

"She had been crippled since we were children."

The older sister sighed and situated her load. "It still hurts when I walk," she grumbled. Her animated face was now more provocative than pretty.

The younger woman quietly shook her head. "She just doesn't see what the Master has done for her, she—"

"Alina! We must go! Hurry before the night falls."

The younger woman bowed her head. "We are Greek,"

she said softly. "My family and I arrived here in Jerusalem a few days ago. We too came to see Jesus."

They're Greek? Van Eaton thought.

"You said you are from Greece?" Paul asked.

"Yes, from Delphi," she answered confidently, as if they should know exactly where it was. "And you?"

"We are from—" Paul turned to Elizabeth, then back. "The West," he answered hesitantly.

"The West?" She brushed a stray lock from her face.

"Actually we're from . . . another country."

"And how is it that you speak my language so well?"

Paul was considering a plausible response when a man appeared at the top of the hill.

"Andra! Alina! Come quickly!" he shouted. "We are almost ready to eat!"

"We must hurry. Would you join us?"

Paul grinned sheepishly, thinking about how long it had been since breakfast. "Yes, thank you. We would love to."

A thick pillar of black smoke billowed from a crackling fire. Rich aromas of pungent herbs saturated the late afternoon air like bouquets of unfamiliar flowers that instantly made memories. Elizabeth and Paul unwittingly hurried their steps without a thought of Van Eaton, who plodded along and drifted even farther behind.

The sun now sank low into the desert sky, melting

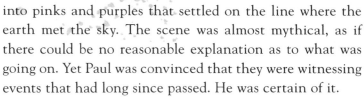

into pinks and purples that settled on the line where the earth met the sky. The scene was almost mythical, as if there could be no reasonable explanation as to what was going on. Yet Paul was convinced that they were witnessing events that had long since passed. He was certain of it.

People buzzed around the blazing fire, hurrying to make their final preparations for the meal. One woman tended slabs of meat that were skewered and roasting over red-hot coals, while a child smuggled a taste. A boy brushed down a donkey while her foal tried to nurse. She nudged him away.

At the same time, children stirred glowing embers with thick branches while clusters of sparks crackled and swirled into the darkening sky. Squeals of delight filled the night air with anticipation, and the little jenny brayed with excitement.

Then they recognized Him. He sat peacefully on a stump in the center of the assembly, listening to the men who sat all around Him. He smiled with deference and nodded kindly at Elizabeth and Paul, then turned back to the conversation.

"Did you see that?" Paul asked.

Elizabeth drew a deep breath and shivered. "He noticed us."

Paul couldn't quite conceive the contentment he felt, while at the same time feeling overcome with excitement. How would he share this with Laura? Would she ever be able to believe him?

Will I ever even see her again? He shook the thought from his mind.

† † †

Elizabeth realized that before anything else, their first priority was to get the professor situated, though it was almost impossible not to drop everything they were doing and join the group. On the other side of the road, she and Paul found a suitable site to make camp. They unfurled their sleep mats, and Elizabeth gently lowered the professor to the ground. He feebly worked his mat up against a smooth stone and positioned himself against it.

From the other camp, the younger of the Greek women made her way across the road, her arms loaded with food.

"Why did you not come? We would have made room."

"No, no, it's fine." Paul took the food and a skin of wine that dangled from her shoulder. He placed it on Elizabeth's mat and they sorted through the food.

Two loaves of bread wrapped loosely in a coarse

napkin were still very hot. There were olives, dates, and all sorts of delectables that smelled wonderful, and Elizabeth was starving. Unwrapping the last of the food, she looked sympathetically at the professor. It was apparent that he wasn't doing well.

"I will bring you a blanket." She spoke softly.

Van Eaton returned her smile without comment.

"The Master will speak to us after the meal," the young Greek woman told them. "We would have you join us."

"We would be honored," Elizabeth said.

She and Paul devoured their food while Van Eaton methodically inspected his. He smelled it, then hesitantly sampled it. To Elizabeth it tasted as good as it smelled—not that the professor would have acknowledged the fact.

† † †

The group stood and moved closer to the fire, which was now more smoke than flame. As Jesus prepared to speak, they spread out on the ground.

"Professor, do you feel like walking over?" Paul asked.

"No. I'm tired and I don't feel good."

""Would you mind if we—"

"Do whatever you like. I've got to get some rest."

Swirls of stratus clouds curled in splendor against rose-pink skies that faded into a colorless canvas. The first of the stars took their place in the heavens as Paul and

Elizabeth crossed the road. They met the young Greek woman halfway. She had three blankets and a container of hot coals.

"I'll attend to the old one." She flashed a smile.

They thanked her and hurried across the road, their faces wreathed with smiles as they found a place and quietly sat down. Sharing the warmth of the fire, they felt a surreal

ambience descend upon the group, and faces glistened with expectancy as the Master began.

The very sound of His voice was melodic and calming, resonating with perfect chords of truth as He uttered words of welcome. He paused long enough to make sure He had their undivided attention. Then, with a surgeon's precision, He pierced their hearts with words so intrinsically poetic that they seemed to spill from His lips effortlessly.

All who were within the sound of His voice feasted upon the morsels of God, there could be no doubt. There was no question as to who this man was or His intentions. His voice would calm the most panic-stricken heart, Paul reflected, and His words were like seeds of hope sprinkled upon the soft, fertile soil of despair.

How is this possible? Paul thought. *"I am in the presence of the living, breathing, Son of God—I am certain of it!* Tears slid down his cheeks as he surrendered to the reality of the moment.

The realization that they were literally in the presence of the human embodiment of the God of the universe was almost too much for him to fathom. Silently, emotion swept over Paul's soul. This was real. For the first time in his life he peered through eyes that now had the scales of doubt removed and replaced with the crystal clarity of God's perfect truth. And he sensed that Elizabeth felt the same way.

As Jesus spoke, Paul noticed that some of the people wept along with him and Elizabeth, while others showed little if any emotion at all. He even noticed one man who was absorbed with a loose thread on his sleeve.

How could this be? he thought. Had they heard Christ speak so often that they were simply accustomed to the poignancy of His message? Perhaps His words and soothing demeanor had become commonplace. After all, they were His disciples, or so it seemed. Or maybe they didn't understand at all.

But for him and Elizabeth, Paul realized, this was hardly the case. They both had an insight that even Jesus' own disciples did not possess—knowing exactly what was going on, and more important, knowing the events that were to come.

"What I wouldn't give for my voice recorder right now," Elizabeth whispered.

Paul nodded. "This is unbelievable. I not only can't believe what I'm hearing, I also can't believe *who* I'm hearing it from!"

Jesus continued speaking. "The hour has come for the Son of Man to be glorified. I tell you the truth, unless a kernel of wheat falls to the ground and dies, it remains

only a single seed, but if it dies, it produces many seeds."
He stirred the dust. "The man who loves his life will lose
it, while the man who hates his life in this world will keep
it for eternal life. He whoever serves me must follow me;
and where I am, my servant will also be." He paused and
glanced into the darkness. "My father will honor the one
who serves me."

Jesus' face took on yet another expression—one that
was humble and warm, though occasionally a piercing
stare pricked the hearts of those around him. To Paul it
was incredibly obvious that this was no ordinary man. The
eloquent message He so fervently delivered was as timeless
and relevant to Paul as it was to the people of Jesus' day,
and the stark reality was that it was being delivered two
thousand years before Paul's own time. The thought
confounded his brain.

As the message reached its crescendo, Jesus gazed
into the star-strewn sky. He drew a deep breath and sighed.
"Now my heart is troubled. And what shall I say—Father
save me from this hour? No, it was for this very reason I
came to this hour."

Paul looked around him, amazed that the group as a
whole seemed oblivious as to what Jesus was saying. Had
He shared so many parables that they assumed this was yet
another? There was no real way of knowing, but the fact
remained that His hour was indeed coming, and this was
only the beginning of sorrows.

Then Jesus stood perfectly still, squinting through

the darkness as if staring a hole right through someone. "Father, glorify your name," He said softly, lifting His hands into the air as He spoke.

The words had barely spilled from His lips when a solemn voice answered. "I have glorified it, and will glorify it again." The words rumbled like thunder from crystal clear skies.

Jesus glanced into the faces of His chosen few, sadness creeping through. "This voice was for your benefit, not mine. Now is the time for judgment on this world; now the prince of this world will be driven out. But when I am lifted up from the earth, I will draw all men to myself."

Suddenly He focused on Paul and Elizabeth as if He knew exactly who they were. Paul froze, felt Elizabeth stiffen beside him, as Jesus pursed His lips to speak. But then He arched His back and yawned. The day had been long, and Paul knew He had to be exhausted.

"We will gather tomorrow," Jesus said. Turning, He whispered to the man closest to Him and gestured toward Elizabeth and Paul. While the group disbanded, He made His way over to them.

"Would you care to sit and talk for a while?" He asked wearily.

Their words were barely audible for their excitement. "We would love to talk to you!"

"I would like that. Perhaps over there." Jesus motioned in the direction of their camp.

A cluster of glowing embers was all that remained of a smoldering fire when they returned to their makeshift camp. Quietly Elizabeth found a place to sit, trying not to disturb the professor, who slept soundly. Glancing over at Van Eaton, Paul cautiously lowered himself beside her.

Jesus leaned back against a large boulder and made Himself comfortable. He seemed more tired than talkative as He prodded a flame to life from the embers. The light danced across His face, quietly setting the mood.

Elizabeth sat nervously erect; her legs tightly crossed—though doing so exposed her modern footwear. She saw that Jesus noticed, but He said nothing. He gazed affectionately from her to Paul.

"Today was a special day," He said softly, "for today the first of Zechariah's prophecies was fulfilled." He stroked His beard and His eyes wandered. "And today brought me one step closer—"

He stopped. Draping His forearms across His knees, He allowed his hands to dangle freely and gazed into the fire, His eyes reflecting the flames. "Still they don't understand."

Elizabeth sat in silence, mesmerized. A thousand questions surfaced in her mind, and a thousand more surely would.

Why had He come to them tonight? And why had He asked them to follow Him? Did He know who they were?

Or why they were even there in the first place? Maybe He knew nothing about them at all. Maybe—

Again, Jesus pursed his lips to speak. "Paul . . . and Elizabeth." A smile captured His face.

Elizabeth's eyes flitted to Paul. With His words, it seemed that all her hopes and dreams had become reality. She felt dazed and confused, as if she had just heard their names read from the Lamb's Book of Life. Judging from his expression, it was clear Paul felt the same.

They both suddenly wept uncontrollably. It was literally all they were capable of doing.

As the moments passed, Elizabeth struggled to gain her composure, saw that Paul was having as little success as she was. The professor, still sleeping soundly, turned and wheezed, but didn't waken. Elizabeth had to admit she was glad they didn't have to deal with his attitude.

She edged closer to Jesus, with Paul crowding close. His words had unmistakably disarmed them of any doubts. And now their only desire was to listen to His every word, to study His face, to understand the things He held as important.

"And the injured man who is sleeping?" Jesus said.

An awkward silence followed. "That's . . . Professor Van Eaton," Paul said timidly. "He joined us in Jerusalem this morning."

Jesus smiled as if He knew the rest of the story. This seemed to please Him.

"You have come for a very specific purpose . . . for

you possess something that none other on earth possesses. Not even my disciples." Craning His neck, He gazed across the road as though to confirm that they were alone. "You bear the knowledge of what will inevitably unfold. The treachery, the deceit, the denials." He stroked his beard and drew a deep breath. "And my path. You know why I am here . . . " His voice trailed off.

Elizabeth studied His face by the glimmering firelight. So many thoughts tumbled through her mind that reading Him should have been difficult, but it was not. She knew unmistakably that He spoke from His heart and that His heart was pure. That had been evident from the very first words she had heard Him speak. That anyone could ever have misinterpreted His words or His motives seemed outrageous to her. Even more than outrageous—ludicrous.

"You have faith because of their faith—a faith, that as of yet, they do not even possess." He pushed His sleeves up over His elbows. "But when I'm gone those things will change. They will become men."

He peered into the darkness and cleared His throat.

"And there is something else you must understand." Now He stared directly into their faces—though it wasn't that He didn't already possess their undivided attention. "There is nothing you can do to change what is about to happen. You must understand this above all else."

Elizabeth stared at Jesus more intently, not fully comprehending what He was saying.

"You said we were here for a specific purpose," Paul

broke in, his voice hoarse. "But what purpose? Are we here to be spectators only, to watch what we know will surely come to pass?" He smeared the tears from his cheeks.

Jesus' expression hardened. "The Father also waits and watches, just as you must do. He, too, understands why I have come and will watch as I take the cup, knowing, as I do, that there is no other way."

Jesus inched closer to the dying fire and quietly scrawled something in the dust with His finger. At last He stood and stretched.

"Your professor sleeps soundly."

He walked over to Van Eaton and knelt quietly by his side. For a moment, He said nothing. He simply caressed the injured limb and combed His fingers through the professor's silver hair. While Van Eaton breathed heavily, Jesus spoke a few inaudible words, then stood.

He returned to Elizabeth and Paul, smiling. "We will be together tomorrow." He extended his arms and pulled them both close to His chest.

"You are why I'm here." His voice broke.

Elizabeth was again swept with emotion, sobbing softly as she embraced Jesus. His thin frame seemed almost frail to her, yet his strapping arms and callused hands held her securely.

He loosened His grip. "There is much to do, these next few days."

Paul hesitated, and then drew back. Elizabeth was reluctant to let go, but finally did as well.

"I love you," He said tenderly, his eyes wet with tears, "and I'm glad you're here."

Both were speechless. Elizabeth knew that this was where they were supposed to be. There could be no doubt.

"But what about—"

Jesus placed a finger to His pursed lips. "Shh—have patience. The answers to your questions will be made known."

Paul nodded gently. "Lord, we are so honored to be with you, here in this place."

Jesus smiled at both of them, then turned and disappeared into the darkness. Impulsively Elizabeth reached out to Paul and, weeping, they embraced. They had finally met Jesus!

TWELVE

(12 Nisan)

The first glimmer of dawn silently shed its light on the makeshift camp. Embers from the campfire, now cold and gray, lay dormant. The three travelers slept soundly, all thoughts of the previous night, for now, forgotten.

To keep things respectable, Paul and Elizabeth had decided to sleep with the fire between them—not so much for their benefit, but one never knew who might drop in. And since they really didn't know how men and women traveled together at this point in history, it only seemed logical that they were separated.

Van Eaton woke up first. For some time he sat confounded after discovering that his arm had somehow miraculously healed during the night. Once he realized the import of it, he found it hard to go back to sleep.

Staring into the still blackness, he watched while the night sky slowly began to take on color again. He blinked and refocused, scarcely making out a thin layer of fog that blanketed the ridge to the east. He remembered his office back at home and how the cigar smoke hung in the air in much the same way. Holding his knees to his chest, he rocked back and forth in a daze.

How could this be? He pressed his forehead to his knees and sighed. *Something has happened here that makes no sense. Paranormal psychosis? Perhaps. But the truth is, my arm was broken. Severely broken.*

He smeared the sleep from his eyes and rubbed his

arm. *I remember the pain, the bone that moved within the wound, and the young doctor—how she pushed it back into place.*

He glanced at his tunic. The dried blood was still on his sleeve. He squeezed his eyes shut and convinced himself that he was dreaming or even hallucinating. Finally he drifted off to sleep.

† † †

The morning sun peeked silently over the eastern ridge and found the three fast asleep, nestled under thick, borrowed blankets. The morning air was cool but dry, and the only sounds were the crickets playing their morning serenade.

Suddenly, in the distance, the rattle of wooden wheels and horses' hooves cut the morning solitude like a knife. Elizabeth's eyes sprang open, and she bolted upright.

"Someone's coming!" She crawled cautiously around the campfire and shook Paul.

Paul scrambled to his feet and squinted to focus. He scratched his increasingly bearded face.

Those are soldiers.

As the party neared the camp, it became alarmingly apparent that they were not the elite Roman army that Paul had pictured they would be. They were seemingly undisciplined men with no coherence as a group, a filthy horde to the point that one man urinated right from his horse as he rode, never blinking an eye.

These are the kind of moments you don't read about in history class, Paul reflected wryly.

The horses slowed, grunting and snorting in protest as they pulled to a halt. A cloud of dust engulfed the riders, adding yet another layer of dirt to the already grungy men. As the air cleared, the lead rider motioned to Paul.

"You! We seek the men from Nazareth." He spat on the ground and wiped his mouth with the back of his hand.

Paul blinked and glanced across the road to where Jesus and His disciples had been only hours before. They were not there.

"What men?"

The man's expression hardened. "That lot that came through Jerusalem yesterday causing all the commotion." He glanced at Paul, then cast a stony eye at Elizabeth.

Paul shrugged.

"What about him?" The man motioned toward Van Eaton.

"He's been here with us all night."

The man turned and mumbled something inaudible, and several riders laughed. He glanced at Elizabeth again

149

and slapped his mount. They disappeared in a cloud of dust.

"Who were they?"

"Those . . . were soldiers," Paul said, his voice hesitant. "*Roman* soldiers."

Elizabeth glanced across the road, then back at Paul. "I wonder where *they* went."

Paul rolled his belongings into his mat. "I don't know, but they couldn't have gone far."

Van Eaton stirred and sat up slowly. "Who . . . were those men?" His voice was raspy with sleep.

"We're not exactly sure," Elizabeth admitted.

Van Eaton rubbed his day-old beard. "Well, what did they want?"

Elizabeth looked at Paul, feeling oddly as if she needed his permission for what she was about to say. "They were looking for . . . They were looking for Jesus." The words felt strange.

Van Eaton rolled to his knees and staggered to his feet. "So where is he?" He brushed off the backside of his tunic with the hand that had been injured.

"Professor, why haven't you said anything about your arm?" Paul asked.

Van Eaton looked at his hand, clenched his fist, then relaxed. "What do you want me to say? That I don't know any more about what's going on here than you do?" He smirked. "Well, I don't, but I'm going to find out."

An awkward silence followed his remark. Elizabeth knew that arguing with him was pointless.

"This is crazy," she whispered under her breath to Paul. "He didn't even seem that surprised."

"You know, you're right. But he obviously knows something very out of the ordinary has happened here. And while we're talking about it, I'm pretty darned amazed myself! The man was healed by Jesus Christ!"

"But I think that even as cynical as he is, he'll have

to come around."

"You know, I've often wondered why people in Jesus' day had such a hard time believing in Him—especially when they witnessed His miracles," Paul responded. "And now, this very thing happens, and there is still unbelief. It's beyond me."

Something caught Elizabeth's eye. "Wasn't this where Jesus was sitting last night?"

"I think so. Why?"

"Look at this. There's something written here in the dust."

She pointed to a series of strange symbols:

תמאה תא אצמת םש ,המוניהה ךרד

Paul knelt and studied the writing. "This is Hebrew. Professor, take a look at this."

Van Eaton ambled over reluctantly.

"What do you make of this?" Paul traced the letters with his index finger.

"If you're going to do it, do it correctly," Van Eaton

said. "It reads from right to left."

He studied the message. *"Through the veil, you will see—"* He stopped. "Who wrote this?"

"Who do you think?" Paul gave him a spontaneous smile.

Van Eaton smoothed his eyebrow. "This means nothing." He scuffed the writings with his foot and

sauntered back to his mat.

Paul tensed, then caught himself before he did something he would have regretted. Elizabeth took him by the arm.

"You know, we figured that by all indications yesterday was Palm Sunday."

Paul crossed his arms and widened his stance. "Yeah, that much makes sense."

"Well, if that's the case, then where would He be today—the day after He entered Jerusalem?" Elizabeth's eyes wandered for a moment, then widened. "Wait a minute!"

She tore open her backpack and rifled through its contents until she found her leather-bound Bible. She thumbed through the pages and stopped at Matthew 21, staring in disbelief.

"What is this?"

She quickly thumbed through the Gospel of Mark, and again the pages followed the same strange sequence: Following the triumphal entry into Jerusalem, the pages were all blank, as if they had never been printed on at all.

Paul took the book and found that the remaining

Gospels followed the same pattern. And from those books forward, the pages were void of print altogether.

"Where are the other books?" Elizabeth asked. "Paul's epistles, Hebrews, Revelation?"

Paul flipped back through the Old Testament. "I don't know, but look at this."

Every chapter was in place.

"It doesn't make any sense," Elizabeth said.

"No, it makes perfect sense. Look, it's all here. All of the Old Testament and even part of the new, everything up to the point of where we are—or where we think we are now!"

Elizabeth took the book from him. "Then . . . what is not written, hasn't happened yet?" She felt the hair on the back of her neck prickle. "I can't believe it. Professor, what do you make of this?"

She handed the book to Van Eaton, who scanned the pages. He handed it back to her.

"So?" he said smugly.

"So? Come on, Professor. How long are you going to deny what is happening here? Even Einstein believed time travel was possible."

Van Eaton's eyes narrowed. "The future is nebulous, and the asymmetry of remembering past events along with future events is completely illogical. But for the sake of argument, let's suppose this is the case. What happens next, provided Einstein's theory is correct?"

Putting his hand to his forehead and closing his

eyes, Paul said tentatively, "Well . . . after His triumphal entry, Jesus went to the Temple. Yes," he said with greater assurance. "Yes, that's right, He cleared the Temple."

Van Eaton folded his cloak and stuffed it under his arm. As though suddenly realizing it was the previously injured one, he switched to the other side. He even favored the arm as if it were still hurt.

"This is ridiculous. And I'm not going to sit here and listen to the two of you fantasize."

"But Prof—"

"Besides, if things are as you say they are, I won't be hard to find. Jerusalem wasn't that big in Jesus' day." He turned and started down the road.

Paul took a step after him, but Elizabeth put her hand on his arm. "Let him go. He'll be all right."

"I wasn't worried about him. I was thinking about all of those poor, unsuspecting people."

Elizabeth let out a laugh. "Oh boy. Let's go find the Temple."

Thirteen

(12 Nisan)

The morning sun inched higher in the eastern sky as Van Eaton followed the road that led back to the city. The air was still and cool, filled with aromas of spice and charred wood.

He recalled the previous night's events. And though he had been asleep through most of it and so had no idea exactly what had happened, he knew something very strange had occurred.

In truth, the whole chain of events followed such an odd twist that he wasn't exactly sure what was going on or what he was supposed to do, if anything at all. And then there were the words scrawled in the dust.

Through the veil—

The words cut deep into his conscious. *No! I won't be caught up in this! I will not!*

He pushed on toward the city, and the sights grew even more mesmerizing. He had been under the influence of so much medication the day before that he'd had trouble discerning fact from fiction, and now being coherent added yet another dimension to the saga. He stared stupefied at the skyline. It was crude, with no modern architecture to be seen.

Where are the buildings I saw yesterday?

He gazed across the wide expanse of desert toward the southernmost walls of the city, trying in vain to catch a glimpse of anything vaguely familiar. But there was nothing. This was not the city he remembered from only two nights before, though he couldn't bring himself to admit it to the others.

Surely the city will yield the answers.

† † †

"Did you notice anything strange about what He—what Jesus said last night about the professor?" Paul shifted his load as he walked.

"What do you mean?"

"Well, He knew our names, but He didn't seem to know the professor's name."

Elizabeth's gaze fell to the ground. "I didn't even think about that."

"I wonder if he is a part of all this?"

"I don't know. I just know I want to find Jesus again."

Paul beamed. "Amen to that, sister."

† † †

A lush stand of olive trees blanketed the rolling hillside that spanned as far as the eye could see to the south. To the north, the road descended into a shallow valley that dissolved into the trees, then surfaced again on the far side before vanishing over the next rise. Above that, the walls of the ancient city jutted skyward, looming against swirling stratus clouds that streaked azure blue skies in

every direction. The setting was surreal, but very real.

Nearing the larger of the two gates in the eastern wall, the two time travelers mingled unnoticed with the flood of people that filed through the massive entrance.

Spanning as much as one hundred feet from end to end, the double-portal gate stood almost as high as it was wide. The openings themselves spanned perhaps forty feet across and were supported in the center by a stone column that crumbled slightly at its base. Even now the walls looked ancient. As far as Paul recollected from his studies, they would already have been nearly five hundred years old.

"What if he's driving out the money changers?" A wily smile washed Elizabeth's face.

Paul heaved an enormous breath. "Wouldn't that be something to see?"

Filtering deeper into the city, the two blended well with their surroundings and with those around them. Only Paul's stubbled face and fair skin stood out. A few days in the sun would hopefully solve that problem as well. And though their clothing turned away suspicious eyes, they still drew a few wary stares.

"We're going to have to get rid of these shoes."

Elizabeth glanced at her feet. "Yeah, you're right. Good thing I didn't go all Hollywood and wear my heels when we set out on this tour. That would really have raised some eyebrows."

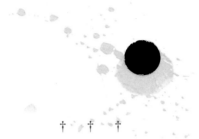

† † †

Meandering through the crowded streets, they quickly found themselves in a busy marketplace. Colorful tents of jade and crimson scantly shaded vendors and their homespun merchandise from the elements.

They shuffled past untold numbers of merchants hawking their wares before they happened upon a shoe vendor. Sifting through the assortment he offered, they both found sandals they thought would fit.

The pudgy merchant stepped closer, bowed, and hitched up his tunic by the belt. "You honor my humble establishment. What might I offer you today?" He fumbled through his goods, offering them as quality merchandise, which, sadly, they were not.

"We were looking for shoe—for sandals," Paul said. He pulled a pair from the pile and squirmed his foot into one.

Elizabeth noticed the merchant peering over the edge of the table at their shoes with a strange expression.

"These will do fine," Paul said as he put on the other

sandal and laced them up.

"Yes, my friend, a fine choice—a fine choice indeed. And, ah, what do you plan to do with the bleached footwear you now possess?" he asked curiously.

Elizabeth cleared her throat in warning, but Paul appeared not to notice.

"Well . . . we thought we might possibly barter for the

sandals," he said.

The man's eyes widened, then narrowed, but it was already too late.

"I tell you what. We'll swap you even for the sandals," Elizabeth said, matter-of-factly.

The merchant scratched his head and giggled. "I don't know," he whined. "I take special care to produce fine goods."

Paul knelt and began to unlace one sandal.

"No, no—wait," the merchant pleaded. "I suppose I will deal," he said with a wink. He took the sneakers, reveling at their light weight.

Elizabeth was suddenly uncomfortably aware of her backpack. She held it behind her and went to where a selection of fabrics billowed. She chose a plain hemp pattern and marched back to Paul and the merchant.

"Is there anything else I can do for you my friends?" the merchant asked. He ran his finger over the swoosh and slipped the sneakers along with Elizabeth's Sperrys under his table.

"Yes, add this fabric to our choices," she said.

The merchant nodded in affirmation.

"We are looking for the Temple," Paul broke in.

"The Temple? Ah yes, it is just ahead, past the end of the market. But I would be careful. There was a disturbance there earlier today. They say the Nazarene caused it."

They thanked him and hurried down the street, but it didn't take long for them to realize the sandals were a far cry from their shoes.

† † †

The massive flight of steps that marked the entrance of the Temple was littered with goods. Some people were gathering what was theirs, while others stole what was not.

"Who does he think he is?" an irritated woman grumbled. She gathered the shards of a broken pot and dropped them into a pile on the street. "That piece had been in my family for generations."

Elizabeth and Paul ascended the stairs and found even more disorder inside. Tables and benches were snarled with birdcages, and broken pottery lay strewn over most of the courtyard. The square teemed with children chasing and cornering loose animals, while pigeons and doves perched on ledges and watched.

Then, from across the courtyard, Paul spied Jesus. He struggled to keep his composure as they picked their way through the mess and found places next to a man they'd met the day before.

"I am glad you came." He extended his hand to Paul.

"I am Simon Bar Jona."

Chill bumps coated Paul's arms when he took Peter's hand. Elizabeth nodded demurely to Simon and smiled. They both sat down.

Jesus paused long enough to acknowledge the two, then He continued, "To gain, you must freely give. To receive forgiveness, likewise you must truly forgive those who are against you. And to live, you must surely die."

Paul listened intently, captivated with the simple, yet poignant words. And, as on the night before, he understood because he knew the whole story.

Paul closed his eyes and focused solely on Jesus' voice, the tone of every syllable and the syllable of every word. They were words that kindled fires of devotion and service, while at the same time quenching the spirit of pride and selfishness. Every word from Jesus' lips felt like a seed falling onto Paul's fertile heart.

"There was a landowner who planted a vineyard," Jesus said. "He put a wall around it, dug a winepress in it, and built a watchtower. Then he rented the vineyard to some farmers and went away on a journey. When the harvest time approached, he sent his servants to the tenants to collect his fruit. The tenants seized his servants; they beat one, killed another, and stoned a third. Then he sent other servants to them, more than the first time, and the tenants treated them the same way." Jesus' eyes swept the room, and he smoothed his beard.

"Last of all, he sent his son to them. 'They will respect

my son,' he said, but when the tenants saw the son, they said to each other, 'This is the heir. Come, let us kill him and take his inheritance.' So they took him and threw him out of the vineyard and killed him." Jesus' gaze wandered to the back of the crowd, then He continued, "Therefore, when the owner of the vineyard comes, what will he do to those tenants?"

A voice echoed from the back. "He will give those murderers what they deserve," the man said dryly. "Then he will lease the vineyard to more suitable tenants, who will pay him his fair share of the harvest."

It was apparent from his handsome garment and headdress that the man was a priest. Paul judged him to be a Pharisee.

Peering through the crowd, Jesus made direct eye contact with the man. "The stone the builders rejected has become the cornerstone. The Lord has done this, and it is marvelous in our eyes."

Paul turned to Elizabeth and the two grinned like conspirators. It was as if they were both watching a movie they knew by heart, understanding with a curious knowledge the stage that was being set.

The Pharisees, on the other hand, seemed oblivious to his words. To them, the pendulum swung in only one direction and that was toward the Mosaic Law, Paul thought. Unfortunately, they believed Jesus to be anything but a law abider. And why? The grace and forgiveness He offered were simply too easily attainable.

"Therefore I tell you that the kingdom of God will be taken away from you and given to a people that will produce its fruit." Jesus spoke without blinking, His eyes cold. "He who falls on this stone will be broken to pieces, but he on whom it falls will be crushed."

Now the Pharisees grasped what Jesus was saying—that he referred specifically to them. But though their faces contorted with anger and hatred, they remained silent, covertly darting glances around them at the crowd that greatly outnumbered them.

In the still of the moment, a shrill cry echoed over the assembly as a gaunt figure awkwardly topped the stairs. The crowd parted and made way for the man.

Propped against a rough wooden crutch he gripped tightly with skeletal fingers, he inched his way to within a few feet of Jesus. "I . . . have been crippled since birth," he muttered.

He balanced precariously on his one good leg and steadied himself with his crutch. The other leg, twisting inward almost 90 degrees, hung limp, the leathery skin stretching tight over swollen joints. The top of his foot was raw, oozing with infection, and two toes were missing. He moved closer to Jesus, quivering slightly as he spoke.

"My father is given to wine, and my mother . . . my mother cares only for herself." He sighed. "I have no one."

Tears traversed the sun-baked wrinkles that lined his face. "Lord, please help me," he pleaded, "I cannot go on this way!"

A stony silence fell over the assembly. Jesus cradled the man's face in His hands while he sobbed.

"Blessed are those who call on my name. And woe unto those who have not helped carry your burden. For it would have been better if they had never been born."

The man's crutch slipped from his arm, but there was now no need for it. Nestled in the arms of the Savior, he

watched in awe as his twisted limb suddenly flushed with warmth.

Paul's heart hammered his chest as he watched the crippled leg miraculously straighten and regain its color.

The man rubbed his eyes and focused again. For the first time in his life, he was whole.

Gradually he lifted his head from Jesus' hands and stepped backward. He placed his weight on the healed limb and stepped forward with the same dubious step, obviously expecting to fall flat on his face. He did not.

Again he stepped forward, and again, each step confirming the next, until finally he leapt into the air and cried for all to hear, "You are the Son of the living God!"

Jesus smiled and His countenance revealed His heart. He was pleased the man had confirmed His deity.

In the midst of the moment, another man maneuvered through the crowd, his movements guarded and his steps unsure. Paul's gaze followed the man until he reached the outermost circle of the assembly a short distance from where he and Elizabeth sat. Suddenly he realized the man was blind.

The man brushed against one of the onlookers and noticed his garment, then gave a sniff. It was smooth and carried the pungent scent of smoke and of blood, and he realized it was the robe of a priest.

"This is blasphemous," the priest hissed. "These people think this man is from God!"

"Yes, but what are we to do?" another man asked in a

low voice. "We are greatly outnumbered."

"In due time," a more solemn voice responded. "In due time."

"Who does this infidel claim to be?"

"He calls himself Jesus of Nazareth," the priest answered.

"Jesus of Nazareth?" Suddenly the blind man straightened and shouldered his way through the crowd. "Jesus, son of David," he cried, "have mercy on me!"

At the call of His name, Jesus found the man among the many faces. "I am here."

The timbre of His voice appeared to calm the man. He turned toward the sound, his face brightening.

The former cripple pressed through the crowd and took the man by the hand. "Don't be afraid. This man is from God, there is no doubt. Come and see." With confident steps, he led the man to Jesus.

The Master gently took him by the hand and spoke with an easy familiarity. The man sank to the ground, and Jesus knelt in front of him. Then He spit on the ground, gathered the spittle and dirt into His hand and made a paste.

He pulled closer to the man, who flinched initially at His touch, then steadied himself against Him. Jesus brushed the man's hair from his face and gently swabbed his eyes with the mixture. Then He stood and backed away.

Moments passed, then the blind man's face flushed red. He rubbed his eyes, screaming. Something was happening!

Pins of light swirled in his clenched eyes. There was a strange flash of light and suddenly the darkness he had known every second of his life gave way to a sensation he had never known.

What is this? he thought. He squinted and shielded his face against the light. Opening his eyes, he gazed toward the warmth he had known so well over the years, but now reckoned it with hues and tints he never knew existed.

Now shapes and forms blurred into vision. He rubbed his eyes and reached for a wall across the courtyard. He had no perception of depth.

The man blinked hard and focused again. His gaze swept the crowd until he came to Jesus. And even though he couldn't have known who He was, he knew just the same.

He stepped awkwardly toward Jesus and kneeled at his feet.

"Master," he cried.

Jesus took him by the hand and raised him to his feet as the crowd erupted into cheers and crowded around him.

The religious assembly quietly made their way out of the Temple. As they left, more than one glanced back at Jesus, rage and malice clearly reflected in their stares—angered not only at how the people revered Jesus, but how Jesus Himself hadn't acknowledged them for who they were.

They were the religious voice of the people, they reasoned. They were not to be questioned, and certainly

not to be accused of anything other than righteousness. How could this sinner from Nazareth work miracles or understand anything of a spiritual nature?

† † †

On the other side of the city, the professor had little trouble mingling with the crowds. Interestingly enough, he had also found that he could speak either language, Aramaic or English, and was understood either way. This phenomenon only proved to complicate matters since he still refused to accept what was happening.

Mopping his brow, he ambled along the street and pretended to look at the vendors' goods. He was beginning to feel flushed. His pulse raced, and a wave of nausea flashed through his gut. He was looking for a place to get out of the sun when he noticed a group of men filing through the doorway at the corner of the street. He used the walk to collect his thoughts.

The events of the past twenty-four hours had raised more questions than answers. And the harder he looked for the answers, the farther away they seemed to be. On the broader front, the whole language thing was about to drive him crazy, and then there was his arm. His sleeve was stained with dried blood, and yet there was no wound—not even a scar! It simply didn't make any sense. But then again, considering everything else that was going on, what did?

Reaching the door, Van Eaton covered his head and

shuffled through with the pious group, virtually unnoticed. The heavy scent of olive oil permeated the stale air from several pint-sized clay lamps lining a ledge that ran the length of the shadowy room. Their flickering shadows danced eerily with every wisp of air. There was scarcely enough light to see at the front of the room, and little reached the back at all. It was the perfect place to hide. Van Eaton found a seat and quietly shrank into the shadows.

The room settled and a lone figure stood. He was clad in an ornate, multi-colored robe the professor knew to be an ephod, the vestment of a high priest. Methodically he unfurled a weighty scroll, and then cleared his throat. Holding the scroll high enough for all to see, he stood erect, making sure that everyone in the room understood that he was about to start. Then he lowered the parchments and placed them on the stand in front of him. He struggled to focus in the dim light.

As the professor strained to hear the priest's words, he reached in vain to adjust his hearing aid before remembering. He sighed, but something else pricked his curiosity.

The scrolls. They were made of a pliable papyrus

or hemp he supposed, and they were coiled around two wooden rods nearly three feet in length. At the top of each rod dangled gold cords tipped with tassels that shimmered in the lamplight.

As far as he knew, the oldest Torah manuscripts that were intact in the twenty-first century dated back to well after the advent of Christianity. The exception was the

Dead Sea scrolls, which were only fragments and in very poor condition.

To possess such a set of documents would be the archeological find of the century. That is, if I am where I think I am. Greed fueled his thoughts. *If I could get my hands on those scrolls, and if, by the same strange twist of fate, I was able to find my way back to my own time, I could stun the academic community.*

Van Eaton studied the room. There were only two entrances: the one through which he had entered and one at the front. There were no windows, and thick, woven hemp curtains hung from a header above each doorway.

When the priest brought the service to a close, he meticulously rerolled the scrolls and slid them into a narrow brass box at the base of the podium. Then with a hallowed spirit, he continued his valediction.

"We are the Sons of Zadok, the Essenes, the chosen seed of Yahweh."

The room chorused with amens, and they all stood.

Essenes? the professor thought. *These are the Essenes?*

† † †

The crowd of as many as a hundred people had thinned to perhaps half that and only a handful of people still hovered around Jesus. Paul rose with Elizabeth as two men approached.

"Tell us more of yourself and your . . . companion."

The first man's question seemed to indicate suspicion. Appearing undaunted, Elizabeth looked the man squarely in the eye.

Paul, stymied for an answer, wavered for an uncomfortable moment, then Peter intervened. "They are friends of the Master. Jesus introduced us yesterday in the city."

"And are you from this region?" the second man asked, again implying distrust.

"Brothers! Brothers, please, you question our friends as if they were our adversaries, and I can assure you, they are not," Peter said.

A hand dropped heavily on both men's shoulders. "I see you have met my friends," Jesus said. "Elizabeth and Paul, may I introduce Thomas, whom you may wish to call Didymas."

Paul took Thomas by the hand and forearm, as he had seen the others greet one another. Thomas turned to Elizabeth and nodded respectfully.

"And this is Judas Iscariot," Jesus said.

Incredibly, there was not a semblance of animosity

in His words. This was hardly the case for Paul, and beside him he felt Elizabeth stiffen as well. The awkwardness was more than evident as they were introduced and there was no hiding their emotion. Paul could taste the bile of hatred rise in his throat.

Judas extended his hand to Paul with a scant smile and nodded at Elizabeth. She froze, but Paul pushed through his emotions and grasped Judas' hand.

It was cold and moist. Or maybe it wasn't. Maybe he just thought it would be.

Others gathered around.

"This is James," Jesus said, "a son of Zebedee."

James appeared to be in his late teens. He had a medium build and stood maybe five and a half feet tall. His boyish face was lightly bearded, and he spoke with a slight lisp.

"And this is Andrew, the brother of Peter." Jesus winked playfully.

He too was a young man, even younger than James, it seemed. He was short and well-muscled, and he strode confidently forward and embraced Paul heartily. Then he smiled and nodded gingerly to Elizabeth.

"This is John, the older son of Zebedee; Philip; Bartholomew, who also answers to Nathanael, of the house of Naphtali; and Levi, whom we call Matthew."

Matthew was tall and loose-limbed. He ambled over to them.

"And this is James, Matthew's brother." Jesus mussed

the hair of the younger man. "And Jude, whose surname is Thaddaeus; and Simon the Zealot."

Simon beamed. "And proud to be," he said. Laughter followed.

"And you have already met Simon Peter. We welcome you with open arms." Jesus pulled both Elizabeth and Paul to His chest.

The mosaic is beginning to take shape, Paul thought.

Fourteen

(12 Nisan)

Only a few oil lamps still burned. They flickered with movement as the pious entourage of Essenes left the room. When the last man passed through the door, Van Eaton crouched in the shadows. Nervously he assessed the situation.

The scrolls of the Essenes. Any museum would pay dearly for such a find.

He swallowed hard. His disbelief was ebbing, and the reality was slowly gaining a foothold. But this wasn't like him at all. He had always lived inside the box, he reasoned. What had changed?

Again the priest entered the room. He dropped the curtain behind him and moved along the wall, methodically extinguishing all but one lamp.

Van Eaton held perfectly still, his eyes clenched tightly shut, stinging sweat creeping into their corners. The priest ambled through the shadows and stopped at the door. His gaze swept the room one last time, and he drew back the curtain.

Stark sunlight momentarily flooded the room, shining directly in Van Eaton's face. He lay frozen as the priest stepped through the doorway and let the curtain drop behind him.

Van Eaton exhaled nervously. Now was his chance. Slipping through the shadows, he knelt at the brass box. He reached in, gingerly removed two weighty parchments, and spread them open. Even by the dim light, he could tell they were exquisite. He quickly rerolled and gathered the rest. There were five in all.

With hushed excitement, he unrolled his sleep mat and placed the scrolls in the center. He tied the bundle at both ends and clambered to his feet. He was dizzy, and it wasn't the Mepergan. He hadn't taken any all day, and besides, he didn't need it anyway. Pain wasn't the problem. He felt unsteady, and it was apparent that he was growing increasingly ill.

He stepped awkwardly toward the rear door and stumbled headlong over the brass container. The crash ricocheted off the walls.

Oh my God!

He scrambled to his feet and rushed toward the rear door. As he pushed his way past the curtain, he heard someone enter through the front door.

He darted around the building's corner and melted into the crowd clustered around a merchant's tent. Cautiously he looked back the way he had come and noticed two Essenes rounding the corner. As Van Eaton worked his way deeper into the crowd, one of the men pulled a shofar from his belt and blew into it. The blare sounded in every direction.

† † †

Gathered in a modest shanty on the outskirts of the city, Jesus and His chosen few had just sat down to eat when the shrill tone of a ram's horn echoed over the chatter. Jesus leaned close to Elizabeth and Paul.

"Pray for your friend," he whispered before moving away.

Elizabeth shot Paul a blank look. "Is he talking about . . . the professor?"

"I guess so."

"What do you think is going on?"

Paul shrugged. "There's no telling what he might have gotten into."

Elizabeth prayed silently.

After the meal Jesus and His entourage, now more subdued than talkative, passed through the Eastern Gate and headed toward Bethany. Following the beaten path that led through the Kidron Valley, Jesus instructed Andrew and the younger James to return the donkey and foal they had borrowed the day before.

Elizabeth slowed her steps and fell in with John. Paul lagged behind to join them.

"Have you known the Master long?" John asked. He was gracious almost to a fault.

"Since I was a child, I guess," said Paul. "And you?"

John picked up a stone and skipped it across the sand. "Since the Baptist," he said. "Sometimes I wonder how all things truly work together for good. The Baptist was God's man, and he believed so much in the one we now follow . . . " His voice broke and the words trailed off.

Impulsively Elizabeth touched his arm, remembering the Bible's account of John the Baptist's beheading at the hand of Herod. From John's expression it was obvious that he still carried the memory of the rugged prophet close to his heart. His brutal end must have been especially painful for the young disciple.

"What do you remember the most about him?" she asked softly.

John's face warmed in a smile. "His face. And his eyes, piercing and convicting. But most of all, I remember how he had a manner like no other. He was direct. Sometimes painfully so, even to the point of offending—but he always spoke the truth, no matter what the cost. That was what Herod hated most about him."

For some moments they walked along in silence. Then in the distance, Elizabeth caught a glimpse of a familiar face sporting sunglasses. She put her hand over her mouth to hide a grin.

"Ah, shalom my friends. Shalom," the merchant greeted them cheerfully as they approached. "And where is your injured friend?"

"Ah . . . he's in the city, somewhere," Paul said casually.

"And have you lost a lens from your . . . your spectacles?"

"Spek-tak-els," the man repeated, "Is that what you call these?" He pulled the frames from his face. "I know only that I can see as well as when I was a child, though it is more difficult at night."

Laughter rippled between Elizabeth and Paul.

"So what happened to the other lens?" Elizabeth asked.

"Well . . ." He grinned sheepishly. "I could not help myself. Do you have any idea how many denari I received for that one?" He clicked his tongue between his teeth, "Linz?" His grin protracted into a jagged-tooth smile. "I am talking gold denari!"

Elizabeth wagged her head. *Once a salesman.*

"Joseph!" Jesus clapped the wry merchant on the back.

"Jesus," he said happily. The two men embraced.

"Did I tell you that I met the rabbi at my niece's wedding?" He slipped his arm around Jesus as if they were old friends. "And the wine you brought—they talk about it still!" Turning to Elizabeth, he said, "In fact, the skin of wine you purchased from me yesterday? That was his doing. It was new wine then but, you know, it tastes as good today—maybe even better!"

She patted the wineskin that dangled from her shoulder and grinned at Paul, who shrank into the background. Suddenly his doctrinal ties were feeling a bit heavy.

"Come with us to Bethany," Jesus said.

Joseph smiled. "Oh thank you, sir, but no. I have appointments in the city. But I will see you soon. I pledge it."

Jesus turned and they continued down the road. "He doesn't know me, not really. So many know *of* the truth." His gaze fell to the ground, and He sighed.

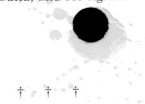

† † †

Van Eaton sat with his bounty between a thatch roofed shanty and the city wall. He wheezed heavily and set aside the sacred parchments, desperately seeking what, at the moment, was equally important. He removed the cap from his inhaler and sprayed the healing mist into his lungs.

Now, if I only had something for this nausea.

He replaced the cap and tried to think about anything other than how bad he felt. He carefully rerolled the scrolls and looked over the other writings that were there. These documents seemed more fragile than the scrolls but were still in considerably better shape than any of the ancient documents he'd seen on display in the States. Peeling open the parchments one by one, he read the Hebrew titles: Exodus, Isaiah, Deuteronomy, and Esther.

Esther?

Van Eaton stood and touched his forehead. His fever was climbing, and he knew there was nothing he could do about it. He stepped back and studied the wall that loomed in front of him. It seemed to touch the sky. Foreboding, ominous, magnificent.

Suddenly he spied a child step through a cleft at the wall's base and disappear. A moment later, another appeared from the same spot and darted into the street.

An opening.

He moved closer and gauged its size. Then he glanced

in both directions and crawled awkwardly through to the other side.

† † †

On the road to Bethany, Jesus and His followers forged past their camp from the night before. Ashes now lay cold where luminous fires had burned, and now only footprints were evidence of the memories.

Paul and Elizabeth reminisced over the previous night and their first encounter with the Savior. There were a thousand questions they still craved answers for.

"Lord, how is it that we are able to speak to those around us in their own native tongue, and yet, we don't even know the language?" Elizabeth whispered.

For a moment, Jesus said nothing. Paul had noticed this particular trait more than once—that He never responded quickly.

"Would your reason for being here have made sense lest you had the tools to comprehend?" He asked.

Paul tried to stifle a grin. Talking with Jesus released

a strange sort of freedom and spontaneity that he had noticed from their first encounter. It was almost like talking to one's own conscience, though there was never a hint of censure or criticism. Jesus never berated or spoke with an incriminating tone. He always seemed objective and transparent, though Paul knew His followers didn't always think so.

Oftentimes, the parables He spoke seemed to cloud what He was really trying to say, but this too couldn't have been further from the truth. His parables had a way of perfectly correlating scripture with life. In fact, it was one of His most amazing attributes.

"Martha will have prepared a meal for us," Jesus mentioned. "She is always good to take care of us."

"Mary and Lazarus will be there too," Peter assured Paul and Elizabeth. "They'll be glad to meet you."

"This is so unbelievable!" Elizabeth whispered to Paul. "Thank God we have this opportunity!"

He returned her exuberant smile, but suddenly he was keenly aware of the watchful eyes of Thomas and Judas, who walked not far behind them.

† † †

A trail of shallow footprints etched into the blistering sand was the only link to where the professor had been. Soon the desert winds would solve that problem as well.

Van Eaton staggered and caught himself. Dizzying images danced whimsically through his head.

I've got to get farther away.

With every step, bile crept slowly into his throat, piercing the corners of his jaws. His pulse raced. His mind numbed. A moment later, he was on his knees and heaving uncontrollably.

He wiped his mouth on his sleeve and swallowed saliva with grains of sand. He was flushed with fever and in a cold sweat. Raising his head, he squinted beneath cupped fingers at the brown-capped range that spanned the horizon. He shuddered.

Have I completely lost my mind?

Now driven solely by greed, the ailing professor was determined to grind on. He envisioned the scrolls and how they appeared to be identical to the samples he had studied at Chicago's Field Museum. He'd been one of only three people in the country selected to take part in an exhaustive study of the scrolls that included encryption decoding as well as carbon 214 dating. The scrolls he carried, as far as he could remember, had many of the same markings, though they were vastly more legible.

† † †

The afternoon sun burned right through his clothing as Van Eaton slowed to a shuffle. He smeared the sweat from his brow and caught a glimpse of something on the horizon.

There on the line where the sand touched the sky, a head flashed between the dunes. It was there—then it was not. Then again he saw it, and again it was gone. Curiosity now guided his steps. He worked his way to, and crested the ridge. He couldn't believe his eyes.

A dozen camels and half as many donkeys laden with goods and riders traipsed along in a single file. Van Eaton counted six riders and a boy on foot. He wondered if they were friendly.

Waiting until the last man was nearly past, he mustered enough courage to flag him down. The man tugged the reins and pulled to a stop.

"Could I . . . possibly have a lift?" Van Eaton squinted through one eye and tried to smile.

The man looked curiously at him. "A lift?"

"I mean, may I travel with you?"

"How is it that you are here without a mount?" The man squirmed in his seat as he spoke.

Van Eaton stood still without saying a word, not really knowing what to say. Finally, the man motioned toward a camel at the rear of the pack.

It soon became obvious that Van Eaton knew nothing about camels, but somehow he managed to crawl on. He balanced precariously and took the reins.

The animal stank to high heaven! Its hair was stiff and matted with a stench of perspiration that stirred a swarm of flies. Not to mention that it was a flea-infested carpet.

The weary professor synced his cadence with the group and settled in for the ride . . . but to where? Having been so eager to escape, he hadn't even considered where they were going, though as it was, it really didn't matter. They were heading away from the city, and at the moment that was what was important.

Fifteen

(13 Nisan)

The home of Mary and Martha was unadorned and spoke of simple comfort and solace. Standing alone on a rock-strewn hillside off the beaten path that joined Bethany to Jerusalem, it was well known to everyone who lived in the area, Elizabeth had learned from John.

Two twisted acacia trees stood on one side of the paltry mud-brick house, and an undernourished row of shrubbery lined the front wall. On the other side, a crude, split-rail fence hemmed in a handful of sheep and a milk goat. A stone well was located halfway between the house and the road and a trough beside that. They were the only structures standing in the otherwise barren landscape, and Elizabeth regarded them with interest.

As she and Paul followed the disciples into the house, the sweet aroma of a feast wafted through the doorway, pervading their senses. The center wall divided the interior into two main rooms of equal size and also supported the large, flat-top roof. John confided to her in an undertone that Jesus and His disciples had spent many nights there, sleeping under the stars.

"Martha!"

Martha glanced past Mary to Peter, and then quickly checked the table setting. "You are early," she said with an artificial smile. "It will be some time before we are ready." She began to grind meal heavily with a stone pestle.

"There is no hurry," Peter said. He slipped a date from a dish on the table and popped it into his mouth, ignoring

Martha's irritated glance.

"Mary, this is Elizabeth," he said, motioning her and Paul forward.

Mary smiled and dipped her head in the traditional manner, then looked up through dark lashes.

"And this is Paul. They joined us yesterday in the city."

Mary's dark eyes flashed as they were introduced.

"And this is Lazarus," Peter went on.

Standing maybe five-foot-two and sporting a lean build, Lazarus had a head full of curly black hair and a thick beard. He barely smiled when introduced, seeming preoccupied. Through the montage of faces, he caught Jesus' eye and went to Him. The two men embraced.

"My brother has been waiting all day for the Master's return from Jerusalem," Mary explained, keeping an affectionate eye on Lazarus. "He wanted nothing more than to be with the disciples, but although he's getting stronger every day, Mary and I didn't think he was quite ready to go so far from home."

Elizabeth exchanged a glance with Paul and saw that

he too was thinking of the illness that had ultimately led to Lazarus's death and the miracle of his resurrection there in Bethany. Undoubtedly he still tired more easily than before, but it was clear his sisters doted on him.

While Jesus mingled further, Elizabeth followed Paul over to join Peter and Lazarus. "The Master seems troubled," Lazarus said, frowning.

"We had a run-in at the Temple today," Peter confided.

Lazarus stood with arms crossed, searching the larger man's eyes while he spoke.

"The Master was angry as angry as I've ever seen Him."

"What happened?"

"We went to the Temple, and the merchants had set up on both sides of the entrance there at the stairway."

"You mean the bazaar?"

"Yes, the bazaar. Well, imagine this: They have moved it inside! They were set up in the Court of the Gentiles!"

"You jest! Surely you are not serious."

"As I am standing here," Peter said. "And the Master was furious! He overturned all their tables, spilling everything on the floor. It was the biggest mess!"

Lazarus' eyes widened, and he smoothed his beard thoughtfully. "I heard some time back that the merchants struck a deal with Annas to supply the sacrificial animals for the Temple. I wish I could have been there."

"So do I," Elizabeth whispered to Paul behind her hand. 'That's one scene I would love to have witnessed."

Paul shook his head. "Wouldn't you know we'd miss it."

Peter sighed. "It was all so unexpected. We just stood and watched at first. We didn't know what to do."

Lazarus shook his head. "And nobody tried to stop Him?"

Peter thought for a moment. "You know, now that I think of it, no one lifted a finger to stop Him. Not one man even tried, as I remember." Peter's eyes narrowed. "Not one."

"Then what happened?" Lazarus hung on Peter's every word, as did Elizabeth and Paul.

"Well, after He ran most of them off, Jesus taught the ones who remained and—"

"Peter!" a voice called out. "The Master would have us outside."

† † †

In the shade of the acacia tree, they gathered. James and Andrew had already found a seat and sat together, as did Matthew and Simon.

Now there's a twosome, Paul thought, *Matthew and Simon the Zealot. Such an awkward pairing: Matthew, a tax-gathering Roman sympathizer; and Simon, a Jewish Zealot!*

Were not these Zealots bound by oath to purge their country of any foreign oppression? And would not these same two men on any other terms have been mortal enemies? Would Simon not have been ready to bury a knife in the back of this traitorous Jew?

Yet they seemed to share one common bond: Jesus. How could such a lack of malicious aversion be explained any other way?

Then there were Bartholomew and Thomas, who sat together and talked. From all indications, Bartholomew, or

Nathanael as he preferred to be called, seemed to always accept everything at face value. There never seemed to be a point of contention between him and any other man. And he had the faith of a child. It was an attribute that seemed to please Jesus, Paul reflected.

There was Thomas, or Didymas, who answered to both. Thomas seemed more highly educated and more analytical than the other disciples, relying more on his own reasoning abilities. Paul had noticed that he appeared to have a great deal of discernment in many areas, but there were times when he appeared to lack real spiritual depth. This idea was manifested in his relationship with Judas—or maybe that was simply how Paul perceived it. His foreknowledge of the situation had created such a strange perspective that he had difficulty in dealing with it.

Then there was John. The older of the two apostle brothers seemed more introverted than his younger sibling. He was reserved, resolute, almost too old for his years. But he had a rapport with Christ that was clear to everyone.

And finally, the big fisherman. Peter was just as Paul had pictured he would be—and the exact opposite of John.

He spoke his mind. And he did so with little regard for who was listening. But that's what made Peter so special, Paul felt. He had a genuine fervor for Christ, an infectious zeal that he exuded in the presence of one—or a hundred.

As the disciples gathered on the shady side of the house, they all knew that they were there to listen and to learn from the one they knew to be the Messiah. But there was a problem, at least as the two time travelers saw it: Judas.

How could Jesus stay so adamantly focused on His mission, knowing all along that there was a devil in their midst? And yet Judas' eloquent demeanor seemed to defy Paul's preconceptions. In fact, he seemed to be a likable fellow.

While Paul considered all of the possibilities surrounding Judas, Jesus walked to the sheep pen and opened the gate. He knelt and gently took a lamb into his arms, kneading His fingers in its soft wool while He walked back to the group.

"I tell you the truth, a man who does not enter the sheep pen by the gate, but climbs in some other way, is a thief and a robber." He leaned against the wall of the house and looked out over the plain. He considered His words before continuing.

"The man who enters by the gate is the shepherd of

his sheep. The watchman opens the gate for him, and the sheep listen to his voice as he calls his own sheep by name and leads them out."

Jesus put the lamb on the ground at His feet. "Andrew, call the sheep."

Andrew smiled and called out playfully, "Heeere, sheep!"

Snickers chorused through the group, but the lamb didn't budge. This brought on even more laughter.

Jesus then motioned to Matthew. "And you, Levi, make him come to you."

Matthew turned from his sitting position and kneeled, calling softly to the lamb. He received the same response.

After another moment, Jesus turned to the owner of the sheep. "Now, Lazarus, call your lamb."

Lazarus stood and brushed off the back of his tunic, then sank to his knees. "Come on—come on, little one," he called softly. "Come on."

At first, the lamb didn't move, he only quivered and twitched his tail. Again, Lazarus called softly. "Come on, little one. Come on."

Now the lamb turned toward the voice of his master. And though his eyesight was less than perfect, he inched toward the voice. Lazarus called softly again as the lamb crept toward him. A few more steps, and he was close enough to see that it was indeed his master. He leapt into his lap, and laughter and applause followed while the lamb licked every inch of Lazarus' face.

Jesus smiled at the sight. "When he has brought out all his own, he goes on ahead of them, and the sheep follow him because they know his voice." The lamb laid his chin on Lazarus's knee and closed his eyes as Jesus continued, "But they will never follow a stranger. In fact, they will run away from him because they do not recognize a stranger's voice."

Jesus took in all their faces and held their gaze for a several long seconds. "I tell you the truth, I am the gate for the sheep. All who ever came before me were thieves and robbers, but the sheep did not listen to them. I am the gate. Whoever enters through me will be saved. He will come in and out, and find pasture, but the thief comes only to steal and kill and destroy. I have come that they may have life, and have it to the fullest. I am the good shepherd, and the good shepherd lays down his life for the sheep."

Peter leaned close enough to Paul to speak for his ears alone. "Why does the Master speak so often of His dying?" He quizzed Paul as if he knew more than he let on.

Paul stared straight ahead, numbed by Peter's words and amazed at his candor.

"I've seen Him look at you both," Peter continued, "and there is something there."

Paul was taken aback, and knew it showed on his face.

"I thought He would establish His kingdom here," Peter muttered. He hushed when Jesus cleared his throat.

"I am the good shepherd. I know my sheep and my sheep know me just as the Father knows me and I know the

Father, and I lay down my life for the sheep."

Again Peter glanced at Paul, but Paul quickly looked away.

"I have other sheep that are not of this sheep pen." Jesus stared directly at Elizabeth and Paul. "I must bring them also. They, too, will listen to my voice, and there shall be one flock and one shepherd."

Peter glanced a third time at Paul, whose face was now wet with tears. He suspected Peter wondered what the Lord was saying to him and Elizabeth, the two most recent additions to the fold, that He was not saying to Peter—or any of the others.

†   †   †

"Ain Feshkha," the lead rider announced.

He threw one leg over his mount and artfully slid to the ground. His feet sank deep in the sand as two women ran to him from the stand of mud-brick shanties. The caravan was home.

Van Eaton awkwardly slid to the ground while the rest of the party dismounted and began to unload.

The boy who had walked beside him most of the afternoon tugged at his tunic. "This is Qumran," he said. His large brown eyes sparkled.

Qumran. Van Eaton sighed. *How ironic. The Dead Sea Scrolls were found there.*

He considered the thought, then it blurred. He was

happy to be on his feet again. Though his fever had cooled, he was still a bit queasy.

By now, the afternoon sun had slipped behind the ochre-brown dunes. The men loosened their cargo and began to unload. Children playfully lined up and waited their turn to transport the goods, each one eventually running with everything he could carry and disappearing

through amber-lit doorways. In the process Van Eaton slipped away and hid between two of the shanties.

Easing to the back of the house, he noticed a slab of meat on a spit roasting over a bed of red-hot coals. The desert breeze wafted the aroma past his nostrils, and his incredible hunger overcame his slight nausea.

First the scrolls and now food, he thought, salivating. *I am turning into a common thief!*

He crept toward the fire. Grabbing the steak, spit and all, he fled into the darkness.

Earlier, he had noticed a cave in the foothills just before they reached Ain Feshkha. He figured that if he could make it there, he could get some much needed rest. Now he just had to get there.

† † †

When Jesus finished His teaching, the group prayed, and then entered the house, drawn by the alluring fragrance. Peter leaned in to Paul as they walked inside.

"What did the Master say that stirred you so?"

After a moment of reasoning, Paul looked directly at Elizabeth while he spoke to Peter. "Could we . . . talk in private a little later?"

"I would like that," Peter said. "After dinner, then?"

Paul nodded.

"Oh, the dinner!" Peter whispered. "Mary and Martha have planned a special feast to honor the Master." He put a finger to his lips. "He knows nothing of it either. And Mary—she has the finest gift of all, just wait and see."

Paul was pleased that Peter had taken them into his confidence, and he was equally relieved that he had stopped asking questions. Elizabeth though, was clearly worried. She drew him aside.

"What are you doing?" she hissed.

"I don't know—buying time, I guess."

"You're not considering telling him anything, are you?"

"I don't know." Paul combed his fingers through his hair and backed away. "I just don't know."

When Jesus entered the room, He was ushered to the head of the table. Everything was exquisitely prepared. There were clumps of dates and figs, oranges and apricots all arranged in the center, and sliced pomegranates nestled in a circle around a mound of purple grapes. On each end of the table platters held mounds of smoked fish fillets. A bowl of sweet figs boiled in grape molasses sat beside each plate, and there were two clay flasks of new wine.

While the men assembled around the table, Mary

entered from behind Jesus and quietly traversed the crowded room. The room fell silent, and all eyes fixed on the young woman. Her face beamed as she knelt beside the Savior and opened the small, alabaster jar.

Lifting the top, she carefully poured the contents onto Jesus' feet. The room was filled with the sweet fragrance of nard as she meticulously massaged in the ointment from

His soles to His ankles. When she was finished, she pulled the covering from her head and dried His feet with her hair.

Jesus smiled, clearly pleased with what she had done. Paul marveled at the sight. Glancing at Elizabeth, he saw that her eyes were bright with unshed tears. They both sat in awe, motionless and watching in silence as the story they had heard since they were children unfolded.

At the end of the table, Judas sipped his wine and dabbed his lips. "Why wasn't this perfume sold and the money given to the poor? It had to have been worth a year's wages."

Frowns and murmurs of agreement followed his words.

Jesus' gaze went from one face to the next around the table, his expression turning sour. "Leave her alone. It was intended that she should save this perfume for the day of my burial." He stared directly at Judas as He spoke. "You will always have the poor among you, but you will not always have me."

Again Jesus' words seemed to pass right over their heads. Christ's death and burial was not an issue with these men, Paul reflected. It wasn't even a consideration. Jesus had already overcome death with one that was in their very midst. Lazarus was living proof that death had no sting. And yet Jesus seemed to allude to the subject on a regular basis, and even Peter and John, His closest disciples, were none the wiser.

Jesus sat quietly and savored the moment. He, most of all, realized that no one in the room, save Paul and Elizabeth, had a clue as to what would soon transpire. He knew His disciples weren't looking for a lamb to be sacrificed, but a king who would deliver them from the tyranny of Rome.

As His eyes wandered the room, Jesus studied the faces of those He had known since the beginning of His ministry. He had spent so much of his time preparing them for these last days—and for the days when He would be present in Spirit only.

For three years He had grown accustomed to each man's distinctive persona, from Peter's raspy laughter, to the childlike faith of John. He remembered how Bartholomew had wept when called to follow Him. Then there was the Zealot. He had so much to offer, so much fervor, so much passion. Jesus was pleased that he had redirected those emotions toward the kingdom.

All of his disciples held such a special place in His heart—yes, even the betrayer, though as of yet he was not. Jesus watched as Judas pulled a piece of fish onto his plate. He licked his fingers and casually wiped them on his tunic, then cut his eyes around the room. He seemed preoccupied. Even suspicious. And while Jesus was fully aware of the deed that would eventually entangle Judas and ultimately lead to his ruin, He loved him deeply.

Jesus' eyes now rested on Paul and Elizabeth. They too realized that the story was drawing to a close, that Jesus only had three days before He faced the cross. He also knew from the look on their faces that He was going to have to talk with them. For He knew they were hurting, though it really didn't take deity to see it.

†   †   †

The firelight chased shadows across the jagged rocks, dancing eerily up the walls and across the ceiling of his hiding place. Van Eaton wondered if the glow would be noticed from the outside. He also wondered what the family would do when they discovered their main course was missing.

That steak hit the spot. Thank heaven I finally got past that nausea; my strength was waning dangerously low.

To add to his good fortune, there was a freshwater spring in the cave that emptied into a tub-sized basin from a fissure in the wall. It was the ideal spot to bed down. He had journeyed in the hot sun most of the day, and though his fever was gone, he was worn out. He cleared a spot and drifted off to sleep easily.

† † †

The weary disciples stepped into the brisk desert air. The night was tranquil, and the moon, almost in full bloom, appeared over the chain of mountains to the east. In the distance a donkey brayed and a dog barked. Another replied. A dove called to her lost mate and silence

answered. She knew that silence was death. The soft breeze changed direction and the faint cries of a child were now discernable. He was hungry.

Jesus listened intently to the sounds that filled the night. He heard the cries of the weak, the whines of the hungry, and the laments for the dead. For they were all His creatures and He alone heard every one. Not even the travelers from the future perceived what was going on. They too had stepped outside to discuss a real problem—at least as they saw it.

† † †

"But he hasn't done anything yet! The only evidence we have is in the Bible, which we don't actually have." Elizabeth glanced at her backpack, still wrapped in its disguise and propped against the corner of the house.

"All I'm saying is that if you could go back say, twenty years or so, would you not change some of the things in your life if you could?"

Elizabeth answered without hesitation, "Well, sure I

would, but—" She stopped. "What are you up to?"

"We're responsible for what we know, are we not?"

"I don't think we're supposed to interfere with any of this."

Paul shook his head. "Indulge me for a minute, please. Why do you think we're here?"

"He said we came for a specific purpose—"

"And what do you think that purpose is?"

"I . . . I don't know. To watch, I guess."

"I just can't believe that." Paul plucked a rock from the dirt and flung it into the darkness. "I want to ask you something." He looked around and made sure they were alone. "In light of what's happened to us over the past forty-eight hours, if you knew beyond a shadow of a doubt that someone was going to hurt or even murder someone close to you—if you knew for a fact that this was going to happen—what would you do?"

Elizabeth thought for a moment. "Under the circumstances, nothing I guess."

"How can you say that?" Paul stopped short and glanced warily around. Satisfied no one had heard him, he whispered sternly, "How can you say that?"

"What do you think we're supposed to do?"

"I don't know! I just want to spend as much time with Jesus as I can. I want to know everything I can about Him, and there just aren't enough hours in the day."

"Don't you think I'm torn too?" Elizabeth asked. "It's not like I do a quick time travel all the time, much less back to the time of Christ. In fact, if I stop and think about it, I'm pretty freaked about the whole thing!"

"I know. I am too. It's just that . . . it's just that I feel like Judas is cutting us out of what little time we have left to be with the Master."

While they sat in momentary silence, Paul could feel the tears trickle down his cheeks. He reached through the darkness and touched Elizabeth on the arm, knowing full well that she was hurting as much as he was, but what could they do? They both felt an overwhelming sense of helplessness.

All they knew for sure was that they had just begun to know the Savior. And there wasn't much time left.

Sixteen

(13 Nisan)

The early morning hours were a silent witness to Paul, who sat in a corner of the flat-top roof under the stars. Reflecting on the previous day's events he melted into the velvet blackness and listened while the band of weary disciples lay sleeping around him.

Somehow they had managed to slip backward into another time, to an era filled with beginnings as well as endings. This was decidedly the most momentous of all occasions in the history of mankind. A new promise was being introduced. A New Testament to the world! The old way was passing, and soon Jesus would take His place as the ultimate atonement.

How strange it felt to be in the midst of it all. To hear *Him* speak, to witness the miracles *He* performed, to talk with *Him* face to face. It was all a dream. It was all very real.

A single oil lamp glimmered with the night breeze as Paul sat in the tranquil darkness and watched the Savior while He slept. The man Paul knew most assuredly to be the living, breathing Son of God seemed strangely uneasy. He turned restlessly, pulled a tattered blanket over His shoulder, and clenched it close to His chest. Paul wondered if Jesus might be dreaming, and if so, what were His dreams? Was it possible that He agonized over what He knew would surely come to pass? Or perhaps God the Father spoke to Him even in His sleep. And though Paul didn't know for

sure, it was certainly worth considering.

How wonderful to be in the presence of so many illustrious men of God—men who had given up everything to follow this one called Jesus, and one day would give their lives for Him. Sadly, they were also men who had no concept as to how their world was about to change. They had no idea that the man they had followed faithfully for the past three years would suddenly be snatched from them, leaving them as sheep for the slaughter.

And what's our part in all of this?

Jesus really hadn't explained in any great detail to either Paul or Elizabeth. He simply had said that the answers to their questions would be made known. That was it. He didn't seem to worry about explaining any further than that. In truth, He didn't seem to feel the need to explain much of anything He did.

Our answers will be made known. But what are our questions?

Suddenly the lamp's flame flickered and died. Paul ran his hand blindly across the floor and pulled his watch from his things. Pressing the indicator, he illuminated the face. It was April 7, and it was already a quarter till five. He hadn't slept a wink, nor was he the least bit tired.

Shadows were now faint and long as the moon hung low in the western sky. Paul sat in silence, enamored with a stillness so tranquil that every sound was distinct, down to the beating of his own heart.

His mind reeled. The idea of physically meeting Jesus

Christ in the flesh still played heavily upon his emotions. In all his hopes and dreams, he would never have believed that it could be possible. There was nothing that could ever have pleased him more than meeting the Savior—nothing. It was as if God had taken all his hopes and dreams and rolled them into one. Jesus was everything Paul hoped He would be, and though Paul savored every moment, he knew Christ agonized with the very knowledge He possessed.

This greatly distressed Paul. How would he have the fortitude to sit and watch without lifting a finger as his Savior was murdered? How would he be able to watch while they hammered the nails into His feet and hands? Was this how it was supposed to be? Were they really there to be spectators only? Were they?

Although Jesus had been specific in that they would not be able to stop what was going to happen, what about their interaction with those around them? Was there anything they could do that would change things? Had they already done something that might, in some way, have already affected the future? Neither Paul nor Elizabeth knew for sure.

And what about the professor? Jesus had asked them to pray for him. Was Van Eaton in some kind of trouble? Would they ever even see him again? There was no clear answer.

Through the shadows, Paul watched as Jesus curled into a fetal position and massaged His palm. It was as if He already considered the pain, envisioned the scourging, the

beatings, the rusty nails that would pierce His flesh. These were all atrocities of man's twisted fantasies. And the very sacrifice Jesus would pay would be for those who carried out this hideous task.

Paul watched another disciple turn restlessly in the shadows. Knowing specifically the role Judas Iscariot would play wore heavily on his heart. It was all he could do to keep from exposing the man's treachery himself, yet he knew this was the way it had to be.

Jesus' unprecedented love was now more evident than ever to Paul. He couldn't bring himself to even look at Judas without contempt—and yet, Jesus seemed to care for him as deeply as He did all of his disciples. It was a realm in which only the Son of God could possibly dwell.

Again Paul considered his and Elizabeth's reason for being there. This whole idea of witnessing events already ingrained into history and yet not lifting a finger was the most agonizing situation either of them had ever faced.

Bearing the burden of such knowledge was almost like a curse, he reasoned. To remain passive in the midst of a battle that was surely imminent would take them both to their ultimate limits. And Paul didn't know if they had the strength to endure it.

Suddenly Jesus stirred and gingerly sat up. He wiped the sleep from His eyes and yawned. He had been asleep almost five hours.

He stood and girded Himself with His belt, then descended the stairway, stopping at the bottom to slide on His sandals. Paul watched as He was reduced to a shadow and disappeared into the darkness.

Paul slid on his shoes and hurried down the stairs. He woke Elizabeth who was instantly alert.

"What's happened?" she whispered.

"Jesus just left. He headed out that way." Paul motioned into the darkness.

† † †

The eastern sky slowly blushed with color. Birds and creatures that had spent the night in relative silence stirred and filled the air with their medleys. But on this particular morning, Jesus heard very little. The light of heaven found him solidly on His knees, bound in impassioned prayer to the Father.

Elizabeth was the first to spot Him. He was there in the distance, perfectly poised and facing away from them. As the sun crested the ridge, He stood wearily.

The sight was surreal. Mist from the valley rose between the two slopes, enveloping Him like a cloud so that pale streams of light from the morning sun radiated past His body and burst in all directions. It was Jesus Christ in all His splendor—a more beautiful portrait than any artist had endeavored to paint.

"Do you think we should we bother him?" Elizabeth asked.

"I think He wants us to."

Paul almost reached for her hand to lead her up the hill, but stopped, fearing it could be misinterpreted. Their relationship was burgeoning into a pure friendship that he knew he would never experience with anyone else. Sharing these days with Christ was creating a bond that could not be described.

He brushed past her and started up the hill. "Come on!"

† † †

Paul caught the first glimpse of the majestic sight: Jerusalem, ancient and unadorned in all its rustic grandeur. The sun cast its light across the walled fortress, accenting the distinct skyline that for centuries had defined the eastern wall. Standing beside Elizabeth, he watched columns of smoke rising from numerous fires throughout and heard an occasional donkey bray, but the city as a whole was still asleep.

Paul gazed at the Master in awe, feeling a twinge of foreboding. Jesus seemed disconnected, even muddled, though He was lucid. It was as if He was putting His affairs into order, preparing Himself for that single momentous instant when He would give His life for all mankind. Thirty-plus tumultuous years on earth were drawing to a close—and Paul and Elizabeth knew it. And though they had only known the Savior on such a personal level for two short days, a strange sort of clairvoyant link had been

established between their hearts and His.

The oneness made perfect sense to Paul, and he and Elizabeth never questioned it. They merely stood with Him in silence, recognizing the gravity of the moment and sharing the inexplicable affirmation. This was as close to heaven as they had ever been.

Jesus stood, the sweet smell of perfume from Mary's anointing still very present. Paul had seen what a special time that had been for Jesus, and how Mary had been honored that He'd accepted her exquisite gift in spite of the critical remarks of some of the disciples. Jesus had known she gave solely from her heart, and there was nothing more He could have asked than that.

"Jerusalem," He sighed. "If you—even if you had only known on this day what would bring you peace. But now it is hidden from your eyes." His hands clenched into fists.

"The days will come upon you when your enemies will build an embankment against you and encircle you, hemming you in on every side. They will throw you to the ground, you and the children within your walls. They will not leave one stone upon another because you did not recognize the time of God's coming to you." His face tensed with the agonizing prediction.

Paul reflected on his studies. "The fall of Jerusalem. But that's not for . . . another forty years."

Jesus turned, His face glistening with tears. "Time is not what is important. You of all people should know that."

He stepped closer to Paul, and His face took on a

different expression. "For you are here with me, and yet, at this very moment, I am with you two millennia from now." His eyes burned into Paul's. "From the day you were conceived, I was there. And the day you preached your first sermon—you entitled it 'Payday Someday' did you not?"

Tears suddenly spilled from Paul's eyes, and Jesus clutched his shoulder. "Paul—" He smiled thinly, and Paul's heart fluttered at the sound of his name. "You worry over so many things, my son, your church—and your father, Robert."

Paul heaved a sigh as thoughts of his stepfather wove into His conscious. "I—I don't know if I'm ready for this—"

Elizabeth stepped away and looked out over the valley to give them some privacy.

Jesus cupped one hand at the nape of Paul's neck and squeezed gently. "Worry will neither add one member to my church, nor will it heal a sick man. Worry only brings tomorrow's difficulty into today, and God didn't give you grace for tomorrow's difficulties. He gave you grace for today. Worry takes not the sorrow out of tomorrow; but the strength out of today."

Paul saw that tears swelled in Jesus' eyes. A long pause fell between them that Paul didn't want to end.

"And I want you to know," He said softly, "that Robert is mine."

Paul beamed and pulled Jesus to his chest. "Thank you, Lord," he sobbed. "Thank you."

Elizabeth too was stirred by Jesus' words, though the impact on Paul was considerably greater. But that was about to change. Jesus stepped toward the young doctor.

"Elizabeth," He said, "there is something you, too, must try to understand." Jesus drew a deep breath and sighed as He let it out, His gaze piercing Elizabeth's. "Death is not a punishment but, rather, a door. A door through which we all must surely pass."

Elizabeth smiled timidly. She was an accomplished woman, and in all of her life, she had never been in such a precarious place as this.

With gentle deftness, Jesus continued. "You lament over your brother, Thomas." His words penetrated deep into her soul, echoing in her ears and injecting her heart with pain.

She furrowed her brow as she spoke. "My brother . . . " She cleared her throat, not really knowing how to respond. "My brother . . . is homosexual. Or was. And I hate what it's done to him."

Jesus' face was passive, though He listened intently.

"But he wasn't always that way. He . . . he just . . . took a wrong turn, I guess. He never really seemed to get a handle on life."

Jesus' expression suddenly indicated His distaste for Elizabeth's rationale. "The same sun that melts the wax . . . does is not also harden the clay?"

Elizabeth considered the Master's words.

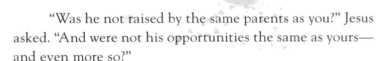

"Was he not raised by the same parents as you?" Jesus asked. "And were not his opportunities the same as yours—and even more so?"

She listened without comment, knowing full well to what Jesus alluded. If anything, she should have been the one to have problems. She hadn't been the favored of the two. For whatever reason, it had always been Tom. But it still didn't matter. That was just the way it was, and she had accepted it long ago.

In the quiet of the moment, her mind reeled to her last meeting with her brother. How his life had changed, virtually overnight. How Tom had reached out for God, and God had answered.

"I want to tell you a story," Jesus said. He settled back to the ground and appeared to gather His thoughts. "There were two brothers. They were twins—identical, in fact."

Elizabeth glanced at Paul as Jesus continued. "They were both raised in the same house, living and growing together equally and without favor. Then one day their father walked out on them, never to return, and left their mother to the task of raising the family." Jesus let the words sink in.

"Both children were loved equally by their mother, and both were raised without preference or precedence. Eventually the two boys grew into men and went their separate ways." Jesus tipped His head to one side for emphasis. "As time passed, the one man gained prominence and great wealth, while the other became a beggar."

Tears pooled in Elizabeth's eyes as she listened.

"One day the beggar was asked why he lived in such a way, sleeping with the swine and eating from the garbage in the street. 'When I was a child,' the man explained, 'my father abandoned us and never returned. I never forgave him for that. How could a man do such a thing to his family?' "

Jesus faced Elizabeth. "The same question was posed to the wealthy brother. 'And to what do you attribute your success,' he was asked? The man thought for a moment, then replied, 'When I was a child, my father abandoned us, and I knew I had to take care of my family.' " Jesus waited while the message took hold.

Suddenly Elizabeth was flooded with emotion.

Jesus had made His point, and had done so with a surgeon's precision. Perhaps she had been blaming herself all these years for her brother's downfall, Elizabeth thought, though she really didn't know why. But then again, that was just her way. She often took responsibility for things she had no control over—such as losing young accident victims.

But there's more to this story, she thought.

"The day before I left, Tom gave his life—" She stopped mid-sentence.

Jesus gave her a warm smile, the sun-browned skin at the corners of His eyes and mouth wrinkling.

"But you already knew that, didn't you?" she whispered.

Jesus' smile broadened.

"Why is it that sometimes we have to hit rock bottom before we find the truth?" she asked, her face now splotched with tears. "And then it seems that God opens the door."

Jesus stroked His beard while He considered the question. "Do you not think the door was always open, and you just went your own way to find it?"

Elizabeth smiled, marveling at the Master's words. Life suddenly seemed to make perfect sense when He told the story. And though these were different times, they seemed very much the same.

"I know you're hurting, but try to understand that Thomas of all people knows what he has done, and he has accepted the consequences." Jesus flashed a compassionate smile. "But more important, that single act of accepting God's call outweighs the multitude of sins he has committed, and the consequences of that decision will reap unimaginable returns."

Elizabeth nodded slowly. She only hoped that one day she would see her brother again and be able to share with Tom the amazing experience of this day.

Suddenly, Peter appeared at the top of the hill. "Lord—" he huffed, winded from the walk. "I've been . . . looking all over for you. We've got trouble."

Jesus glanced at Elizabeth and Paul and rolled His eyes.

† † †

Voices caromed off the cold, dark walls, shocking the professor awake. He had been asleep for nearly nine hours. As on the night before, jet lag had taken its toll on the elderly professor, and he awoke just as puzzled as when he had drifted off, though the nausea was still completely gone. That was a good thing.

He watched as two figures entered the cave, both carrying clay jars. They were women, and both had come for the same reason.

While they filled their jars, they talked of the day's events. Van Eaton instinctively reached to turn up his hearing aid and again remembered losing it in the well room. He swore. Then he cupped his hand to his ear and caught most of the conversation.

The women spoke in a form of old Arabic, which was odd enough, but then again, not as strange as the two languages he had heard when Elizabeth and Paul talked with the locals.

He wondered if he'd made the right decision leaving them that way. He also considered the words that had been scrawled in the dust at the campsite.

Through the veil you will see the truth.

As strange as it seemed, he felt the words were somehow meant for him, though he didn't know why or understand their relevance. Finally the women finished and left. Van Eaton bided his time in the cave until they were well away.

† † †

Elizabeth and Paul slowed their pace, falling farther behind Peter and Jesus. She opened her pocket Bible and flipped through the pages.

"Look at this. Matthew stopped at twenty-one yesterday—remember? And now look!"

Words, even complete chapters, filled pages that were previously blank. Their theory was right. Quite a drama was unfolding. The perfectly orchestrated last days of Christ were now intertwined with their own presence. And though they weren't able to use her Bible as a key to coming events, it allowed them to validate the events after the fact.

She slid the Bible under her belt, then tried to put her feelings into words. "You know, these things are happening. We've even met the Lord. But it all still seems like a dream."

Paul was still distracted. "You know, since this is God's plan, is there anything we could do to mess things up anyway?"

Elizabeth didn't respond. Truthfully, she hadn't even considered that idea.

Paul pushed farther. "I mean, is our memory of biblical history still a reliable source to draw from, or are we remembering from a future that could now be uncertain?"

"You mean quantum mechanics, like the professor was talking about?"

"I . . . I don't know. I guess so. Have we done one thing or changed anything, for that matter, that would possibly change something about the future?"

Elizabeth shrugged and shook her head.

"It just seems to me that if we base our knowledge on what we think happened, do we know for sure that it is going to happen that way? Or has our presence here already changed something in the future?"

"Don't even go there," she chided. "You're making my head hurt."

"I can't help it," Paul whispered heavily. "It makes too much sense."

"But didn't He say that there is nothing we could do to change what was about to happen?"

"Yes, He did, but didn't He also say that we had come for a very specific purpose?"

Elizabeth listened while Paul tried to make his point. "Okay, I understand what you're saying, but what have we done?"

"I don't know. Maybe nothing . . . but maybe more than we think."

Elizabeth searched Paul's eyes. "Does the Bible say anything that might indicate that there were any outsiders involved with Jesus in those last days?"

"Not that I can remember."

"What about those Greeks we met yesterday?"

"They were supposed to be there," he said.

"Well, maybe we just need to make sure we *don't* do

something that might change things, you think?"

Paul stared vacantly at Elizabeth. "Maybe so."

Elizabeth's mind reeled with the thought of witnessing the crucifixion—and doing so without recourse. Staring into Paul's eyes, she read the same emotion in their depths.

SEVENTEEN

(14 Nisan)

The two-mile trek from Bethany to Jerusalem seemed to take twice as long as it had the day before. The band of itinerant disciples all maintained less of a hurried pace. Even Jesus didn't have the usual spring in His step, Paul noted, and yet still He pressed on. Retiring late as He had the last several nights and rising well before sunrise had become the norm for the Master, and though it had begun to take its toll, He never complained. Paul sensed that He wanted to make the most of every minute.

Paul was dragging too. He hadn't slept a wink the night before, and now he too was beginning to pay for it. Instinctively he glanced at his wrist for the time, and smiled to himself. It was interesting to live without telephones—cell phones and otherwise—and realize that there was no real lack of communication; to live without electricity, and yet there seemed to be no real need. There wasn't even a good way to tell time, but it really didn't seem to matter. There were no board meetings or planes to catch, no clock to live by or Internet to dictate your day. It was all so simple, even primitive—and yet, there was a wondrous freedom.

This was the time Christ had chosen to live, and though He could have chosen any other time in history, He stopped here. But what if He had chosen the twenty-first century? Would things have been different? Would modern man have been more apt to recognize the truth? To find the deeper meanings of Jesus' words, His thoughts, and why

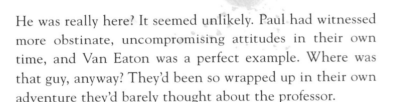

He was really here? It seemed unlikely. Paul had witnessed more obstinate, uncompromising attitudes in their own time, and Van Eaton was a perfect example. Where was that guy, anyway? They'd been so wrapped up in their own adventure they'd barely thought about the professor.

Apparently Elizabeth was reading his mind. "Paul, do you think we should ask Jesus about the professor? I mean, he wasn't in the best shape when he left us. I feel kinda guilty just blowing him off. I did take an oath, you know."

"I guess so, but I'm not leaving Jesus to go after him." The conversation hung in the air without resolution.

For Paul this was more than just an incomparable life event. This was his life. Like Jesus, Paul was a shepherd, and he hoped Elizabeth didn't blame him for being single minded about it.

I guess, even Elizabeth, right in the midst of it, doesn't realize how important it is, Paul thought. Not her, and not even these men who had spent virtually every minute of the last three years with Jesus, could interpret the signs or even the very words of Jesus, for that matter. Had He not already revealed the plan repeatedly? What was it about

"My kingdom is not of this world" and "I go to prepare a place for you," that they didn't get?

Were their preconceived hopes of an earthly kingdom outweighing their own spiritual discernment? Paul wasn't sure. And even if that was the case, what about Judas? The man both he and Elizabeth knew would eventually commit the heinous act of sedition seemed as oblivious as the rest,

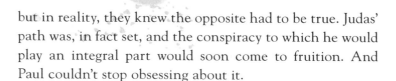

but in reality, they knew the opposite had to be true. Judas' path was, in fact set, and the conspiracy to which he would play an integral part would soon come to fruition. And Paul couldn't stop obsessing about it.

† † †

Peter slipped closer to Paul. "Last night, you said you wanted to talk." His tone was frank.

Elizabeth, only a few steps behind, coughed and cleared her throat, then fell in step with Nathanael. The older disciple smiled and nodded to her.

"Have you known the Master long?" he asked pushing his sleeves up over his elbows.

Elizabeth circled the question. "A few years I suppose. And you?"

Nathanael smiled and stroked his beard. "It's been three years." He glanced toward the sun. "And a month. Funny how I remember that. I was in Galilee when Jesus called me. It was the strangest thing too. He knew me before I knew Him. I'll never forget as long as I live." He spoke with passion, savoring the moment.

"The night before we met, I had had the strangest dream," he explained. "Actually, I don't remember all of it, but I remember standing under a tree—a fig tree in the midst of the desert. I was alone and yet . . . I was not. I must sound like an old fool."

"No. Not at all."

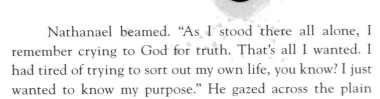

Nathanael beamed. "As I stood there all alone, I remember crying to God for truth. That's all I wanted. I had tired of trying to sort out my own life, you know? I just wanted to know my purpose." He gazed across the plain and sighed. "I wasn't a young man even then, yet I knew there was more to life than what I was living."

Elizabeth nodded as they walked on common ground.

"The very next morning, Jesus was there in the city. He had already called Andrew and Peter—and John, as I remember. Then Philip came over to me." Nathanael brushed the tears from his eyes. "He said he had found the one Moses had written about, that He was the carpenter from Nazareth. I remember asking him if anything good ever came from Nazareth! Can you believe I said these words?"

Elizabeth laughed with him. Nathanael was so transparent—and incontestably honest. It was obvious that Jesus knew of this attribute from the start.

"Nevertheless, I followed Philip," he continued. "And when I met Him, the Master already knew who I was! He called me an honest man and told me He had seen me under the tree—the tree I dreamed about! I had told no one of that dream. Not a soul."

He stopped in the road and looked directly at Elizabeth. "I just wanted to know the truth. And now I have been following the truth for three years."

"And a month," she added.

Nathanael touched her on the shoulder. "Yes, my friend, and a month."

† † †

Quantum mechanics. Quantum mechanics, indeed.

The professor re-rolled the scrolls. He recalled his undergraduate work at MIT and how his professor had hammered him. Now he tried desperately to recall his studies.

Directly related to quantum physics, quantum mechanics was born out of the idea that if one could actually travel backward into time, as quantum physics suggests, and change one minute detail, it would constitute an alternate future. That much Van Eaton did remember. It was a logical deduction from an illogical concept, or so he'd always thought. Then there was Planck's Hypothesis of Discrete Units, Heisenberg's Theory of something or other, and of course, there was Einstein.

"God does not play dice," Einstein had once said.

Van Eaton combed his fingers through his oily, silver hair. *God doesn't need to* play *dice. He's a master at it.*

Crunching over shards of broken pottery, he moved to the edge of the pool and knelt. Drinking from cupped hands he splashed his face and noticed his blood-stained sleeve. Phantom pain suddenly riddled his arm, but he knew it wasn't real.

He stood and noticed several broken clay jars beside the pool, and some that were still intact. Good. Actually, none of them would have held water, which was why they were probably there in the first place. But they would certainly do for what he needed.

The light of the morning sun drove shadows from the cave as the professor examined his surroundings. There was any number of suitable hiding places. He only had to choose one and then remember which it was. Finally he found just the spot.

He coiled the scrolls carefully and slid them into the jar. They disappeared below the rim and uncoiled slightly as they came to rest. He lifted the clay jar into the cleft and placed a stone in front of it. It was the perfect place.

I shouldn't have left the city in the first place. He stepped outside and gazed across the desert plain. *Besides, it's less than a day's journey, and there are too many questions still unanswered. Far too many.*

† † †

Paul was tormented by thoughts of the man walking ahead

of him and how He would soon hang from a wooden cross. But he was even more tormented by thoughts of the one who would sell him out.

The others were in yet another place—a place with visions of affluence and grandeur, while ideas of commonwealth clouded their thinking. There was no cross to consider, no suffering, and certainly no death.

Paul searched Peter's eyes as he wrestled with his words. "Peter," he stammered, "please try to understand . . . I . . . I just want to help." His eyes flashed desperation.

Jesus glanced back as Paul's heart cried for wisdom, but there seemed to be no clear answer. Jesus turned away and walked on ahead.

"I don't understand why you are hurting, but I want to help," Peter offered. He clasped Paul's shoulder. "Denial is not a good thing."

Without speaking, Paul considered the irony.

† † †

In the distance Elizabeth noticed a lone figure descending from a paltry brick house perched in a clearing on the hill to her immediate right. While Jesus and most of the group walked on ahead, she slowed her pace and watched.

The woman appeared to be middle aged. She was hunchbacked and hobbled unsteadily with a crutch. Elizabeth walked toward the woman, who cowered and stepped backward.

"Unclean!" she cried. "I am unclean!"

Elizabeth hesitated, then stepped closer. "Don't be afraid. I'm not going to hurt you."

"No! Don't you see I am a leper?" the woman cried.

Her cadaverous face was pasty, her eyes red veined. She quivered slightly. Elizabeth guessed that no one had dared come this close to her for a long time.

Elizabeth could feel Peter watching with amazement as she moved toward the ghostly figure. He certainly knew that leprosy was deadly and believed it to be extremely contagious, but at the moment Elizabeth was more concerned about the woman than about what he might think. After a cursory examination, she gently pulled the woman's sleeve above her elbow and touched her scaly skin. The woman winced at the touch.

"It's all right." Elizabeth said.

She dropped her backpack to the ground, and Paul's video camera spilled out along with the nails from the well room. She stuffed them back into the bag, but not before Peter had noticed. She glanced up to find him staring at her, mouth open.

"What can we do to help?" Paul asked, clearly making an effort to steer the conversation away from dangerous territory.

Shaking her head, Elizabeth sifted through the case. She found what she was looking for, took the tube, and squeezed ointment onto her fingertips.

At first the woman winced when the cool cream

contacted her skin, but a moment later she relaxed and allowed Elizabeth do whatever she wished.

It was clear Peter thought she had lost her mind. No one touched lepers other than Jesus.

"She doesn't have leprosy," Elizabeth told the two men. "It's ichthyosis."

"It's what?" Peter asked.

"She has ichthyosis. Granted it's the worst case I've ever seen, but I believe that's all it is. She's not contagious."

Elizabeth turned toward Peter, not realizing what she had shared.

"How do you know these things?" Peter asked.

Oh well. "I learned of it in my training as a physician." Elizabeth prayed that Peter wouldn't ask any more questions.

The big fisherman watched, his expression reflecting total dismay, while she massaged the woman's reptilian skin. She could almost hear him thinking, *A woman physician?*

"This cream will help." Elizabeth replaced the cap and handed the tube to the woman. "Put this on every day until it's all gone."

The woman eagerly took the tube and peered at the strange script written on it. "Thank you, my friend. You are truly a physician?"

Elizabeth laughed. "Yes. And you don't have leprosy."

"Thank you—thank you!" she cried. She threw her arms around Elizabeth's neck and wept. "I will never forget what you have done for me! Never!"

Elizabeth watched the woman hurry up the path to her

house and disappear through the door. Repacking her bag, she contemplated a whole laundry list of drugs she wished she'd brought. She smiled to herself, wondering what Peter might have done with a few milligrams of Ritalin, and what John might have reaped from a week or two on Prozac.

She turned as Thomas and Judas joined them.

"What did you do to her?" Judas asked. An air of

distrust mingled with his words.

Beside her, Paul bristled. His prejudice was more than obvious, and he wasn't doing a very good job of controlling it. It was obvious Thomas sensed it as well, but he kept this thoughts to himself.

"I gave her a sort of . . . healing agent," Elizabeth said, choosing her words carefully.

Raising an eyebrow, Judas shot Thomas a meaningful look.

"Come on!" Andrew called out. "We're meeting at the Olive Mount."

She wrapped the cloth around her backpack and heaved it to her shoulder, hurrying ahead as Peter and Paul trailed behind. "Don't worry about him," she heard Peter say. "Sometimes Judas wears his heart on his sleeve, but he's a good man."

Good people go to hell too, Elizabeth thought.

✝ ✝ ✝

The mottled stone walls that surrounded the ancient city

followed the jagged contour of the rocky slope, looming against powder blue skies and accenting the landscape with ancient motifs—or modern as the case might be.

Peter pointed. "That is the Dung Gate." He scrunched his nose and grinned. "We will follow the valley to the north around the southeast corner of the city, and then up to the Mount of Olives.

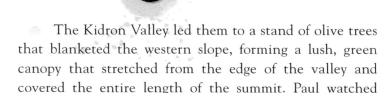

The Kidron Valley led them to a stand of olive trees that blanketed the western slope, forming a lush, green canopy that stretched from the edge of the valley and covered the entire length of the summit. Paul watched while the group filtered into the trees and disappeared along with others who had joined the assembly.

"Come on!" Excitement hurried his steps. "I don't want to lose them!"

"Slow . . . your pace," Peter huffed. "I know . . . where . . . they're going."

Pressing toward the wooded slope at a steady clip, Paul and Elizabeth followed Peter's lead. But someone was missing.

"Where is Judas?" Paul's suspicion went unnoticed.

"He will be along," Thomas answered innocently. "He had business in the city."

Paul drilled Elizabeth with a stare. *I'll bet he does.*

Paul was amazed at Thomas' indifference, and yet it seemed to be the general consensus of the entire group. No one seemed to be at all suspicious of Judas.

In a small clearing in the olive copse, the group, now

doubled in size, gathered and sat as Jesus prepared to teach. Paul and Elizabeth joined the assembly with the other disciples. Save Judas.

Jesus bowed his head, which was His signal to begin. The assembly hushed.

"For the kingdom of heaven is like a landowner who went out early in the morning to hire men to work in his vineyard."

Jesus waited long enough for them to still, then he continued. "He agreed to pay them a denarius for the day and sent them into his vineyard. About the third hour, he went out and saw others standing in the marketplace doing nothing. He told them, 'You also go and work in my vineyard, and I will pay you whatever is right.' So they went."

Jesus glanced quickly around the group, which was nearly twice the usual size. "He went out again about the sixth hour and the ninth hour and did the same thing. About the eleventh hour, he went out and found still others standing around. He asked them, 'Why have you been standing here all day long doing nothing?' 'Because no one has hired us,' they answered. He said to them, 'You also go and work in my vineyard.'"

Jesus spoke with controlled passion. "When evening came, the owner of the vineyard said to his foreman, 'Call the workers and pay them their wages, beginning with the last ones hired and going on to the first.' The workers who were hired about the eleventh hour came and each received a denarius. So when those came who were hired first, they expected to receive more, but each one of them also received a denarius. When they received it, they grumbled against the landowner. 'These men who were hired last worked only one hour, and you have made them equal to us, who have borne the burden of the work and the heat of the day.'

"But he answered them, 'Friend, I am not being unfair to you. Didn't you agree to work for a denarius? Take your pay and go. I want to pay the man I hired last the same as I gave you. Don't I have the right to do what I want with my own money? Or are you envious because I am generous?' "

Jesus stroked his beard while He spoke. "So the last will be first and the first will be last." Again He paused to iterate the message.

As before, Paul knew well the story Jesus shared, but the most amazing part of all was to watch Christ while He shared it, watching his eyes as they pierced the facades of pride and vanity. It was as if angels whispered on the breeze that sifted through the trees.

Then suddenly a figure stepped from behind a tree and stood at the rear of the group. And though he said nothing, all eyes were drawn to him. Even Jesus stopped speaking.

The man stood transfixed, arms crossed at his chest as though he sized up the gathering, counting their strength while considering his own. He knew he was well outnumbered, but he was unmistakably a Roman, and the sword he carried made his odds much more favorable.

Paul could feel a wave of emotion sweep over the group as each man weighed the situation. Would he arrest the whole group or simply slay them where they stood? Was he alone or were others waiting in the trees? After a few anxious moments, he spoke.

"You are the rabble," he spit in the dust, "that's been

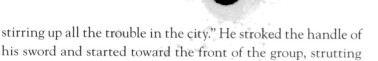

stirring up all the trouble in the city." He stroked the handle of his sword and started toward the front of the group, strutting with an arrogant gait.

"His face seems vaguely familiar," Peter told Paul in a low voice, "but I cannot place it."

Jesus stood without comment and watched as the man worked his way toward Him.

"I will make you a proposition," the man said in a gruff voice heavy with malevolence. He paused and wiped the sweat from his acne-pocked face. "If there is anyone here, who is not part of this seditious group, I will allow you to leave." He slapped his fist into his open palm.

A deafening silence fell on the group. Stirring nervously, each man pondered the offer and its underlying threat. Even Paul was shaken, and he saw that all the color had drained from Elizabeth's face.

"Well?" the Roman shouted.

One man quietly rose to a crouch and eased toward the path that led back to the city. Another followed, then another. Man after man disappeared through the trees, leaving only the Savior, the disciples, and the two from the future.

Peter's eyes were fixed on the lone warrior. Shafts of sunlight pierced the trees and crisscrossed the man's face as he strode toward Jesus, pulling his sword from its scabbard.

His heart pounding, Peter jumped to his feet, along with Matthew and Thomas. Jesus immediately stepped between them and the intruder, staring directly into the Roman's eyes.

With the tip of his sword, the soldier methodically carved an arch in the dust at his feet. Jesus paused for a moment, then with the toe of his sandal struck a second arch, forming the sign of the fish.

A smile crept slowly across the Master's face.

"Marcus," he said softly.

"Lord." The two men embraced. "I'm sorry I had to do that, but the eyes of Jerusalem are not without deceit."

"You are wise. Brothers, this is our friend Marcus Altus. Remember—in Capernaum?"

Then Peter remembered. *This man came to Jesus nearly two years ago when his servant took ill and called upon the Master to heal him. It was of him that Jesus said, "I have not found anyone in Israel with such great faith."*

"You charlatan!" Peter embraced the centurion. "Rabble?" he teased.

Marcus shook his head and grinned. "Forgive me, Peter," he said, returning the embrace.

"And where have you been these past two years?"

Marcus peered at the ground. "I was assigned to the

Praetorian Guard here in Jerusalem nearly a year ago."

"Pontius Pilate?" Peter asked hesitantly.

"Yes."

"And your servant—he lives still?"

"Now more so than ever."

Elizabeth peered at Paul. "Pontius Pilate?" she

whispered.

His expression grim, Paul nodded.

Gradually the group settled once again, and Jesus returned to his place before them. Her heart aching, Elizabeth leaned forward, listening intently so she would not miss a single word.

"I am sending you out as sheep among wolves," Jesus said softly. "Therefore be as wise as serpents and as harmless as doves. Be on your guard against men; they will hand you over to the local councils and flog you in the synagogues. On my account you will be brought before governors and kings as witnesses to them and to the gentiles. But when they arrest you, do not worry about what to say or how to say it. At that time you will be given what to say, for it will not be you speaking, but the spirit of your Father speaking through you. Brother will betray brother to death."

† † †

The path that led through the Zion Gate on the south wall was littered with travelers from as far south as Eboda and as far north as Sidon, north of Samaria. They had all come as they had every year for the Passover festivities. Now that it was only two days away, the air was electric. People from seemingly every walk of life passed through the gates, many carrying sacrificial lambs over their shoulders like mink stoles in preparation for the religious feast of the year. For the rich as well as the poor, religion permeated every facet of life for the vast majority of people in Israel and this is how it had always been.

Mingling in the crowds, Judas pressed quietly through the street. His movements were fluid, his gait deliberate as he made his way to the home of the high priest. As arranged, he met two Sanhedrin members in the courtyard.

"What would you say if I told you I can turn him over to you?" Judas peered in both directions with deep-set eyes as he spoke, his voice low and contemptuous.

"And what is the price for such a favor?"

Judas considered the question, his eyes narrowing and his face flushing slightly as he licked his lips. "The price of a slave," he answered flatly.

The two priests turned and whispered between themselves. After a moment of division, the larger of the two men agreed. "Thirty pieces of silver it shall be—and not a shekel more."

Judas nodded in agreement. "I will inform you when I know for certain. Give me a day."

† † †

"Get on!" Van Eaton cried. He cleared the phlegm from his throat and tried to spit but swallowed instead.

Crossing the desolate plain of Hebron, east of Qumran, the professor wasn't completely sure that he was going in the right direction. He struggled to maintain his balance while his donkey stumbled across the rocky terrain the professor had hoped would eventually lead him to

Jerusalem. Unfortunately, stealing the animal from a poor family in Qumran would prove to be the easiest task he would perform on this day. Trying to find his way back to Jerusalem—and doing so alone—was beginning to look like a dangerous mistake, but he had gone too far to turn back now.

He strained to catch a glimpse of the city. "I am a fool. I've talked myself into the grave, and for what? Am I to die out here without even knowing what this is all about?"

Quietly in the distance, there appeared a faint silhouette. He wiped the sweat from his eyes and focused on the horizon.

"Those are walls!"

† † †

Following the rocky path around the northern rim of the Kidron Valley, Jesus and His disciples approached Solomon's Porch. There they passed through the Susa Gate and continued into the city. Marcus Altus had said his goodbyes and taken an alternate route to the south, agreeing to meet them later that evening in Bethany.

As they passed through the gate, Eliabeth's attention was drawn to a man at a merchant's tent haggling over a costly tunic. He dropped several silver coins back into his pouch and tugged on the drawstring.

"Judas!" Thomas called out. He motioned to his fellow

disciple, though Judas had already seen them coming.

Judas joined the group without arousing any apparent suspicion. Even Jesus made no comment, though as they walked along it seemed to Elizabeth that He watched Judas with more of a prudent eye.

"Why does he not see it?" she asked Paul in a low tone. She was beginning to feel the difficulty of coping with the knowledge she possessed.

"He sees it," Paul said pointedly. "And it's breaking His heart."

† † †

As Judas filtered into the group, his gait was casual, but his eyes betrayed him. He now seemed diffident. His demeanor had changed, and even the way he carried himself was different. Paul was certain Judas had accomplished what he had been destined to do.

"He's done it," Paul growled.

His throat tightened with malice at the thought, and judging from Elizabeth's expression, she shared his sentiments. Oh, sure, they had expected it, but that didn't make it easier to understand or accept. Jesus was the epitome of love and as compassionate a man as either of them had ever known. What was in Judas's heart that could so blind his eyes to what Jesus had tried to teach them for the last three years?

Neither of them had an answer even after hours of

private discussion over the past few days—and right now, neither cared. Paul's only thought was retribution, and Elizabeth had made it clear that her resentment of Judas's betrayal was growing.

Inching their way closer to the disciple, they moved as one, intent on overhearing his conversation with the Zealot.

"I am a business man." Judas clutched his pouch as he spoke and quieted the contents. "Maybe that's why the Master called me in the first place. I am the only Judean in the group."

Simon clutched the edge of his mantle as he walked, clearly oblivious to Judas' plans. Had he been the practicing Zealot he had been when Jesus called him, Paul reflected, he might have suspected that something was wrong. But as it was, he was totally unaware. When he strolled on ahead, Paul moved closer.

"Judas."

Judas turned. "Yes?"

Paul tried to calm himself by drawing a deep breath and exhaling slowly. "Could we . . . talk with you?" He struggled to keep the anger from his voice.

Judas slowed. "What is wrong with you? You shake as if you are ill."

Paul seethed. He glanced ahead to see if anyone noticed they lagged behind. No one did. Elizabeth stepped back as though she realized what was coming.

Without warning Paul slammed Judas against the stone block wall that lined the pathway, pinning the smaller man at the neck with his forearm. Judas' eyes snapped open wide, and he gasped for breath.

"We know what you're doing," Paul whispered heavily. He rattled the leather pouch on Judas' belt with his free hand. "But you won't get away with it."

The color drained from Judas' face, and he shuddered.

"We know about all of it," Paul hissed. "The deal with the priests, the silver! Everything!"

Judas made an ineffectual attempt to break free. As Paul's grip tightened, Judas gurgled, and then went limp, his eyes rolling back in his head.

Then, as suddenly as he had started, Paul released his grip, and Judas slid to the ground.

For some moments, the disciple huddled at their feet. Then finally he stood, massaging his throat and coughing. He forced a perfunctory smile.

"My friends," he said penitently, his voice raspy, "have I in some way offended you?"

Paul recoiled. This was hardly the response he had expected.

Eying the two of them warily, Judas brushed the dust off his mantle. "Why would you accuse me of such a thing? I have been in the city on business."

Elizabeth rolled her eyes, but Paul stared fixedly at Judas. He wasn't buying the tale.

"Let's dispense with the small talk," Paul snapped.

This elicited a glare from Judas. *Small talk?*

Just then Thomas walked back toward the three of them.

"Judas! The Master needs us."

His smile smooth, Judas stepped between them and hurried toward Thomas, straightening his cloak as he walked.

"Well, he got lucky," Elizabeth drawled.

Paul brushed off his sleeves. "Let's go. It'll be night soon, and we've got a lot of thinking to do."

EIGHTEEN

(14 Nisan)

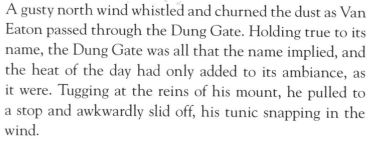

A gusty north wind whistled and churned the dust as Van Eaton passed through the Dung Gate. Holding true to its name, the Dung Gate was all that the name implied, and the heat of the day had only added to its ambiance, as it were. Tugging at the reins of his mount, he pulled to a stop and awkwardly slid off, his tunic snapping in the wind.

This part of the city was different, relatively quiet compared with where he'd been two days before. Good thing. Now that he was, in all truth, a thief, he wanted nothing more than to remain anonymous.

He wandered the narrow streets with no particular agenda other than blending with the crowd. But the chill in the air—who knew the desert could be so cold—drove him to seek warmth by a crackling fire where a few others huddled. After a moment he felt a tug at his sleeve.

"You are the one." A scraggly looking boy stood at his elbow, his brown eyes sparkling with the reflection of the flames.

"You are the one!" His voice grew louder and more insistent. "The one they were looking for yesterday! You were there at the wall!"

Van Eaton's adrenaline pumped. He drew a trembling breath and nervously backed away from the fire.

"He is the one!"

† † †

In a narrow courtyard along the path that led to the washing pools, a fire blazed. The disciples crowded close and soaked up its warmth. Peter found a place near the back, while Paul and Elizabeth sat on either side of him. As so many times before, they all waited expectantly for Jesus to share His heart. They never tired of listening to Him, and there was always something more to learn.

"The Master seems uneasy," Peter worried. He pulled his sleeves to his wrists and moved closer to the fire. "I don't understand. Passover is at hand."

What could either of them say that would possibly help the big fisherman understand, and would it really matter anyway? Paul wondered. Weren't these events already indelibly ingrained into history? And the squabble with Judas? Paul might have killed him— or was it even possible for him to do so?

Taking matters into their own hands had simply

been a reaction to the treachery they knew was afoot. So maybe they had made a difference. They had drawn the line, and Judas now knew they were on to him.

Jesus rose to speak. "I tell you the truth, you will weep and mourn while the world rejoices." His voice echoed in the cove in an eerie sort of way. "You will grieve, but your grief will turn to joy." He flashed a warm smile, though it was short lived.

"A woman giving birth to a child has pain because her time has come, but when her baby is born, she forgets the anguish because of her joy that a child is born into the world. So with you." He peered somberly into their faces. "Now is your time of grief."

Peter blanched at Jesus' words and the urgency in His voice. He turned to Paul. "Why does the Master speak in this way?"

Elizabeth held his gaze but said nothing. Paul looked away. An awkward silence fell between them.

"The device that fell from your bag on the road today—what was it?"

Elizabeth directed an alarmed glance at Paul. Paul nudged Peter and nodded toward Jesus.

"Now I am going away to the one who sent me," Jesus continued. "And none of you asks me where I am going. Instead, you are filled with grief. But I tell you the truth: It is for your good that I am going away."

Peter laid his hand on Paul's arm. "What is going on here?"

Again Paul could not come up with a response.

Peter was becoming increasingly agitated. "You *do* know something, I fear—"

Paul brought a finger to his pursed lips.

"Unless I go away, the Counselor will not come to you," Jesus told them. "But if I go, I will send Him to you."

"Counselor?" Peter whispered, straightening and looking up.

"There is so much more I want to tell you," Jesus said. "But you can't bear it now." His eyes swept the group. "When the Spirit of truth comes, He will guide you into all truth. He will not present His own ideas; He will tell you what He has heard, and He will tell you about the future."

Jesus stared directly at Paul and Elizabeth, and Peter noticed the exchange. Paul sensed that Peter's fear was rapidly turning to exasperation.

† † †

The professor lurked in and out of the shadows, inching deeper into the heart of the city. *Somehow I've got to avoid people as much as possible. And that's not easy with this Passover melee. Let's just hope I don't run across anyone else who can connect me with the scrolls.*

He wondered if taking the scrolls would be worth all of the trouble. How could he prove their provenance and explain where he got them? Oh well, he'd figure that out when it was time. Right now, hiding the scrolls in the cave until things settled down seemed to make as much sense as anything else, if there was any sense to be made at all.

Gazing into the star-strewn sky, he felt uncertainty steal over him. He no more understood what was going on now than when he'd stepped into the street three days earlier. This stirred him deeply. He also wondered where his friends might be and if they still followed their Jesus?

When he thought about what his feelings were at the start of this trip, he could hardly believe he now considered these people friends. And he couldn't help but recall the girl in his class who had irked him so much with her unflinching religious beliefs. Experience was certainly changing him, though he wasn't sure to what degree or where it might all end up.

He wasn't even sure who he was anymore. And he could only imagine what Carolyn's reaction would have been. If only she were here to share his journey.

† † †

The disciples were all tired and yawning, and looked forward to a decent night's sleep there in the city. On more than one occasion they had made their beds in this courtyard, and tonight they would do the same.

Returning to Bethany after dark was completely out of the question.

Peter brushed the dirt from his tunic and headed into the shadows. Paul and Elizabeth followed, and the three gathered at the stone wall bordering the courtyard. They stood in reflective silence for several moments.

"What did the Master mean when He said He was sending someone else—a . . . a Counselor?"

Paul glanced at Elizabeth as if seeking her approval. She shot him a look she hoped communicated that he was on his own.

As though getting the message, Paul studied Peter, clearly searching for the words that would somehow touch the disciple's heart. Elizabeth knew how deeply Paul wanted to share the truth with Peter and somehow make him understand what was about to take place.

Elizabeth, on the other hand, didn't know what to say. She found herself rethinking and reconsidering everything. Now she was thinking it was a bad idea to share what they knew with people who would undoubtedly consider them lunatics. Surely even Paul had to admit their situation was implausible, to say the least. And these people—these simple, primitive people—they didn't know about even basic things like radio waves. How could they conceive of time travel? It was irrational to think they could grasp it. Nope, she and Paul needed to just keep their mouths shut.

Peter stepped between them and propped his back against the wall. He plucked a piece of a withered vine from a crevice and stuck it between his teeth.

"Well?"

"Peter . . . we are not who you think we are," Paul said.

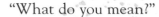

"What do you mean?"

Paul took a deep breath. "We're from the future."

So much for rational behavior, Elizabeth thought.

Peter straightened and measured the gravity of Paul's words. "It is as I thought. You are the Counselor!"

Paul gave Peter a peculiar glance. "No, we are not."

"No? But I saw how the Master looked at you when He spoke of it tonight."

Paul gave him a tight-lipped smile. "You don't understand."

"So help me understand."

Paul reached for Elizabeth's backpack. She flinched, then loosened her grip. Paul took the bag, peeled open the Velcro flap, and pulled out her Bible.

"Don't!" she whispered.

Ignoring her, Paul thumbed through the pages. Elizabeth shouldered her bag and flounced off.

He's hopeless!

Peter waited anxiously.

"There is a traitor here in our midst." His voice dry, Paul spoke just above a whisper.

Peter stared through blank eyes as if he hadn't heard the words at all. Paul wondered if he had.

"How do you know this?"

Paul handed Peter the book. "This is how." He pointed to a passage that specifically named Judas. Peter took the book and pulled it close to his face. He stared at it in stunned silence.

"What manner of writing is this? I . . . don't understand."

Paul took back the book, feeling ashamed. "I'm sorry." He closed it and stared down at the cover. "I should've known better."

"You should have known?"

Paul slipped the book under his belt. "It's not important."

"Simon, the Master needs all of us." The voice was John's.

"I'll be right along." Peter turned back to Paul. "I'm sorry, my friend, but I must go."

Paul's smile deflated as Peter walked away. He stood motionless in the shadows and wept.

Elizabeth came quietly to join him. "I'm—" They spoke in unison, and both recovered with a smile.

"I'm sorry, I don't know what's wrong with me," Paul said. "I just can't keep avoiding his questions. He's been so close to Jesus, and I know he feels left out."

"No, I'm sorry. You're the one with the courage. My ignorance is the only thing that keeps me from saying any more than I do."

"But I'm a pastor."

She smiled sympathetically. "All the more reason. You have so much more knowledge about all of this.

It's got to be harder on you."

Paul brushed the tears from his eyes. "Thank you. But it's only going to get worse, I'm afraid. Passover begins at sundown tomorrow, and if the pieces come together the way they're supposed to, tomorrow night will be the Last Supper. Then Gethsemane—and the cross." Paul's eyes shifted toward Jesus. "And He knows it all."

Elizabeth slipped her hand over Paul's.

"Seeing all of this is so different from what I'd imagined. Jesus knows every detail of what's about to unfold, and yet He nurtures everyone around him." Paul caught another glimpse of Christ, and his heart clenched. "He's the sheep who knows He's about to be slaughtered, and yet He still goes."

She grimaced. "I never really thought about it like that."

Paul pulled her close. "I don't know if I'm going to make it through all this." He drew a shuddering breath.

Elizabeth's gaze fell to the ground.

There really was nothing more either of them could say, Paul thought. They were there, and, for whatever reason, it was supposed to be that way.

Wandering into a small stable, the professor headed for a mound of hay piled high in one corner of the lean-to. The animals inside, mostly lambs, brayed a warning at the intruder. Nervously they shifted to the other end of the stable.

Van Eaton picked a spot and unrolled his bedroll. Wiggling into the soft, dusty hay, he made himself as comfortable as possible. Lying there, he listened to the sounds of people passing in the street.

"Every Nisan it's the same: more people, longer lines, more sacrifices. It's a wonder . . . " The words faded away.

Nisan. It's April, he thought. He slid his watch down to his wrist and pressed the indicator. It read 4/7. He made a mental note and shifted deeper into the coarse hay. Drifting off to sleep, he dreamed of a cigar—and tasted it.

The still dawn ushered in a cool breeze as Elizabeth

coaxed a blaze to life with a handful twigs. In the midst of the slumbering group, a quart-sized copper pot dangled unsteadily above the fire. She added more brush to the fire and steadied the pot.

Paul awoke and sat up. He noticed an aroma he knew all too well. Elizabeth stirred the remainder of the packet's contents into the pot and glanced at Paul with raised eyebrows.

"I found a packet of coffee in my things," she whispered. "It's instant, but what the heck." She poured a clay cup half full and handed it to him.

Paul puffed at the steam and sipped. "Oh man," he whispered. He cuddled the warm cup and settled back onto his bedroll.

It was the fourteenth day of Nisan, or so Peter had mentioned in passing the night before. And it was the celebrated beginning of Passover. Nisan was the first month of the Jewish calendar, and Passover was traditionally celebrated on the fourteenth day after the new moon.

Now Peter stirred and rolled over. He yawned and wiped the sleep from his eyes, then pointed to the cup Paul was cradling.

"What is that?"

"What?"

"The smell. What is that?"

"Oh, it's just a little something we brought from home."

Peter sat up and extended his hand, and Paul gave him the cup. Peter sniffed the steam and pressed it to his lips.

"What *is* this?"

Elizabeth glanced at Paul and shrugged. "It's coffee."

When Peter returned Paul's cup, she poured a second cup and handed it to him. The disciple took it.

Again he sipped, enamored with the new taste.

"Where is home?"

Paul stared into his coffee. "Home is not where you might think."

Peter looked curiously at them both. "But your accents . . . They are Galilean."

Elizabeth exchanged a wry look with Paul. In truth, they could only speculate as to what Peter was actually hearing. They no more knew what they sounded like to him than his real language did to them.

"No matter." Peter slipped one sandal on and tied it. "Sometimes I miss Capernaum." He stared into the distance for a moment. "My wife tends to her mother there. She has taken ill."

Paul reeled as thoughts of Laura flooded his mind. He wondered if he would ever see her again, and then there was his stepfather, Robert. Had his condition changed? More than likely. But if it had, he feared it was for the worst.

Peter grinned and handed Elizabeth his cup. "More kofey?"

† † †

A host of disciples rose as the morning sun promised a new day. It was indeed the first day of Passover, and it was a day that Paul realized would be the last the Savior would spend with them. And though none of the disciples had spoken of it specifically, the Passover supper would be this very night.

Paul watched as John stood and arched his back, then went to talk with Judas and Peter. "Last night the Master asked me to make arrangements for the Passover feast tonight. We'll have to journey back to Bethany for the lamb, and we'll need money."

Judas sighed and reached for the purse laced to his belt. "How much?"

Peter stared strangely at Judas. "Does it matter?"

"Well, no. But I want to make sure we get what we pay for."

Combing His fingers through His hair, Jesus sat up and yawned. He slowly gained His cognizance and stood.

"Mas-ter," Judas called—as if a dear old friend, Paul thought with disgust. Jesus now seemed indifferent.

"Master," John echoed, "we were planning to go into the city this morning to make preparations for the Passover."

Jesus nodded without speaking.

"We also wondered if, rather than going to Bethany, we might purchase a lamb from the bazaar."

Jesus brushed his hair from his face. "No, I will send Andrew for the lamb. Now remember what I told you. When you go into the city, you will find a certain man carrying a water jar. Follow him, and he will lead you to a house. When the owner comes out, tell him the Teacher wishes to eat the Passover meal there with His disciples."

"How will we know this man?" John asked.

Jesus smiled. "You will know."

John and Peter exchanged glances and shrugged.

"Judas," Jesus said, gently pulling him aside, "why are you troubled?"

Judas stroked his beard, and sighed. "Why am I about the petty chores of our group?" he asked indignantly. "Am I not the keeper of the funds?" He shook the purse that dangled from his side. "My talent is wasted."

"God delights not in talent," Jesus said, "but in likeness to Himself. For talent is God given, but likeness to God is a choice."

"Are you coming, Judas?" Peter called.

Turning with a scowl, Judas loosened the purse from his side and poured three coins into his hand. "No. This should be all you need."

Peter slid the silver into his own pouch. He glanced at Paul and Elizabeth. "Will you join us?"

† † †

A coarse tongue swiped across the professor's face. "Huh . . . what?"

His senses dulled, he slowly sat up. The stench of manure was strong as he awkwardly struggled to one

knee. He'd only slept a few hours, but it was the best sleep he'd had in days.

From inside the stall's meager, split-rail walls, the professor watched activity stir in the street. The morning air was still, and though it was cool, for the first time in as many days it carried a hint of humidity. This only worsened his disposition as his clothes had already begun to smell. He rarely noticed his own odor, but it was now powerfully present. And he couldn't even think about his breath. Going days without a toothbrush was awful.

He watched a woman carrying her infant son and considered his next move. There seemed to be thousands upon thousands of people in the city. He had no money, no place to stay for any length of time, and no food. Not to mention that finding his cohorts seemed increasingly unlikely with every passing moment. And though he had only known the reverend and the young doctor for a short time, their faces would be a welcome sight.

Then suddenly, he froze. Fear invaded his senses.

On the far side of the street, he caught sight of one of the men who had chased him through the streets two days earlier. He backed into the shadows.

Time to go, he thought.

Awkwardly, Van Eaton worked his way to the gate and pulled a large clay jar from beside the water trough. He coolly stepped into the street and lifted the jar onto his shoulder, shielding his face.

Shouldering through the crowd, he made his way down the street and rounded the corner. He drew short, nervous breaths, struggling to balance the jar with one hand while he popped the cap of his inhaler with the other. He shot the mist into his mouth and sighed, wondering what he was going to do when he ran out.

Nervously he balanced the jar and replaced the inhaler, when a hand fell heavily on his shoulder. Every muscle in his body tightened. He squeezed his eyes shut, fearing at any moment he would feel a knife pierce his back.

"Professor!"

Van Eaton recognized Paul's voice immediately and wheeled around. "What are you doing here?"

"What am I doing here?" Paul chided. "What are you doing here?"

"Is this the man we seek?" Peter interrupted.

Paul exchanged glances with Elizabeth, and then with Van. "This is our friend."

Van Eaton grimaced. "Excuse me?"

"We were sent to find a man with a water pot," Paul explained. "But surely you're not the one."

"And why not?" John asked. "This is the only

man we have seen with a water jar since we've been here."

Paul looked at Van Eaton, suddenly inundated with John's words. *Is it possible that the professor is somehow a part of all of this? The story of the man and the water pot has been in the scripture from the beginning, but this—this is too much for words.*

"Well, we're glad to see you just the same, Professor," Elizabeth broke in. "Oh, and Professor, this is John, and Peter—Simon Peter," she said with a smile.

Van Eaton seemed unmoved and kept perusing the crowd.

"What are you looking for?" Elizabeth asked.

"Nothing. Did you find the Nazarene?"

Paul's face brightened. "Oh, yeah."

"So . . . where is He?"

"We made camp just outside the city," Paul explained. "We're going back there later."

Van Eaton nodded, keeping one eye on the street.

"What are you looking for?"

"Nothing. We need to go."

"What's wrong with you?"

"Just come on."

Van Eaton led the way down the street. Finally he stopped long enough to catch his breath. He pulled the jar from his shoulder and leaned against a doorpost. Immediately a man stepped outside.

"May I help you?"

John stepped forward. "The Teacher has sent us and asks where we may eat the Passover meal."

The man nodded as if expecting them. He motioned them inside and led them up a shadowy stairway to a room that was being prepared.

"How did you know this was the place?" Paul asked.

"I didn't," John said.

†   †   †

Atop the massive staircase, two scribes stood on either side, perched on granite pedestals and sounding their shofars. The blasts resounded, appealing to all pilgrims to bring their offerings. Standing at the foot of the stairs, John spotted Andrew, who was leading a lamb by a rope.

"Andrew!"

The young disciple waved when he recognized the familiar face. He tugged gently on the rope and patted the lamb.

"I'm glad I don't have to do this," he admitted. He

handed the leash to John. "This little fellow is cute."

John took the rope and hurriedly scaled the stairs, with the lamb stumbling up after him. Peter followed along with Paul and Elizabeth, while Andrew disappeared into the crowd.

"Are you coming, Professor?"

Van Eaton glanced nervously over the crowd. "No,

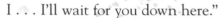

I . . . I'll wait for you down here."

"What's up with him?" Elizabeth asked.

"I don't know, but we can't worry about it right now."

† † †

The courtyard inside the Temple was crowded with hundreds, even thousands of people, all waiting to bring their offerings to the priests. Droves of men young and old stood in lines that snaked up a massive stairway to a long stone platform where a myriad of priests stoically performed their rituals. The fearful brays of countless lambs were the most evident of all, even above the dull roar of the crowd. They sounded almost like cruel warnings to their counterparts as they too awaited their fates.

Over the next hour, the professor lurked in the shadows of the Temple walls, trying to blend with the crowd and hoping that at any moment his friends would rejoin him.

Feeling a tap on his shoulder, he sighed, "Well, it's about time." But before he could turn, there was a dull thud and everything went black.

† † †

"Nicodemus! Joseph!" John motioned to the elder rabbis.

The two men shouldered their way through the crowd, their faces somber.

"This is Nicodemus, a friend of the cause—and Joseph, of Arimathea," Peter told Paul and Elizabeth. "They are both friends of the Master."

Elizabeth looked from the two men to Paul, her eyes widening. He returned a wide grin.

Nicodemus leaned close, then hesitated, frowning at their unfamiliar faces.

"They can be trusted," John assured him.

Nicodemus' eyes flitted in both directions. "We've just come from a meeting of the Sanhedrin. I'm afraid Caiaphas is up to something."

"What do you mean?" Peter asked.

"He said that we would have answers this very night and that the Nazarene would present his own case." Joseph shifted uneasily from one foot to the other. "I can only suppose he was talking about Jesus."

"But we know nothing of this." Peter protested.

Nicodemus stroked his beard. "I thought as much. Where will you celebrate Passover?"

Tipping his head toward the sinking sun, John said, "There is a house on the west side near the Jaffa Gate."

"Who else knows of this?" Joseph asked, his eyes narrowing.

"No one, save the four of us—and the Master," Peter said.

Nicodemus exchanged a meaningful glance with Joseph, then nodded. "Good. Tell no one else. As soon as we know more, we'll send word. Agreed?"

"Yes."

"Shalom."

"Shalom, my friends."

As the two rabbis walked away, a priest called from the top of the stairs, "Your lamb! Bring the lamb!"

John led the animal to the top of the stairs and handed the rope to the priest. Showing no emotion, the priest seized the bleating lamb and laid it on the massive stone altar. After a cursory examination, he pinned its neck to the stone altar, recited a short prayer, then with a swift and sure motion dragged a cold blade across its throat. Instantly a river of blood spilled across the altar. The bleating stopped, and the lamb went limp. It quivered for a moment, then lay still.

When the last bit of blood had dripped from the wound, the priest quickly handed the animal to John and wiped the altar clean.

"Next!"

Soberly, John took the lifeless lamb and descended the stairs. "Let's get out of here."

While the four of them picked their way through the crowd, Elizabeth spoke quietly with Paul. "Did you think that he would have a part in all this?"

"Who?"

"Van Eaton. Did Jesus know that he would be there in the city with the water pot?"

"Well . . . I guess He did."

Then suddenly she gawked at Paul. "You know, I just had a terrible thought. Could Satan somehow use us as well, maybe even to change things? Or is that even possible?

Paul considered her words. "Dear God, I hope not."

As the four descended the flight of stairs and stepped into the street, they all searched for the professor.

"Where is your friend?" Peter asked.

"I don't know," Elizabeth said, her eyes darting from face to face. "He was supposed to be right here!"

Nineteen
(14 Nisan)

Jesus led his chosen few from Solomon's Porch into the city, forging up the rocky path and through the massive Susa Gate. Pressing through the relentless Passover crowds that flooded the city, He felt a great burden of loneliness. Peering into the nameless faces of those He passed in the street, He felt compelled to speak—though He did not—obliged to teach—yet He knew His time had passed. But most of all, He was moved by an unyielding compassion simply because He loved them all, and He did so without limit or restraint.

† † †

Peter and John followed directly behind Jesus while He walked, and Elizabeth and Paul trailed them, each one following the other blindly along with the other disciples. They snaked their way through the crowds toward the place they knew only as the upper room.

It had been late in the afternoon when the four returned from their preparations for the Passover feast.

John had spent the majority of his time meticulously preparing the lamb according to Jewish tradition, while Paul and Elizabeth shopped with Simon Peter for fruit and other incidentals. The day had been long, and though Van Eaton's strange disappearance remained a mystery, there was little time to worry about it. More pressing issues had surfaced.

"I've been thinking about what you said last night." Peter had said, stopping beside a market stand to pick through a mixture of fruit. "You spoke of a traitor." He dropped a handful of dates into a hemp sack and tied it off. "So who is this man?"

Paul sighed, wishing he hadn't broached the subject. He rubbed his four-day beard. "Maybe I shouldn't have said anything."

Peter bristled, his eyes flashing at Paul. "Oh no," he snapped. "What you have started you cannot stop."

Peter's glare cut deep into Paul. It was the first time he had seen this side of the big fisherman.

Peter handed the merchant a bronze coin, which the man bit, then dropped into his pouch. Peter stepped into the street, with Paul reluctantly following.

"And there is something else I fail to understand. Where is the Master going?"

Peter now seemed more curious than suspicious. Paul scratched his head and stalled. It was as if Peter hadn't heard a word Jesus had been saying for the past week, but that didn't make a bit of sense. If two strangers from the future who had only known Him for a few days could understand, why wouldn't His closest companions have an inkling? Well, sure he and Elizabeth did have the benefit of having read the history, but still. There was so much the apostles had to learn, so many circumstances they all still had to face, and Peter especially.

Paul simultaneously felt anguish and awe. Was it a

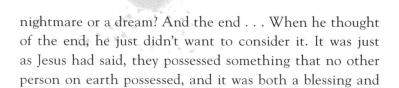

nightmare or a dream? And the end . . . When he thought of the end, he just didn't want to consider it. It was just as Jesus had said, they possessed something that no other person on earth possessed, and it was both a blessing and a curse.

† † †

Through a fog of confusion, both hands bound tightly behind his back and secured to a leather strap wrapped around his throat, Van Eaton awkwardly worked his way across the room in the darkness, trying not to choke himself to death in the process. Sweat streaked his face and pooled at his chin, and he paused long enough to press his forehead against the floor. The cool stones felt good against his brow. As he lay in the stillness, the only perceptible sounds were those of his own labored breathing, echoing off the bare walls.

What happened? One minute I'm waiting for those guys to return, and the next here I am in this predicament.

When he reached a corner of the room, he began to

inch his shoulders up the wall. Exerting all his strength, he finally managed to wriggle into a sitting position.

So far so good, he thought, though he was feeling every bit of his sixty-three years.

He twisted his wrists against the sweaty leather straps until they felt hot, then pulled with every ounce of his strength. It was no use. The straps were just too strong.

Feeling defeated, yet almost giddy with exhaustion, he laughed to himself, thinking that whoever had tied them would make a good Boy Scout.

† † †

As the afternoon sun settled lower into the western sky, a sliver of sunlight slipped through a narrow gap between two mismatched stones in the wall and pierced the musty darkness. Van Eaton blinked and squinted to focus on his surroundings. The room was small, maybe ten feet square, with a thick thatch roof and a rough-hewn wooden door with no handle.

His mind raced. *What am I going to do?*

Suddenly, the door rattled and cut the stillness like a knife. Van Eaton drew a short breath and held it nervously. His heart hammered in his chest.

"He is obviously a spy," one voice accused. "How could it be anything else? He took the scrolls right out from under our noses!"

"There is no doubt of it," another agreed.

"I wager he is a Sadducee—"

"Or worse, a Samaritan!"

There was laughter and the voices trailed away. The professor now shook uncontrollably.

They were talking about me.

† † †

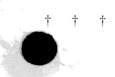

The passage through the back streets of the old city to the upper room had become an emotional pilgrimage, especially to those who already knew the story. Ecstasy and torment merged into one as the two time travelers walked in silence behind Jesus—and watched. And even though Jesus seemed undisturbed by the coming events, Elizabeth wondered if this was truly the case. The knowledge He carried had to be unbearable. It simply had to be.

Shouldering his way deeper into the inner city, Jesus directed His steps through the crowds as if disconnected from His surroundings altogether. Then, in the midst of the moment, Paul reached out and gently touched Him on the sleeve.

"Lord—"

Jesus turned and met Paul's eyes. Even in the darkness, Paul could see Jesus' face glistening with tears. It finally hit Paul that he really might not be capable of coping with what he knew was to come. The imminent death of God's only Son was now an actual personal event.

This is happening! This is really happening!

Yet he also recognized that Jesus had carried the

shadow of these last days since His birth. It was unthinkable!

As they walked, Paul noticed the place where they had begun their journey. *The well room.* He motioned to Elizabeth who raised her eyebrows as if to say, *Boy, if only we'd known.* The room appeared exactly as it had five days earlier, the tattered wooden door flapping in the desert breeze.

"How much farther?" a man called from behind.

Paul immediately knew the voice.

Again, he called out, and this time Jesus cut him off. "Judas," He said, never turning or missing a beat, "just follow me."

The irony cut deep. *If this weren't so pitiful I'd be tempted to laugh,* Paul thought. *Just follow me . . .*

Paul considered how many times Jesus had voiced those very words to Judas. In truth, if Judas had known where the Passover meal would take place, he would have alerted the chief priests, and this all-important occasion might not have taken place at all. But Jesus knew this would be a pivotal time of transformation. The Passover of the Old Covenant and the shedding of a lamb's blood was about to be replaced with a New Covenant—and this doorpost would be stained with His own blood.

† † †

Judas. From a small leather pouch dangling precariously from his belt, coins jingled with every step he took.

Step after grueling step, the sound rang louder and more offensively until finally Paul turned and blocked the path.

Elizabeth turned with him, but she managed to stay in character, submissive and passive, as a first century Jewish woman could have been, though she was sure she could take him—and wanted to. Judas smirked and tried to pass, but Paul obviously had no intention of letting him.

"Why do you insist on making things difficult, my friends?" Judas kept his words lively for the ears around him.

A few uneasy moments passed until Paul turned away. Elizabeth followed on his heels as he made his way toward Jesus. Glancing over her shoulder, she saw that Judas fell back and joined Thomas.

"Do I wear phylacteries or boast of being a Judean?" Judas asked indignantly, his voice just loud enough for her to hear. "No! I am a simple man."

"These two—" Judas motioned toward her and Paul as though unaware of her scrutiny. "Have you noticed anything significant about them?"

Turning her back on the two men, Elizabeth lagged several steps behind Paul so she could catch the two disciples' conversation.

"What do you mean?" Thomas asked, his tone puzzled.

"Doesn't it seem strange that they appeared less than a week ago and now they have the Master's ears?"

"Well, I hadn't thought of it," Thomas admitted. "But now that you say it—"

"And why is it that both have Galilean accents,

and yet they know nothing of the region? And they are certainly not Jews."

Thomas said slowly, "It does seem peculiar."

Elizabeth threw a quick glance back in time to see Judas clap Thomas on the back and smile. "No matter my friend," he said.

She hurried to catch up with Paul, her stomach clenched with the sinking feeling. The consummate deceiver had planted yet another the seed of deceit.

† † †

Ascending the narrow corridor that led up the darkened stairway, Jesus led his chosen few up the stone steps that eventually emptied into a shadowy room. The air hung thick and blanketed the room like a fog. Elizabeth breathed in the aromas of a sumptuous feast. Clay lamps perched on the tables and in the corners of the modestly adorned room glimmered, and their smoke rose gently and emptied through a single window on the far wall.

She could feel a suppressed sense of passion filling the room as the last man quietly approached the Passover table. Each disciple found his place as if he had done this before—and surely they all had, though not for a year.

This would be the third Passover they would spend with the Master. But what they didn't know was that it would also be their last. How strange she found it to watch them as they chatted with each other, smiling with expectancy and savoring the lavish table setting.

"I almost feel like an intruder," she said under her breath.

Beside her, Paul shifted uneasily. "I know."

As though sensing their discomfort, Jesus wrapped his arms around their shoulders and guided them to a table near the window. Tears sprang to Elizabeth's eyes. Obviously

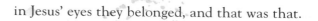

in Jesus' eyes they belonged, and that was that.

† † †

Softly Matthew began to hum a melodic tune as the others at the table quieted. Smiles crept across faces, and they all eventually chimed in. Some were magnificently off key, but it didn't matter. It was Passover, the beginning of the Feast of Unleavened Bread, and they were all together.

Jesus sat quietly, His gaze methodically covering the room. He studied each man's face as He sang. Paul knew it had to be an emotional time for all of them, but especially for the Lord Jesus, who mouthed the words, but barely focused on the events in the room. Even as He prepared to share the Passover meal, He surely knew that other plans were being made, that Judas had prepared his own agenda, already striking a deal with the Sanhedrin and peddling away his soul in the process.

From across the room, Paul watched Judas press a clay cup to his lips and drink. He appeared nonchalant, as if he was just one of the twelve joining in the festivities. And other than the two souls from the future, none was the wiser except Jesus.

Finally Jesus cleared His throat and the room fell silent. Until now, He had seemed to be in relatively good spirits, but His eyes now spoke a different message. Sitting straight, He stared steadily into each man's eyes and thus into their hearts. One by one, He was saying goodbye to them—and not one knew.

To Paul it was as if he was watching a movie he had seen before. In fact, he had seen a number of movies about Jesus, all such hollow recreations of these most powerful moments in history.

Somehow, deep within him, he knew they would eventually return to their own time and that each measured the effect this experience would have. He thought of their roles in saving lives, but knew that for each of them it would be in a different way.

My ministry can actually be life saving and life changing if I live up to what I know is possible! My role model quite literally has shown me the value of my path!

His thoughts ceased to wander as Jesus stood, preparing to speak. This was it. The story that he had heard since he was old enough to understand was unfolding right before his eyes—and they were fixed on Him.

"What I am about to do you will not understand now," Jesus explained, "but you will later."

He removed his outer garment, folded it in half, then in half again, and laid it at His feet. Taking a towel, He tied it loosely around His waist, then pulled a pitcher from the table and filled a small wooden basin half full of water. Without comment He began to wash the disciples' feet.

At first they all seemed to be stunned at the prospect of their Master serving them in such a way. Despite what they were thinking, Jesus continued. One by one, He took each man by the ankle and gently turned the dirt to mud,

carefully wiping away the excess and emptying the basin each time. He repeated the procedure again and again. Every man had his turn and no one was left, not even Judas.

Paul's heart contracted as Jesus came to Judas. He seemed to be careful to follow the same scrupulous procedure He had taken with every other man in the room. With humility He knelt and carefully washed Judas' feet—feet that had traveled the very same dusty roads as He had for nearly three years. Feet that had initially seemed so eager to follow this radical prophet from Galilee, but through the process of time had yielded to a different course altogether.

Guilt gnawed at his Judas' soul as he stared stoically into the shadows. He couldn't bring himself to look at Jesus as He performed the servant's rite. And though he was visibly shaken at what the Master was doing, there was nothing that was going to keep him from collecting the bounty he had been promised. *True kings don't wash feet*, he reflected.

Jesus brushed the hair away from His face as a single tear dropped unnoticed into the dirty water, "Not every one of you is clean."

The statement hung in the air for a moment while He emptied the basin and returned to the table. "In truth, I say that one of you will betray me."

Suddenly Judas' face paled. and his stomach tightened to a knot. *Surely, He couldn't know.* He glanced nervously to his right and then his left. Fortunately, there was no more concern for him than for any other person in the room. He

relaxed, though only slightly, as uncertainty suddenly and tenaciously invaded the room. Doubt germinated in every man's heart as each one quietly questioned his own motives.

Elizabeth turned nervously where she sat, fearful that she and Paul would be prime suspects. Paul, appearing unconcerned, stared daggers at Judas in hopes the others might read his mind and discover the traitor.

"Is it I?" Matthew asked.

Andrew echoed. then Nathanael and Thomas. Each man posed the question, but Jesus said nothing.

Finally Peter touched John's shoulder. "Ask Him who it is," he whispered urgently.

John pushed back from the table and leaned close to Jesus. "Lord . . . who is it?"

Jesus stared away, then pulled a crusty flat loaf from the table and tore off a piece. He turned to John, and John leaned closer.

"I will dip this morsel and give it to him," He said in a low voice meant only for John's ears.

Jesus dipped the bread into the bitter sauce, then

handed the sop to Judas. John glanced at Judas, then at Peter. Both appeared to be dumbfounded.

Elizabeth watched as Judas took the bread and stuffed it in his mouth. He smiled a conspiratorial smile and licked his fingers as he glanced at Jesus.

Beside her, she could hear Paul grind his teeth. "Is every man in this room blind?" he hissed to her, clenching

his hands. "His arrogance makes it clear he has no regard for Jesus or for the sanctity of this hour. Why can they not see it?"

Her heart clenching, Elizabeth glanced back at Jesus.

"What you are about to do, do it quickly." Jesus' eyes never strayed from Judas.

Judas choked on the morsel of bread. It seemed to Elizabeth that his face became visibly gaunt and hollow-eyed while he surveyed the room as if he was accounting for everyone there. After a moment he abruptly rose, strode across the room, and disappeared through the doorway.

A silence heavy with emotion descended over the room, and Elizabeth's breath caught. Jesus looked around the table into the faces of these loyal men with a deep love she could feel to her marrow.

"Now is the Son of Man glorified," He said, "and God is glorified in Him. If God is glorified in Him, He will glorify the Son in Himself and will glorify Him at once.

"I will be with you only a little longer," He added softly. "You will look for me, but where I am going, you cannot come."

Peter glanced at John, then at Jesus. "Lord, where are you going?"

Jesus' chin settled to his chest, and He closed His eyes. "Where I am going, you cannot follow now. But you will follow later."

"Lord, why can't I follow you now? I will lay down my life for you."

Straightening, Jesus regarded Peter sadly. "Will you really? I tell you the truth—before the cock crows this night, you will have denied three times that you even know me."

† † †

Eyes open or closed, it made no difference. If the professor's captor had been standing one inch from his nose, he wouldn't even have known he was there.

Van Eaton's wrists were raw from the fight he had waged for hours trying to free himself. He would lie down until he couldn't stand it, then he would work himself into a frenzy trying to pull his wrists free. Again he would realize the futility and stop. He had repeated the sequence well into the night, and he was still strung up like a trussed bird.

During the process, Van Eaton had wiggled around the perimeter of the room and discovered that it had only one entrance. It seemed to be a solid wooden door, and it was pulled snugly against the jamb on all sides. He worked his way up one side and could feel a pair of crude metal hinges. The other side bore no handle.

Then he had an idea.

With his shoulder planted against the door, he maneuvered his watch down to his wrist. With both hands, slowly and clumsily, he took the stem of the watch, and pressing against the bottom of the hinge pin, he worked it far enough through the knuckles of the hinge to get his

thumbnail under the cap. He worked out the rusty pin, and with it tediously picked apart the straps on his wrists.

He stood, followed the jamb with his fingers and found a second hinge. Carefully he removed the hinge pin using the first, and then hoisted the door from the frame. He was free.

† † †

Peter was clearly stunned by Jesus' words. Paul found it impossible to look him in the face. Instead he stared down at his clenched hands, his heart aching for the disciple— and for his Master.

Haltingly, as though movement pained him, Jesus took a small, flat loaf of unleavened bread and held it up for everyone to see. He gave thanks and broke it, then gave half to John and the other half to Peter. The two men broke it into smaller pieces and passed them around.

Paul took a piece from Peter. He broke it in half and handed half to Elizabeth. They both sat in silence, staring at the bread.

They had both done this hundreds of times in their lifetimes, Paul reflected, and all had been meaningful. But this? This was too much to fathom. They were here at the Last Supper of Christ! Sharing the meal. Surreal couldn't touch this.

Peter finished sharing the bread and sat back down, his expression blank. Jesus gripped his shoulder, then released him and continued.

"Take it; this is my body." He placed the bread in His mouth, and the others followed his example.

Tears streamed down Paul's face as he slipped the bread into his mouth. He didn't dare to look at Elizabeth, to see her tears, for fear of completely breaking down.

Jesus took the cup and again gave thanks. For a suspended moment He gazed into the cup, holding it as though it were too heavy for him. At last He drank. He turned and offered the cup to Peter, who drank and handed the cup to Andrew. Around the room, the cup slowly passed, even to Paul and Elizabeth.

Paul took the cup and pressed it to his lips. He felt sweet release as he drank, wanting to swallow every drop but having the presence of mind not to. He handed the cup to Elizabeth, who held it for a moment, then nervously took a sip, all the while staring at Paul. She handed the cup to Nathanael, and it continued around the room until everyone had drunk from it.

"This is My blood of the covenant, which is poured out for many," Jesus said softly. "I tell you the truth, I will not drink again of the fruit of the vine until that day when I drink it anew in the kingdom of God."

† † †

The crowds had dwindled to a fraction of what they had been when Jesus led the group from the upper room and through the streets of Jerusalem. It was well after midnight when He passed through the Eastern Gate and walked through the tangled brush that blanketed the Kidron Valley toward the garden called Gethsemane. The travelers' only light, a brilliant Passover moon, hung in the sky, large and luminous.

Jesus reached for the gate and turned to Peter. "I want you and Andrew to stay here and pray." He raised His hand, inviting Paul and Elizabeth to follow Him farther.

I can understand why Jesus would invite Paul. Elizabeth thought as she stumbled after Him along the uneven, shadowy path that led deeper into the garden. *But I'm just a resident doctor, a normal person. Why would Jesus allow me to share this time with Him?*

Her eyes blurred by tears, she gazed around her at the hallowed landscape she had read about in the Bible but had never believed she would witness in real life. *How can I ever return to my shallow life? The things I thought were so important seem so pointless now. And yet I know deep in my soul that I must still be diligent in trying to save lives, otherwise none of this has any meaning at all.*

† † †

Jesus walked as if He carried a heavy load, and Paul knew that He did. *I cannot believe I will have this time with Him,* he thought, humbled. A deep gratitude washed over him.

Ahead of them, Jesus stopped and gazed across the Kidron, beyond a stand of hundred-year-old olive trees. To the south and west countless flickering fires from the camps of pilgrims who had come to Jerusalem for Passover sprinkled the walled city, gleaming white in the powdery moonlight against the black canvas of sky.

Inevitably Paul's gaze followed Jesus' to the north, past the Damascus Gate, where all was hidden by a solemn blackness. This was Golgotha, the place of the skull. A place Paul knew all too well from his studies, where nameless men slept in nameless graves by way of the cruelest and most sadistic of all punishments known to man. Crucifixion.

Jesus pulled his sleeves to his wrists and shivered slightly, as though haunted by the sight. The air had grown colder as a wisp of wind poetically stirred the olive grove in the valley below. At last he turned to face them.

"Elizabeth, do you really understand why you are here, why the Father has chosen you to be where you are at this particular time and place with me?"

She looked at Jesus, then at Paul. "No . . . I don't think I do."

Jesus glanced at Paul. "There were three men who

had journeyed far from their own lands that year. They all came from different heritages, different countries, different cultures, and yet they all came for the same purpose." Jesus paused thoughtfully. "The scriptures refer to them as Magi. All three were leaders of their people, not simply royalty but, more important, men seeking truth. You are very much like those men, even more than you might imagine."

Paul beamed with surprise and saw that Elizabeth did too.

"You also seek the truth, and while you didn't specifically choose to do so in this way, your ancestors made it possible for you. For you see, you are the direct descendants of those faithful three. The one-hundredth generation of their heritage." Jesus paused as though allowing His words to sink in.

Paul was speechless, his mind racing for answers. This was all so unexpected, so seemingly undeserved.

"Because of your ancestors' faith, you were chosen," He continued, "for you seek answers to questions that have plagued you for years, just as your forefathers did. They too were unrelenting in their quest to find truth, and they found it, just as surely as you."

Jesus flashed an assuring smile and drew them both to his chest. "I love you so much."

Paul sobbed openly, and Elizabeth was unrestrained as well. The three embraced each other tightly. Nothing else mattered now. Nothing at all. Resting in the arms of the Savior was everything. Everything indeed.

After what seemed an eternity, Paul loosened his grip and looked into Jesus' eyes. "Thank you, Lord, for who you are and for what you are about to do."

Jesus cradled their faces in his hands, as His own tears hardened to steel. He then turned and dropped his arms to His sides. His shoulders slumped.

"Death calls to me even in my sleep, and I tremble.

And yet I am not afraid." He gazed up at the sky as if looking to the Father. "It was for this cause I came into the world." His voice broke.

Paul smeared the tears from his cheeks. "I can't even fathom what you are going through, Lord."

Elizabeth nodded soberly. "Thank you, Lord," she whispered, her voice choking.

Jesus turned. "Now I must go to the Father."

Heaving a sigh, He moved away from them and took one last look at the city. Then He quietly shrank into the darkness and toward His destiny.

† † †

For a long time the two stood in silence, unable to speak. "I can't believe He took this time with *us*," Elizabeth said finally. "I'm so confused by everything. The way He talks, it's as if we were always supposed to live *then* and travel back to . . . *now*."

Paul nodded. "How could we have known that we were the ones chosen for these moments? Do you realize how important it is for us to fully understand His message? And how important it is for us to *do* something with it?"

"I don't know how I can ever live up to His example."

"Well, it's not over yet." Paul hesitated. "We are still facing the hardest part."

Behind them, the sound of footsteps crunched through the brush, and they heard a familiar voice grumbling.

Paul swung around. "Professor?"

Twenty

(14 Nisan)

"I thought I'd find you here." Van Eaton's breath fogged the dank air as he spoke.

"Professor, where have you been?" Paul asked.

Van Eaton eased his bulky body to the ground. "I just came from the city." He paused to catch his breath.

"Where in the city?"

"That's not important. But what is important is the conversation I just overheard." He looked around to be sure they were alone and lowered his voice even more. "Thank goodness I found you."

"But how did you know we'd be here?

Van Eaton smirked. "How do you think I got a Ph.D. in religious studies? According to the story—in case you've forgotten—the Sanhedrin will dispatch their temple guards here to Gethsemane and take—" He paused and nodded into the darkness. "And take him."

Stark silence met his words.

"Did you hear what I said? They're on their way here."

"We know," Paul said curtly.

"Well, did you know that they're after you too?"

Paul's eyes widened. "What are you talking about?"

Van Eaton scratched the arm that had been broken and looked at it with amazement, as he had many times over the previous days. "There were three, maybe four men, as far as I could tell. There was no mistaking what they were talking about."

Elizabeth bent over him. "Go on."

"They were talking about Jesus—well, they called him the Nazarene, but it was obvious who they were talking about. And they said they knew the whole bunch was here at Gethsemane."

Van Eaton focused on Paul, in the darkness no more than a silhouette. "Given your affinity for the man, I assumed you were part of the bunch they were talking about. One of them mentioned that there were foreigners with the group and that there might be trouble. One thing led to another, and they agreed that they would take the whole lot of you to the Sanhedrin."

"But . . . that's not how it's supposed to happen," Elizabeth protested, sounding breathless.

"Yeah, but it is happening," Paul said. "And we're part of it."

"Well, you're not supposed to be," Van Eaton shot back.

"What do you mean?"

"You know very well that you're no more supposed to be a part of this than I am." Van Eaton considered the irony of his words since he had stolen the scrolls of the Essenes.

"That's not true, Professor," Paul said. "If you had been with us you'd understand that."

"Will you never learn?"

"Excuse me, but we have—"

"It was a rhetorical question." Van Eaton rolled his

eyes.

"Okay, well, you're as much a part of this as we are," Elizabeth broke in. "You were the 'certain man,' for Heaven's sake!"

"The what?"

"You were the certain man with the water pot there in the city. It's in the scriptures, *Professor*," Paul said sarcastically.

Van Eaton scowled at Paul. "You're insane. You're sticking your nose where it doesn't belong, and you're going to get hurt! Both of you! Can't you get it through your thick skulls? We. Do. Not. Belong. Here."

Elizabeth took her head between her hands and squeezed for a few seconds, then stood up. "This is crazy. Right, wrong—who cares?"

"Shh! Someone's coming!"

† † †

An aura of lights illuminated high-limbed trees that lined the path to the garden, dancing eerily among the shadows.

Paul could see twenty or more torches approaching the garden. The shapes carrying them became men, and quickly they became men bearing arms. As they drew closer, Paul motioned Elizabeth and the professor to drop to the ground behind a clump of bushes, then crouched beside them.

"Didn't I tell you? Now what?"

Paul fixed Van Eaton in a stern gaze. "Shh! I don't know."

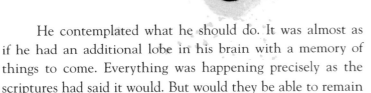

He contemplated what he should do. It was almost as if he had an additional lobe in his brain with a memory of things to come. Everything was happening precisely as the scriptures had said it would. But would they be able to remain uninvolved? There was no way of knowing.

As the torches drew nearer they illuminated a thin layer of fog, only now noticeable. It hovered lazily over the garden, creating the illusion of an eerie abyss that only added to the mystery of the night.

The light also reached farther through the trees, to where Jesus stirred and rose with effort. Unable to turn away, Paul watched as He stepped into the moonlight, His face wet with tears.

Temple guards pushed through the gate, crowding through the narrow opening until the section of the fence collapsed. Hardly a breath between them, the three crouched out of sight, their fear thickening. Then Elizabeth's hand tightened over Paul's arm.

Judas emerged from the mist. He took a torch from another man and ventured farther into the garden. When Jesus stepped into view, he paused, then moved hesitantly toward him. Even through the shadows, Judas could tell it was Him. His stature, the almost ghostly form of His body, even His movements were telling.

"Rabbi." Judas beckoned, his salutation condescending. "Rabbi, is that you?"

Jesus stood motionless while Judas edged closer as if he were an animal moving toward his kill. Stealthy, conniving,

murderous.

Finally Judas stopped an arm's length from Jesus and reached out. Jesus recoiled, then straightened. Judas stepped closer, embraced him, and kissed him on the cheek.

"Master."

Jesus returned the embrace but pulled back enough to look directly into Judas' eyes. It appeared to Paul that Judas tried to break Jesus' hold, but Jesus held him tightly. An awkward moment passed, then He dropped his arms, and Judas backed away.

It's over, Paul thought. *Judas has done what he came to do, and now the consequences will not be his to choose.*

Suddenly two guards shoved past Judas and seized the Master, one man collaring Him around the neck while the other punched Him in the stomach. Jesus crumpled and fell to His knees. Beside him, Paul heard Elizabeth's low cry as one of the guards pinned Him to the ground and wrenched one of Jesus' arms behind His back.

His eyes blinded by tears, Paul pulled her to him. She buried her face against his chest, shoulders heaving.

All at once he heard a rustle, and a shadowy figure punched

through the thicket, clumsily brandishing a broadsword with both hands. Peter screamed, swung, untrained as he was, and connected. The guard cried out, then released Jesus and sprang back, pressing his hand to the side of his head. Just then the remainder of the disciples spilled into view, bewildered but ready to fight.

Jesus struggled to his feet, cradling his arm. "Stop!

Put it back, Simon. For all . . . who draw the sword . . . will die . . . by the sword. Do you think I cannot call on my Father, and He will at once put at my disposal more than twelve legions of angels?"

Peter flinched at Jesus' admonition and stared at him, his expression reflecting frustration and bafflement. Paul knew what he must be feeling. It was as if Jesus didn't even need their help—or want it.

The wounded guard rocked furiously in the shadows, holding his hand to where his ear used to be. Jesus plucked the severed ear from the ground, and after uttering a few inaudible words, He cupped His hand to the man's head, then withdrew it.

For a moment everyone stared as though unable to believe what their eyes told them was true. The guard's ear was again intact, the wound completely fused.

In the confusion of the moment, Peter backed away, looking from Jesus to the guard, then back again. A second later, there was a dull thud and Peter was out cold.

"Seize them all now!" the commander of the temple guards shouted.

"No!" Jesus cried. "You have found who you came for. Let them go."

An eternity passed before the guards reluctantly released the disciples, though not without slipping in a few gratuitous punches in the process. Then in the commotion, the disciples all scattered into the darkness as fast as they could run.

† † †

His wrists and ankles now encumbered with irons laced with rasping chains, Jesus struggled to keep his balance, taking awkward, choppy steps, his body hunched. Infuriated, Elizabeth had to consciously stop herself from using her military arts on these heathens. She could have bloodied at least a few of them before they could restrain her, but she knew that wouldn't please Jesus. Logically, the disciples were outnumbered, and a confrontation would clearly be suicide. Crouching between Paul and Van Eaton, she clenched her fists by her sides and watched in disgust as Jesus was led away.

Once the guards were gone, she and Paul scrambled to their feet and pushed out of the thicket. While they hesitated, wondering what to do next, one by one the disciples filtered back into the clearing.

Elizabeth bit her lip to keep from voicing her opinion of their behavior. It didn't help to remember that she hadn't shown any more courage than they had.

"Where . . . where are they taking him?" Andrew's voice quivered.

James shrugged and shook his head.

Behind him, Matthew stepped out from hiding, his face reflecting the same guilt and shame as the rest. "It was not so long ago that I collected more than my fair share of taxes from virtually every man in that group. And now I—I haven't the courage to face them."

"Well look at me," Simon muttered. "I took the oath of a zealot, and I had not the fortitude to stand for what I truly believe in!" He spat on the ground in disgust.

Nathanael laid a hand on his shoulder. "And why was Judas with them? I don't understand."

Paul had obviously had his fill. "Listen to me!" he shouted. "Listen!" He brushed the grass from his clothing and stepped into the light. "Don't you see what's happening here?"

His tone was heavy, even malicious. Elizabeth sank to the ground, put her head in her hands and cried as much out of frustration as sadness.

Paul glanced over his shoulder, thinking the professor might have followed. So much for that. Turning back to the disciples, he saw they stared at him with mingled shock and curiosity.

"What is it going to take for you people to see?" he pleaded.

"See what?" Phillip asked.

"Jesus has been trying to tell you all week!" Paul felt his words bouncing back at him as the group moved closer.

"Tell us what?"

"Ahh!" Paul threw up his hands and turned away. He rubbed his face with both hands and glared into the night.

"They are taking Jesus to Caiaphas." His gaze fell to the ground as he contemplated whether to continue. "And Caiaphas will in turn send him . . . will send him to Pilate."

A torrent of accusations suddenly spilled from the group. "How is it that you know these things?" James barked. "How *could* you know?"

"And while we're talking of these things," Thomas pointed at Paul, then Elizabeth, "how is it that you and your compatriot both have Galilean accents, and yet neither of you seems to know anything of Galilee?"

Now I know what it feels like to have your blood run cold, Paul thought. He looked at Elizabeth and tried to figure out what to say. *They're going to ask us all the questions we feared, and we sure don't have any plausible answers.*

Then a figure stepped from the shadows. "He speaks the truth, at least in part." Marcus Altus parted the branches and stepped into the moonlight. He was wet with perspiration. "When I learned of their plans, I came as soon as I could."

He glanced curiously at Elizabeth. "He will be taken to Caiaphas, of this I am certain, but to Pilate only if there is division among the Sanhedrin. But I, too, fail to understand how you know these things?"

Suddenly all eyes turned to Paul. He hadn't wanted a confrontation, but he figured it was bound to happen eventually.

"Because he is a spy," a voice accused.

Paul drew a deep breath. "No, I am not. But I tell you this: He will go to Pilate, and Pilate will have Him beaten." His voice broke. "And then He will—" Paul paused and glanced into their faces, his eyes welling with tears. "He will—"

"No!" Van Eaton shot from the shadows. There was a stirring as he stepped out. "This is not right. You don't know what you're getting yourself into."

Paul started to argue, but then glanced at the faces that circled him. "If you had been listening to Jesus you would realize this," he said urgently. "He's been talking about it all week. How many times did He have to say that He was going away? How many?" Tears spilled from his eyes as he spoke. "He is about to be crucified!"

His words struck the group like a whip. They stared at him, incredulous. Even Paul couldn't believe what he had said.

Jesus had shared why the three of them were there and that there was nothing they could to do to alter what was to come, and yet Paul persisted. Why? He knew he shouldn't; he knew what the scriptures told him and that this was what God wanted, but he couldn't stand to see Jesus die at the hands of brutal animals—not without a fight.

"No! This cannot be! How can you know these things? How can you know?" Matthew cried.

Then suddenly, with Matthew's words, fear swarmed like flies, and the band of terrified disciples burst recklessly into the night.

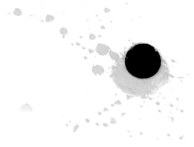

TWENTY-ONE

(15 Nisan)

Peter fingered the goose egg on his head as Elizabeth helped him navigate the shadows toward the firelight. "Wh-what happened?"

Paul prodded the embers. "You got hit." He spoke robotically, as if Peter knew the story as well as he.

Elizabeth eased Peter to the ground. "What about the others?" he asked.

"They ran off."

"And the Master?"

Paul stared at the blaze and sighed. "I will strike the shepherd, and the sheep of the flock will be scattered."

Peter peered curiously at Paul. "You are quoting the scriptures?"

"I am quoting the Master."

The big fisherman pulled his knees to his chest. "Yes, I remember. He spoke those very words at the supper." His countenance changed, as if he recalled a bad dream. "But where . . . where is he now?"

"They took Him to the chief priest. To Annas first,

then to Caiaphas, as I remember."

"I know the home of Caiaphas. It is at the south portal—just inside the Zion gate." Peter straightened. "I know the way there."

Closing his eyes, Peter put his head between his hands. After a moment he looked up and focused on Elizabeth.

"And what manner of clothing is this?" he asked,

frowning.

Elizabeth looked down at her clothes, then to Paul for help.

"Our young physician lost her mantle in the skirmish," Paul said.

"No, they ripped it off me. I'm glad I still had my own clothes underneath."

Elizabeth tucked in her shirt and took in another notch on her belt. Turning, she unclasped the crucifix from around her neck and gathered the chain into her palm. She stared at it for a moment in wonder, then slipped it into her pocket.

"Look, I don't mean to break up your little party," Van Eaton said, "but what are you planning to do?"

Paul stiffened, clearly resenting the authoritarian tone in the professor's voice. "You know, this may fly in the face of everything you believe, Professor, but the world doesn't actually revolve around you."

Van Eaton recoiled. "I'm just concerned about the threat they pose. And I don't want you to get yourself into more trouble," he said hurriedly.

Peter listened without comment, though Elizabeth could see that he was thoroughly confused.

Van Eaton put distance between himself and the others. "But I don't have any intentions of getting any more involved in this than I already have." He plucked his mat from the ground and flung it over his shoulder. "And if you had any sense, you wouldn't either. Neither one of you would." Turning, he stalked away.

Elizabeth watched as he dissolved into the shadows. "He's always running away, isn't he?" she muttered.

Paul shouldered his belongings and helped Peter to his feet. "He won't go far. And that's the least of our worries right now. We need to go."

† † †

It was nearly 2 a.m. when the three passed through the Zion Gate at the southwest corner of the city. Paul discreetly verified the time with his watch, careful that Peter didn't see him do so. He now recognized the fruitlessness of trying to explain anything to anybody. He was only thankful that Peter hadn't heard the fracas he'd had with the other disciples.

"This is Zion," Peter said, "and the home of the chief priest will be just around the corner there." He pointed down a street that arched out of their sight. An eerie glow danced hauntingly off earthen brick facades that lined either side of the street.

When they rounded the corner, they saw that the street emptied into a walled courtyard where two groups huddled around separate fires. No one noticed their approach.

Peter shivered. "The night has grown cold." He walked toward the closer of the two fires, and Elizabeth and Paul followed nervously.

† † †

The palatial home of Caiaphas was packed with well over a hundred bleary-eyed dignitaries and Sanhedrin members, most of whom had been summoned from their beds, attending out of a sense of duty, though curiosity also played a role in the turnout. John, following them since the confrontation in the garden, settled in the shadows and watched nervously.

In awe, his eyes strayed to the four corners of the outer court, adorned with climbing bougainvilleas arranged atop alabaster basins perched on snow white marble pedestals. Spanning the length of the courtyard, fluted stone columns connected by marble arches divided the expansive space into two sections. Armed Temple guards stood between the columns, while behind them the hierarchy of Sanhedrin officials sat in a large semicircle.

In the center stood Jesus.

"Is it truly necessary that this man be bound like a common criminal?" a Sanhedrin member demanded.

The council roared in protest. "He is as much a criminal as any thief," one man shouted.

"He is a heretic!" another screamed.

"But I have heard Him speak, and I find nothing in His teachings that would label Him a heretic."

The familiar voice was that of Nicodemus.

The crowd erupted again, their shouts growing even

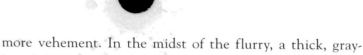

more vehement. In the midst of the flurry, a thick, gray-bearded priest rose with effort, and the noise drained from the courtyard.

Caiaphas strolled the length of the council and stopped in front of Jesus. He cast a steely eye toward Annas.

John knew that the relationship between Caiaphas and Annas was strained to say the least. Of levitical lineage, Caiaphas descended from a long line of Pharisees, but he was not connected with the priestly line of his father-in-law. Annas ben Seth, a Sadducee, had held the position of chief priest for as long as anyone cared to remember, and relinquishing the duties and prestige had been the most difficult challenge of his pseudo-political career.

Although both men had remained cordial through the transition, there was an obvious air of contentiousness when they were both present. But Caiaphas was a wise successor. Over the years, he had built loyalties and, more important, accumulated favors. Now it was time to test the waters.

"Nicodemus, I can appreciate your concern for this man, if for no other reason than that he is a Jew. But if he preaches blasphemy, how could any man defend him?" Caiaphas spoke in the tone of someone accustomed to spouting orders.

Nicodemus hesitated. It was widely known that he greatly respected Caiaphas and the office he held, but he felt certain that the chief priest was wrong. Unfortunately he also knew that sparring with such a man as Caiaphas was neither wise nor sensible, and everyone present knew it.

"Is it not possible that these charges were propagated by those who wish to discredit this man?" Nicodemus stopped abruptly and looked down, as though shocked at his own boldness.

Caiaphas turned deliberately and faced Jesus, his head tilted to one side. "Well. Is this indeed the case?" His words hinted at sarcasm. "Are the charges this council brings against you indeed false?"

Jesus adjusted the ropes on His wrists and sighed. "Why do you ask me?" He asked, the timbre of his voice unshaken. "Why don't you ask those who heard me?"

Caiaphas turned to one of the guards, who stepped forward and slapped Jesus to His knees.

Tears blurred John's eyes as Jesus slowly staggered to his feet and wiped his bloodied mouth on his sleeve.

Caiaphas moved closer. "Well? Are you the Christ?"

Jesus raised His head and met Caiaphas' gaze. "I am, and you will see the Son of Man seated at the right hand of the Father and coming in the clouds of heaven."

The chief priest recoiled as a gasp went up from the onlookers. He turned toward the council and with both hands ripped his vestment from his chest. The crowd exploded into a torrent of accusations.

The guards standing on either side of Jesus began pounding him with their fists, and Jesus crumpled in agony with the blows. All around them, the crowd transformed into a rabid mob.

† † †

Peter stood timidly by the fire. He extended his hands, palms forward, toward the crackling blaze.

"The fire is good, no?"

Elizabeth smiled half-heartedly. Her hands trembled noticeably as she warmed them.

"It doesn't matter," a woman chided. "The fact remains that the Sanhedrin has called a special meeting all because of him. I always wondered what the real story was there. Miracles, raising people from the dead! I knew it couldn't be true."

When she turned toward Peter, he edged toward the shadows.

"What is this? You! I know you! You are one of His disciples!" She grabbed for Peter's arm, but he stepped out of reach.

"Woman, what are you saying? Peter's voice broke.

"I know this man too!" a man chimed in. "He is a

compatriot of the Nazarene. I am certain of it."

Peter's heart pounded at the accusations. "No! It is a lie!" He swore repeatedly.

Instantly the crowd morphed into an angry mob that engulfed the big fisherman, though half of them didn't even know why. The night was so electric with accusations that virtually everyone seemed anxious to come to blows.

"Wait!" Elizabeth screamed. "Let him go!"

Paul reeled back, and the crowd quieted. "Listen to that!" someone yelled. "Are we surrounded by Galileans—with outlandish clothing?" Laughter followed.

"I am not Galilean!" Elizabeth protested.

"I am not Galilean," a man mocked. "Are we all to be taken for fools? Woman, do you think we do not know a Galilean when we hear one?"

Elizabeth's words tasted like ashes in her mouth. She knew well the story of Peter's denial, but watching the scene play out in real life was gut wrenching. She couldn't help but judge what she perceived to be his lack of courage. Then again, he truly feared for his life. And she of all people, who had seen war firsthand, should recognize what people will do when their lives are at stake.

Peter jerked free and muscled his way through the crowd, fleeing into the night.

Amid the commotion, Paul grabbed Elizabeth's hand and nearly jerked her off her feet. "Let's get out of here!"

She didn't have to be asked twice.

† † †

"What are we to do with this man?" a Sanhedrin member asked.

Caiaphas glanced across the courtyard and spied a man standing in the back with whom there had been an arrangement.

"Crucify him!" the man shouted.

The malicious words snaked through the crowd like venom, repeated from mouth to mouth. Caiaphas nodded in approval, though it was hardly noticed.

"Please! Please!" Nicodemus cried. "Surely you cannot be serious! We do not have the right to put a man to death!"

Caiaphas turned and leaned right in Nicodemus's face. "No, we do not. But Pilate does."

† † †

The dusky corridor was deceptively long, but the professor moved with determination, drawn by muted cries that grew louder with every step.

After wandering aimlessly through the cold, dark streets of the city for more than two hours, he had been drawn to a building that stood out noticeably against its surroundings. It was more modern than the common mud-brick structures—Roman, he supposed.

Moving closer, he had counted six—no seven—marble

pillars that formed a stone colonnade atop a massive flight of stairs. Beyond that a gossamer curtain draped the length of the portico, the flowing fabric glistening in the light of oil torches. In the center, on the outside of the curtain, he saw a throne where a robed figure perched motionless.

Drawing closer still, Van Eaton could see that a crowd was gathering at the base of the stairs. Not good. He and crowds hadn't meshed too well lately. He'd quickly worked his way to the back of the building.

When he reached the back he had discovered that, oddly, there were no guards posted, so he easily slipped in unnoticed. Once inside, he followed the long corridor lined with freshly lit torches mounted in ornamental sconces at regular intervals. The scent of olive oil and burnt linen wafted heavily through the hall, and the smoke dimmed the aura of each successive torch a little more than the previous one until he reached the end.

The corridor emptied into a room that was easily eighty feet across and perhaps half as deep. Marble statues stood like guardians along the perimeter walls, and a layered curtain that stretched the entire length of the room divided it in half. It was the curtain he'd seen from the street, but from the inside looking out, it was virtually transparent, resembling a veil.

On the other side of the veil, the throne was clearly silhouetted by torches in stands on either side that flickered with every wisp of wind. He cautiously worked his way across the floor toward the opening.

†   †   †

"Up here," Paul called quietly. "We'll be able to see if anybody is following us from up here." He caught Elizabeth's hand and heaved her over the top.

"Oh, we can see everything from up here." She brushed off her khakis and laid her belongings on the ground. "I wonder where we are."

They made a soft place to sit, and Paul glanced into the night sky. "Well, I know we're on the north side of the city because there's the North Star." He pointed at the familiar sparkle. "Two thousand years ago and it's the same sky."

Elizabeth smiled at the logic as she caught a glimpse of the moon, now low in the western sky. "It'll be light in a couple of hours."

"Yeah, I know." Paul looked toward the city, which was for the most part still asleep. "What are we gonna do?" he asked, shaking his head in resignation.

She smiled sadly at her friend. "I don't know. I just know I'm hurting inside. I feel like we deserted him."

Paul looked out over the city and took a heavy breath. "I do too, but what could we have done?"

"I don't know. As much as we know about this story it just seems crazy to me that we couldn't figure something out. But when that guard grabbed me by the collar in the garden, I only thought one thing: run. And he tore the clothes right off my back."

He smiled faintly. "I know this is hardly the time, but you answered a question I've always wondered."

"What's that?"

He scratched his chin and gazed at her. "The scriptures say that when the guards stormed the garden, that a man ran right out of his clothes. I guess that would have been . . . you."

"A man?"

"Well, it was dark."

"And maybe they weren't talking about me at all."

"That's true."

She grinned and reached for her pocket Bible, but then decided against it. "I wonder were He is now?"

"I was just thinking the same thing. He's probably before Pilate," Paul said.

Elizabeth laid back and put her arm over her eyes. "Dear God."

† † †

Van Eaton decided to do something utterly out of character: a physical act. He'd try to climb one of the marble giants that stood dauntingly on either side of the draped opening. Maybe this way he'd be able to catch a glimpse of what was happening on the other side without being seen.

Jeers from the swelling crowd grew louder, which was a good thing, since he was huffing and puffing, scraping and scrambling trying to scale the statue. He couldn't exactly say it was more difficult than he thought, but he had underestimated his pathetic physical condition. Plainly, he didn't have the upper body strength to pull himself up, and eventually he ended up right back where he started—on the floor.

On the other side of the veil, Jesus stood, beaten, bruised, and obviously in pain. His hands, still shackled, were bleeding from His wrists, and blood swathed both hands, dripping from His fingertips.

Suddenly one of two guards slipped a hemp sack over Jesus' head and the other punched him directly in the face. "Tell us who hit you, *Christ!*" he screamed.

"Yes! Prophesy to us, King Jesus!" the other yelled.

Several in the crowd joined in, but Pilate paid little attention to the goings on. He sat in silence, drumming his fingers nervously while he considered the situation. He loathed the thought of handing down such a cruel sentence as crucifixion—not that he hadn't wished that every Jew in this wretched land were nailed to a cross at one time or another. But this man was different. And a fool could see that the accusations about Him were fabricated. Still, the mob cried for blood, and Pilate felt powerless to stop it.

In all actuality, Pontius Pilate was little more than a figurehead of an unpopular regime in a land where assassinations were commonplace. It was for this reason alone that he was known to be not only cold and calculating, but also evasive and wholly unpredictable. In truth, he appeared evasive because he hadn't the fortitude to make any significant decisions for fear of repercussion, not only from the Jews, but also from the emperor in Rome. Pilate was no ruler; he was merely a coward choosing the

lesser of the evils.

Caesar himself had ordered Pilate to Judea to restore order to the territory, and Pilate knew all too well that it would likely be a death sentence if he did not. He was also well aware that if even a wisp of rebellion made its way to Rome, there would be no questions asked. He would be replaced and reprimanded at best, and he dared not think of the worst. But resistance always came in the form of rebellion, and rebellion had to be crushed.

"Scourge him," Pilate said flatly.

His sentence, more symbolic than punitive, was Pilate's way of skirting the issue. He only hoped that it would be enough.

Immediately the guards led Jesus down the jagged stone stairway to an open courtyard adjacent to the Praetorium. The militant crowd poured in behind.

† † †

In the center of the courtyard, two posts stood, both topped with leather straps smeared with bloodstains and tattered from use. One guard jerked Jesus' robe from His back and lashed His wrist to a post, while another stretched His arm toward the second post just out of reach. He gave a hard yank, and Jesus screamed as both shoulders were wrenched from their sockets, stretching his skin tightly across his back.

Another guard pushed through the crowd and produced a crude whip, its multiple tips clinking with bone and pieces of metal. He shed his cloak and stretched his muscles as if readying for a sporting event. He took steady aim and let the leather tentacles fly, cutting the air like a jagged saw. With murderous precision, fragments of bone shredded Jesus' flesh like paper.

At some point in the ordeal, Jesus drifted away, longing for the Father and realizing that He was almost home, when another slash yanked Him back. He cried out, but it was hardly noticed over the wails of the crowd. Repeatedly the whip came down hard, tearing, severing nerves and blood vessels upon impact, every swing causing more damage than the first, until there was not a single inch of flesh untouched by His blood.

At last the man stopped. "Thirty-nine," he gasped, sweating from the exertion.

The crowd stilled, fully expecting Jesus to remain motionless.

A guard cut the leather strap from His wrist, and Jesus' arm fell limp to the blood-spattered street. When His second wrist was cut free, His arm dropped, but with reluctance. A moment passed, and His chest rose with a shallow breath. Slowly He staggered to His feet.

Then a young Roman guard pushed through the crowd and teasingly flung a tattered robe over Jesus' back, while another slapped a thorn corona on His head.

"Hail king of the Jews!" they chanted.

Jesus barely noticed the sarcasm of the insults.

Tendrils of nightmares flashed through His brain as they led Him up the stairway and back to Pilate.

✝   ✝   ✝

Truly by some miracle of God, Van Eaton made it to the top of the statue and situated himself where he could see over the top of Pilate's throne and down into the crowd. He peered through the veil in disbelief.

Through the veil . . .

Standing in a pool of His own blood, Jesus shook in excruciating pain, tugging at the rough garment that was beginning to fuse to His lacerated back. Pilate appeared composed as he stepped toward Him.

"Here is your king!" he said. "I have no basis for a charge against Him."

"No! Crucify him!" the crowd screamed. "Crucify! Crucify! Crucify!"

Amazed at the cruelty of man, Van Eaton stared in utter disbelief that anyone could ever be so heartless toward another human being.

"Listen to me!" Pilate shouted, but the people chanted and screamed without regard. "Listen to me! I find no fault in this man! But—" Suddenly, the crowd stilled. "But if you are so set on crucifying Him, then do it yourselves!"

"He has claimed to be the Son of God, and according to our law, He must die!" a Sanhedrin member yelled. "But we are not permitted to put a man to death!"

Pilate gathered his cape and sat down again. He gazed at Jesus curiously. "Well? Is it as they say?"

Jesus could barely raise His head. He stared at the blood pooling at His feet.

Van Eaton strained to hear as Pilate leaned toward the commander of his guard and whispered a question. "Yes," the centurion answered. "That custom is still in place."

Pilate's eyes wandered, then he grinned. "Bring him," he said.

As the guards scuttled away, Pilate stood and walked to the edge of the platform, then raised his hand, commanding the crowd's attention. "There is an ancient custom that I should release a criminal to you as an act of benevolence."

A murmur went up from the crowd. Several shouted questions, but Pilate ignored them. In moments the guard returned with a shackled prisoner.

Pilate turned to face the crowd. "I submit to you two men," he said, waving his arm at the prisoners. "Barabbas and Jesus."

"But sire, Barabbas is a murderer, a true enemy of the state!" the centurian grumbled.

A mask of civility swathed Pilate's face. "I wonder who the true enemy really is."

"Barabbas! We want Barabbas!" the crowd screamed.

Pilate glared at the one they called Barabbas. *How can they possibly want such a man set free?*

It didn't matter now. The people had spoken. And though Pilate's plan had backfired, he would honor his word.

He walked back to Jesus and took his seat on the throne. "Your own people condemn you. What have you to say?"

Jesus stood in a daze, as if He hadn't heard a word Pilate said.

"Are you not going to answer me? Don't you realize I have the power to have you crucified?"

Jesus lifted his head weakly and struggled to focus. His eyes were slits. One was swollen completely shut, but the other opened far enough for him to look past Pilate and through the veil at the professor. As their gaze met, Van Eaton froze, possessing neither the strength, nor the inclination to turn away.

Then in the quiet of the moment a voice echoed tenderly in Van Eaton's ears, a voice nearly forty years silent, though instantly familiar, its waters carving a path through the canyons of his mind. Suddenly he was a boy again, cuddled close to his mother's breast as she read from a tattered Bible. A Bible he still possessed. Somewhere.

Then, through the fog of the past, his young bride stepped from the shadows, gently crooning the song he'd heard her sing a thousand times before. *Jesus paid it all, all to Him I owe.*

Tears spilled from his eyes as he reached for her and nearly slipped from his perch. He focused again on Jesus

and suddenly remembered the words Jesus had scrawled in the dust: *Through the veil you will see the truth.*

"Oh, my God. You knew! You knew all along!"

The man once called Van by his beloved wept softly, smearing the tears from his face as he battled to regain his composure. "Lord Jesus," he sobbed, "thank you for holding onto me when I hadn't the sense to hold on to you. I am so sorry to see you like this. So very sorry. Come into my heart, Lord Jesus. Come into my heart, I pray."

He focused again and saw that Jesus appeared to nod in agreement. Then He returned His attention to Pilate, and His face hardened.

"You would have no power over me if it were not given to you from above." Then He bowed his head, and said nothing more.

His heart pounding, Van Eaton watched Pilate rise as though knowing well the conversation was over. He stepped down from his throne and nodded to a servant, who brought a brass bowl filled with water and a towel. Pilate dipped both hands into the bowl and raised them, dripping water.

"I wash my hands of this matter. His blood is on your hands!"

Drying his hands on the towel, he walked to the curtain and pushed his way through. Van Eaton held his breath while Pilate stalked across the room and disappeared down the corridor.

† † †

A perfect full moon hung low in the western sky as Elizabeth slid a smooth, football-sized stone beneath the arch of her back. She gazed up at the stars splashed across the ebony canvas above. The night had grown colder, and other than a chorus of desert locusts pining among themselves, it was relatively quiet.

"What are you thinking?"

Paul sighed and blinked away his thoughts. "What?"

"I was just wondering what our next step is going to be. I mean, Peter is gone . . . and all the others too."

Paul sat up and rubbed his eyes. "Well, I guess John would be with Jesus."

" In front of the Sanhedrin."

"No. By now He'd probably be in front of Pilate. Wherever that is. Or Herod, but not all the Gospels are specific on that part."

Elizabeth peered through the darkness at her friend. "I know you're probably thinking we need to go back, but go back where? Everyone is gone, and now there's a bunch of lunatics after us."

Paul stared into the darkness. "I just wish we had more time with Him. It seems like we just met Him. I want just a little more time."

She smiled dolefully. "I know. I feel the same way, but what can we do?"

Reality slowly began to take hold as they considered their options, but with the blackness of night came the stark realization that it was all about to end. Then, in the quiet of the moment, a meteor streaked across the sky and illuminated an ominous silhouette.

Paul grabbed Elizabeth's arm. "We are here! We are actually here."

He sank to his knees. Elizabeth made her way over and knelt beside him. Slowly her eyes followed a rugged beam upward, then out to both ends and back down again. Even in the darkness, she knew what it was.

"Calvary," she whispered with trepidation. The hair on the back of her neck prickled. "I can't believe we ended up here. I just can't believe it."

Paul sat up and reached for the cross. It was only a few feet from where they had laid and one of several that stood on the hill. The rugged beam, perhaps twelve feet high and nearly a foot thick, was rough-hewn and its corners splintered, but it felt wet, even spongy. He illuminated his watch and held it to his fingers.

Coagulated blood.

He shook nervously, wrestling with his thoughts,

conflicted as they were. Then he jumped to his feet and positioned himself under the massive cross. He wrapped his arms around the vertical beam, which stood loosely in a shallow hole, and lifted with all his might. It loosened, but in the process, he lost his balance, and the cross slammed to the ground, cracking under its own weight.

"Let's pull them all down!" Elizabeth cried.

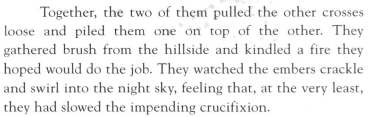

Together, the two of them pulled the other crosses loose and piled them one on top of the other. They gathered brush from the hillside and kindled a fire they hoped would do the job. They watched the embers crackle and swirl into the night sky, feeling that, at the very least, they had slowed the impending crucifixion.

"Paul, I have to tell you something." The fire danced across Elizabeth's face as she spoke. "One day we will go back to our normal lives—whatever normal means—and we'll be forever changed by this. I'm sure of it. But it's going to be the most difficult thing we've ever tried to do because no one other than us will really know, not like we know." She took his hand. "I just want you to know that our friendship is deeper than any I can imagine, and that no matter where we are, I will always be there for you."

"Thank you for saying what I haven't been able to say," he said. "To grow together in faith like this is something that I don't think we could ever explain to anyone. Not to mention they'd think we were nuts! But being here with you has been an honor that I will cherish as long as I live. I'm here for you too."

Silently they looked to the sky, awaiting the inevitable sunrise and the final, most difficult experience either of them would ever face. Together.

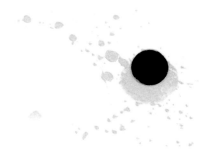

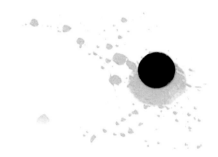

Twenty-two

(15 Nisan)

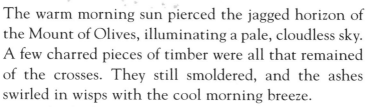

The warm morning sun pierced the jagged horizon of the Mount of Olives, illuminating a pale, cloudless sky. A few charred pieces of timber were all that remained of the crosses. They still smoldered, and the ashes swirled in wisps with the cool morning breeze.

Elizabeth stirred and sat up. She wiped the sleep from her eyes and glanced at Paul. He was already awake.

"I can't believe we fell asleep." He rubbed his face.

"I guess we're no better than those disciples, huh?" Elizabeth's tone was disarming.

"You there!"

Startled, Elizabeth walked to the edge of the crag. Two men sat in a horse-drawn wagon on the road below.

"Might we ask where Skull Hill would be?" one of them asked.

Her eyes cut to Paul, then back. "Right here."

The two men conferred unintelligibly, then the

321

younger man jumped to the ground and loosened his cargo.

"What are you doing?" Elizabeth asked curiously.

"Ah . . . we bring an order the governor placed more than a month ago."

"In Shevat," the driver added. He spit on the ground. "And none too soon, I must admit. We dropped

three of these at the Praetorium on the way here." He threw back a hemp tarp, exposing a stack of wooden crosses.

"It appears Rome's thirst for Jewish blood outweighs its foresight, but they keep the business profitable." Both men laughed harder than the anecdote was worth.

† † †

The narrow cobblestone street that led past the Praetorium swelled with curious onlookers well before daylight as rumors of a crucifixion fluttered through the streets. Pilate had retreated to his quarters under heavy guard nearly an hour earlier, not to be seen again, but for Jesus, the journey of sorrows had only begun. At any moment, he was expected to appear through the thick wooden doors with their hammered iron hinges and rusted handles.

Suddenly there was a rattle of chains and one door creaked open, then the other. The smell of death, putrid and repulsive, spilled into the street like a flood as a gaunt figure emerged from the darkened corridor, filthy and hollow eyed. Shuffling along reluctantly behind armed guards, he stepped into the street, ankles and wrists shackled and scabbed, and disappeared into the crowd.

Behind him another man stepped out, not too dissimilar from the first, though he was taller and more emaciated. He followed his guards into the street, favoring the shackles on his ankles that opened old sores with every step.

Anticipation hung in the air, as if everyone knew what was about to happen. The crowd erupted as Jesus stepped into the flickering light. His face, a bloody mask, still supported the thorned crown, and tears mingled with blood scarred his cheeks, salty and burning. He staggered into the street, pausing to adjust his shackles, when a shove from behind drove him to his knees.

Like a pack of wild dogs, the angry mob surrounded Him A few sought to comfort Him, and even the curious had their place. But by far the vast majority yielded to a twisted form of righteous indignation that had long since defined the people of the day, hurling on Jesus such pitiless abuse that the Romans were forced to intervene, though they were in no real hurry to do so.

Finally the soldiers jerked Him to his feet by the

shackles on his wrists, nearly wrenching His shoulders back out of their sockets. He stifled a scream as the searing pain pummeled His brain and vomited the only contents of His stomach—the Passover bread and wine.

"Bring him here!" the centurion yelled. "We've got a little something for him!"

The crowd parted just enough for Jesus to catch a glimpse of His cross. He winced at the sight.

† † †

"What got into us?" Paul asked. "Did we really think we were going to change anything?"

Elizabeth coaxed a gray ember to life as the thought cut deep into her conscious. "I don't know. I guess I thought that burning the crosses would somehow slow everything down at least—and now look. A wagon full."

One of the men slid a weighty cross to the edge of the wagon, and his partner took the other end. "Seven," he said. "And that makes ten, counting the three at the Praetorium."

Paul's eyes flashed surprise, and he jumped to his feet. "We've got to find the Praetorium," he said in a panic.

Elizabeth brushed off her backpack and reattached the Velcro flap. "I was hoping you'd say that."

† † †

Jesus groaned and pressed His lacerated shoulder into the apex of the two beams. With all of His might He straightened, and the cross rose unsteadily. Drawing a pained breath, He pressed forward, His thighs cramping

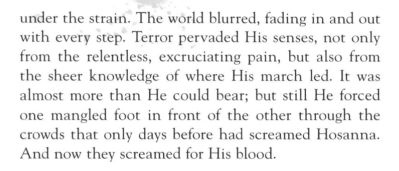

under the strain. The world blurred, fading in and out with every step. Terror pervaded His senses, not only from the relentless, excruciating pain, but also from the sheer knowledge of where His march led. It was almost more than He could bear; but still He forced one mangled foot in front of the other through the crowds that only days before had screamed Hosanna. And now they screamed for His blood.

† † †

A clandestine figure shouldered his way through the masses, following as closely as he dared, driven by nothing more than his newfound faith. But it was more than enough.

Finally he was close enough to see his Savior's face. Horrified and choking back tears, he reached for the Master.

Only a touch.

But he was cut short. Too many guards. Too many people. All he could do was follow. Nothing more. He considered no other course and followed no other plan.

This was hardly the man his students had come to know, he thought, nor even the one he had believed himself to be. But it really didn't matter. Van followed a different Master now, and the need to be near Him far exceeded the risk.

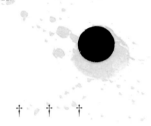

† † †

"Look up there—the crowd." Paul reached for Elizabeth's arm and pulled her close.

"This is it."

She clutched him, and together they made their way up the street until they caught sight of a cross over the heads of the crowd. Then another cross came into view. And another.

"I've got to stop crying. I'm completely useless."

Paul heaved a long breath and wiped his face on his sleeve. "I know the feeling."

Moments later, the crowd swelled against both sides of the street as a Roman guard cleared the way for the first man who dragged his cross past. His eyes were filled with panic as he pressed through the throngs, alternately hurrying or lingering, both equally painful.

The second man appeared, a leather strap pulled tight around his neck. A sneering soldier dragged him along like a terrified animal on a leash. His steps short and hesitant, he lurched through the crowd, his breath rasping with every step.

When Elizabeth saw him she thought his fear could very well be enough to cause heart failure. Judging from his expression, it would have been a welcome demise.

Next, as they feared, Jesus appeared, His body now disfigured, misshapen. His face was swollen beyond recognition, and His eyes burned with sleeplessness and sweat as He struggled to keep His balance while the crowd shoved Him back and forth.

The sight sickened Elizabeth. She had seen more gory trauma at the MED, but at least in those cases she had been able to help. Now she was powerless.

Had they not spent the last several days intently studying the Savior's every physical characteristic and gesture, they would not have recognized Him at all, she reflected. His head and face were swollen to nearly half again their size, so much so that the thorns of His crown wedged tightly into his skull, cutting off the circulation and clearly dulling His senses.

As He passed them, blood and sweat traversed His brow and dripped silently to the stony street, leaving a morbid, bloody trail that went largely unnoticed by the crowd. But Elizabeth knew it would forever be infused into the cobblestone street that would one day be called *Via Dolorosa*. Way of Grief. Way of Suffering.

With every fiber screaming to intervene, she

stood motionless beside Paul and watched as Jesus dragged the cross—*their cross*—through the street. Every step more difficult, every breath more labored, He pushed on.

Then suddenly Paul clutched her arm and motioned toward a familiar figure approaching them through the crowd.

Van forced a smile, though behind it he swallowed hard. He shoved his way through the crowd and reached for Paul, who instinctively recoiled. Finally Van laid hold of him and pulled him to his chest.

"Oh, son, I . . . I don't know what to say." Through his tears Van saw understanding light Paul's face.

"Professor, I'd always hoped—"

Van pushed back and peered at him through glistening eyes. "He saved me! Even through all of this, he saved my soul!"

"Professor—" Elizabeth stopped, clearly speechless.

Beaming, Van pulled her and Paul close. The three genuinely embraced and for a moment time stood still.

† † †

The cobblestone street narrowed and finally ended at the base of the hill known as The Skull. From there, the only way to the top was a rutted path with such a steep vertical grade that even the healthiest of men would have had trouble climbing it.

Jesus appeared to be near total exhaustion as He fell in behind the two thieves and started up the twisting incline. He made it only a few steps before He crumpled under the strain, smashing face down in the dirt, with the cross landing hard across His back.

Angrily, with one fluid motion, the guard on his flank wheeled around and grabbed the first man he saw. He slung him toward the cross.

"Pick it up!" he barked.

Paul stared at the cross for a moment in disbelief.

"Pick it up, I say!" The guard reached for his sword, eyes narrowing.

Paul froze, a million thoughts pounding his brain. He turned and stared at Elizabeth and Van as if seeking direction. They stared blankly back.

"Now!" the guard screamed, his fingers tightening over his sword's hilt.

Paul was about to panic when a husky black man muscled his way to Jesus' side. He reached for the cross, and as he hefted it onto his own shoulder, his eyes met Paul's.

Paul's brain scrambled to place the man. He was sure they had met before, but confusion overcame him. Then slowly the face before him metamorphosed into that of an elderly man.

The burned-out church back home! The man who had insisted he make this journey!

"Pastor Jackson?"

Jackson gave a barely perceptible nod. "This was *my* dream, son." His voice quivering with emotion, he wrestled the cross to his own shoulder, tears spilling from his eyes. "To carry His cross."

His voice cracked, and he sobbed. Groaning, he started up the hill.

Paul knelt and coaxed Jesus to His feet, trying desperately not to add to His pain. But it was impossible. The coarse fibers of Jesus' tunic were blood soaked and rigid, adhering to His wounds so that every movement pulled them open again.

The Master gained His balance and slipped His arm around Paul. "We must . . . make it to the top. For the journey . . . is almost over."

Paul cradled his arm around Jesus and gently levered His weight against his own. With a crack, a whip cut across Paul's back. The pain rifled through his members electrically, and numbness followed.

"Move!" the guard shrieked.

† † †

Following a few steps behind, Elizabeth and Van filtered through the crowd, careful to keep their distance. Elizabeth sensed they were following the

Spirit's lead, though it was not without considerable pain. She wished she was the one helping Jesus. But somehow she knew this was Paul's time. And that was the end of it.

Finally they crested the hill. Partisans of the Sanhedrin began to chant. "Crucify! Crucify! Crucify!" Louder and more vehemently they shouted, inciting the already seething crowd into an even deeper rage.

Without notice, the lead guard tipped the cross from the Cyrenean's shoulder. It slammed the ground with a thud as he stepped between Jesus and Paul. Paul reluctantly withdrew. And though the guard took Jesus by the arm and led Him toward the cross, there was obvious compassion in his movements.

Instantly an officer punched through the crowd, his polished breastplate shimmering in the sun. He backhanded the guard.

"Get out of the way!" he snarled, seizing Jesus by the nape of the neck.

He tore the robe from His back, took hold of His waist, and slammed him down onto the cross. With his foot, he ground His wrist against the crossbeam, then screamed for a nail.

The guard's eyes darted to his partner, then back at his superior.

"You haven't brought nails, you imbecile?"

Suddenly Van raged, flung his bedroll to the ground, and bolted toward the captain of the guard.

With savage intensity he wrapped both arms around the man's neck, squeezing with all his strength. Without hesitation Paul followed, punching the guards closest to Jesus before they knew what had hit them. Even Elizabeth jumped in, slinging her backpack and connecting.

The combat escalated until the crowd parted and more guards poured in. Oddly, though the three were heavily outnumbered, none of the soldiers took lethal action. It was almost as if they had been instructed not to, and whether the Romans feared reprisals by the crowd or God Himself had intervened, they were spared.

In the midst of the mêlée, a guard stumbled over Elizabeth's backpack and the clatter of metal rang loud. He plucked the strange bag from the dust, ripped open the Velcro flap with a crack, and thrust his hand inside.

"I have nails!"

Mortified, Elizabeth groaned, but there was nothing she could do.

Now held at spear point, she and her companions could only watch as the guard again trapped the Master's wrist against the cross and motioned to his underling. "Do it," he said, not a hint of emotion in his voice.

† † †

The guard took the point of the nail and pressed it into the center of Jesus' hand until he found a soft spot. The feel of the metal to his flesh was cold and jagged as it followed the fold in His skin. Jesus cringed as the guard drew back and swung hard, but the hammer skipped off the nail with a spark and smashed

His fingers. Jesus let out an involuntary gasp.

He tensed when the guard drew back again. This time he swung and caught the nail dead center, punching the gnarled steel shaft through Jesus' flesh and wedging it deeply into the wood of the cross, severing nerves and instantly numbing His fingers.

Through blurred vision, Jesus struggled to get a look at the guard who caused Him so much pain. He blinked to clear His eyes, but still saw only shapes. It didn't matter. He knew unequivocally that it was for this man He had come—and for billions more like him across the centuries.

"Did you cut veins?"

"Not one," the guard swore.

"Excellent. The less he bleeds, the longer he suffers."

† † †

Paul shivered. "How can we bear this?"

Elizabeth and Van were without words, only

333

watching in horror and praying that it would soon be over.

The crowd hushed as the guards watching the three time travelers buried the heads of their spears in the ground at their feet and joined a detail of soldiers. Together they wrestled the awkward cross over their heads with Jesus' body affixed and guided the base into

the hole prepared for it.

In the quiet of the moment, Simon Peter emerged from the crowd. Standing behind Paul, he whispered urgently, "My friends, you must follow me quickly while there is still time."

Twenty-three

"Come. We have little time to waste!" Peter hurried at a steady clip farther up the street, frantically searching for somewhere—anywhere—to hide.

"The Master—" He smeared his tears with the back of his hand. "They were so cruel. I cannot believe it. They—they were crucifying him!"

Paul cupped his hand over Peter's shoulder. "I'm so sorry, Peter."

"And they would have killed you too. Those soldiers have been trained to kill, and they are experts at it." Peter drew a deep breath. "Any other time they would have killed the three of you where you stood. But they did not." He searched Paul's face as if he knew the reason for the soldiers' restraint.

Elizabeth's mind reeled. *They could have killed us? I'm not so sure of that. We still have a life in the twenty-first century don't we?*

"But once they have finished . . . once they have finished, they will be back for you. I am certain of this."

As they moved farther away from Golgotha, the crowds thinned until the street was virtually empty. It almost seemed as if everyone was attending the crucifixion. Everyone. Doors to houses were locked. No open windows. No alleys. Nowhere to hide. Farther up the street, a cripple hobbled along. No help there. They hurried farther still.

Then Elizabeth noticed the movement. The door swung back and forth in the breeze, its hinges chirping with each breath of air. It was their door to the past.

Paul noticed it at the same time. "The well room," he shouted. "In here! Hurry!"

Elizabeth ducked inside, followed closely by Paul and Van. Peter pulled the door shut and slid the crossbar into place.

Paul scanned the room and weighed their options. There were few. The only thing in the room was the clutter of wood and debris still on the floor around the well and a collection of clay jars standing against the back wall, where perhaps one man could hide, but only one.

Kneeling, Paul peered over the well's rim and saw the nails he had driven into the wall. They were still in place. And the bottom, still littered with the rotted framework, lay just as they had left it, except that it appeared dry.

He dropped a stone into the pit to confirm it. *Good.* He worked his way around the rim to the nail closest to the top, slid one leg over the edge, and pressed the arch of his foot hard against it. It was solid.

"C'mon guys, let's do it."

Elizabeth and Van automatically followed him over the edge.

When Peter's turn came, he glanced at the door. "Wait. I have an idea."

He looked through the gaps in the door to see if there

was anyone in the street. Nothing. He cracked the door open farther and saw the cripple. He stepped outside.

The cripple hobbled across the street and up to Peter. They spoke for a moment, then Peter stepped back into the room and locked himself in.

Crossing to the edge of the well, he leaned forward and whispered, "My friends, they are coming. I will stay up here."

He scattered rubble to the edge of the well and brushed the footprints from the floor. Then he worked his way across the room to the clay jars and awkwardly crouched behind them.

Outside, muffled voices grew louder as a cluster of men moved up both sides of the street, pushing on every door they came to. Judging from their conversation, they were mostly Roman soldiers and sympathizers.

As they drew closer, outside the door the cripple's hoarse voice bellowed, "Unclean! Unclean!" careening off the walls and echoing through the streets.

The voices grew louder until it sounded as if they were right outside the door. "A leper! I'm not going in there," one man said.

"No one would be fool enough to go there. Let us move on."

As the voices faded away, Peter smiled to himself at the success of his plan.

† † †

An odd stillness washed over the room as the minutes passed. Finally Elizabeth reached blindly through the darkness for Paul. He was still there, and Van was huddled next to him.

It had been nearly an hour since the three had fled the grisly scene of the crucifixion. Sixty incredible minutes since they'd watched in horror as Jesus' hands and feet were nailed to a wooden cross. But time as they knew it had blurred to a conundrum. No longer were there delineations of hours and minutes or even seconds, but of events. And the events, most certainly orchestrated by God the Father, had culminated at the cross. And the irony that Elizabeth had provided the nails weighed heavily upon her conscience.

But there was more—there was most definitely more. Jesus would rise again! As surely as they were there, He would rise again. It was their only solace, but now, right now, their fears were tantamount to what had happened. They were fugitives of the Roman Army, hiding like nocturnal creatures in the shadows of despair and sure to be executed if found.

In the quiet of the moment, Paul stared vacantly into the shadows. He shifted his body to avoid rubbing the bloody welt where the soldier's whip had struck him. He almost felt guilty for considering his own pain, realizing how much worse Jesus' scourging had been.

"It was even worse than I imagined it would be," he sighed. "I know this is the way it is supposed to be, but dear God, I never dreamed it would be like this."

Van pressed his shoulders against the cold stones that formed the circular pit and gazed up at the opening, tears sliding silently down his cheeks. "I . . . ah . . . I don't know quite how to say this." He cleared his throat and struggled to maintain his composure. "But I, ah . . . I'm sorry. I have lived a lie for so long, more than fifty years I suppose. And now to know the truth, to really know the truth—" He quivered and sobbed openly. "I'm so sorry!"

His words were seamlessly stitched into the fabric of all of their hearts as they huddled close to their new brother. How comforting it felt for Paul to embrace him, to stroke his silver gray hair, and to share his heartache.

"You know, deep in my heart I always knew I was wrong," Van sobbed. "Even when I argued the point. But something inside would never let me admit it. I guess I just hoped someone would somehow break through."

Paul smiled and squeezed the professor's neck. "Well, leave it to you to go all the way to the source!"

They all three laughed collectively and embraced even more. There was deference now—unspoken, but mutually understood. And it was such a wonderful feeling. For they had entered this place as strangers, and now they were family.

Paul pulled back enough to make out the professor's face. Even through the darkness, he caught a glint of Van's tears and a beatific smile.

"I want you both to know . . . " Van paused long enough to gather the right words, "that whatever happens, it was all worth it. Even if we don't make it out of here alive, it was worth every minute."

"But there's more," Paul hinted.

For the next hour Van listened as the amazing story unfolded, not once interrupting. And it all made perfect sense. Only where would they go from here? They were on the run from the Roman Army, or at least a small faction of it, and there seemed to be little hope of escape, not to mention that they were 2,000 years from home.

While Paul talked, Elizabeth studied the room. She looked at the nails protruding from the wall like bristles on a brush—single strands of hope that had led them to the Savior and now delivered them from harm's way. She worked one free from the wall and ran her fingers across the cold iron. Her heart fluttered.

"If I hadn't taken those nails . . . "

"If you hadn't taken those nails, it still would have happened," Paul said. "You know that."

"I know. But it's . . . it's so personal now. I really did

have a part in crucifying Him."

"We all did."

The gravity of Paul's words weighed equally on each of their hearts.

"But it's not over," Elizabeth said. She straightened, and a surge of courage suddenly flooded her soul. "We've got to go back." Her words were determined, but cautious.

Van steadied himself against the wall. "I was hoping somebody would say that."

† † †

Several minutes later, Paul wrestled Elizabeth over the top rim, and they repeated the process with Van.

Van grinned when he got to the top. "That was a lot easier than it was the first time."

"You have no idea." Elizabeth laughed. "What do you think happened to Peter?"

Before Van could answer, Paul said uneasily, "I don't know, but what's going on here?" He knelt and brushed his hand across the door. It was cold.

"What is it?"

Paul turned, but before he had the presence of mind to speak, Van finished his thought. "We're back aren't we?"

Paul felt the hair on his arms prickle. "Yes," he said, with both sadness and hope.

There was an awkward silence as the reality slowly took hold.

Elizabeth opened the door far enough to see outside. She squinted through the sunlight and noticed children playing on the other side of the street.

"I wonder what day it is."

Van slid his watch to his wrist and illuminated the face. "It's April 5th. And according to my watch it's almost 9:30."

Elizabeth pulled out her broken watch and glanced at the face. It read 10:35, the exact time they had crashed through the floor, and the date was the same: April 5.

Paul looked down and noticed the key was still in the lock. His face paled.

"We *are* back. But we're early."

Elizabeth scratched her head. "How can you be so sure?"

He ran his fingers across the jagged notches of the brass key, then slid it back into the lock. It turned smoothly.

"When we ducked in here, I broke the key off in the lock. Remember?" Paul glanced across the street again and froze. "Come here! You see the girl? The one with the red scarf?"

Elizabeth looked out. "Yeah."

"That's her." Paul's heart skipped a beat. "That's the girl I saw in the alley. The one the soldiers killed!"

Elizabeth exchanged glances with the professor. "Are you sure?"

"Yes I'm sure!"

There was no mistaking the red scarf, the white cotton

dress that fluttered in the breeze, her bronze complexion. It was the woman Paul had seen murdered. He was sure of it.

Van suddenly caught Paul's arm and the three turned in unison, their thoughts fusing into one salient point. "Isn't it obvious what's going on here?" Van asked.

Paul and Elizabeth waited for the other shoe to drop. "We can save her. Don't you see it?"

"Well, for heaven's sake, let's do it!" said Paul.

Van's expression changed. "But you know, we'll never be the same."

Paul slipped his arm around his newfound friend. "I don't think we're supposed to be."

Van gave a tentative smile "I ramble like an old man."

"You *are* an old man," Paul smiled.

"I am old like wine. You are old like dirt!"

The three time travelers shared a laugh and stepped into the street, fueled with certainly mingled with trepidation as they set out in hopes of stopping a murder.

As they quietly slipped out of sight, the door to the well room creaked open. And Peter peered out.

Coming soon . . .

PETER'S QUEST

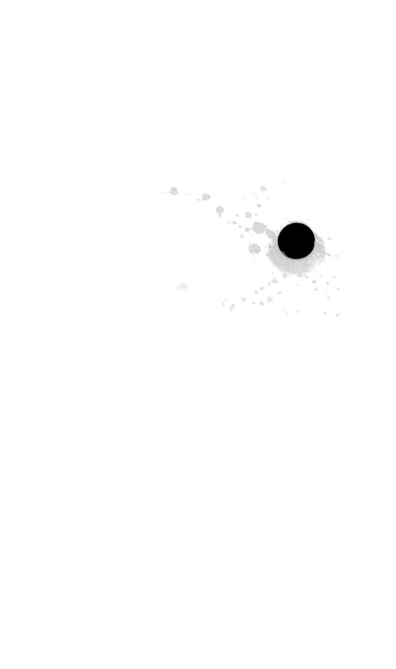

What about you?

Has the Spirit of Christ spoken to you through these pages? Has there been a time in your life when you were ready to stop playing games with God like Professor Van Eaton? Why not today?

Romans 10:10, 13 For it is with your heart that you believe and are justified, and it is with your mouth that you confess and are saved. For, "Everyone who calls on the name of the Lord will be saved."

So it's up to you.

Revelation 3:20 says; "Here I am! I stand at the door and knock. If anyone hears My voice and opens the door, I will come in and eat with him, and he with Me."

So Jesus stands and waits for you to open the door to Him. And if you sincerely ask, He will come into your life. Are you ready to settle it right now? If so, it's as simple as asking.

Here's a suggested prayer: Lord Jesus, I know I am a sinner and do not deserve eternal life. But I believe you died and rose from the grave to purchase a place in heaven for me. Lord Jesus, come into my life. take control of my life, forgive my sins, and save me. I turn away from my sinful ways and place my trust in You for my salvation. Amen.

If this prayer is the sincere desire of your heart, look at what Jesus promises to those who believe in Him.

John 6:47 I tell you the truth, he who believes has everlasting life.

Welcome to God's family, for today is your spiritual birthday, a day you will always want to remember! Now seek out a Bible believing church.

And will you share your decision with us? We would love to hear from you! Please let us know at: questforthenailprints@gmail.com

This salvation outline is based on the Evangelism Explosion program.

ACKNOWLEDGEMENTS

Thirteen years! Thirteen years of writing this story. Whew! I never thought this day would come, but here it is. There were so many people and influences along the way, I dare say I may not remember them all, but I have to give it shot.

First and foremost, to my wife Karen. Honey, you

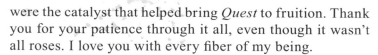

were the catalyst that helped bring *Quest* to fruition. Thank you for your patience through it all, even though it wasn't all roses. I love you with every fiber of my being.

To Randy Malone. Randy, you were the starting point for me. Your passion for writing overflowed to me and I will never forget it. Wherever you are, I love you man. And Mike Volner. Mike you have always been there for me, allowing me to bounce my thoughts off you, and you were always so gracious. You know my heart, brother. And Dr. Joseph Clemmons. Jody! Jerusalem! Need I say more? It changed us, brother. Man, I'll never forget. I love you, my dear friend!

To Jennifer Cortez. Jennifer, you were the first true professional who expressed faith in me, and I will never forget how your words lifted me to new heights. You'll never know how powerful your comments were.

And Patrick Morley. Patrick, thank you, brother, for believing in me and always being completely honest. You are a true friend whom I love and admire greatly. And thank you for the endorsement!

To Marti Thweatt. Marti, you have been such an inspiration to me over the years. You are such a Godsend and an encourager. I can't wait until your book comes out!

Deceptions of Angels is sure to be a hit—I just know it!

There are so many others who allowed themselves to be sounding boards. Brother Joe, you were always a driving inspiration to me. Proverbs 27:17. Dennis and Susan Roaten, dear friends and proofreaders. Did you think I would ever finish? And Don and Nancy Thetford. Your friendship and love have been so greatly appreciated

through these final stages of the book. And Stelian Bizga. Stelly, thank you for your love and friendship, for taking me into your home in Romania and sharing your beautiful country with me!

And, to my first real editor, Susan Drake. Susan, what can I say that would suffice? Your input and expertise were literally invaluable to me. Poring over the book for hours on end, through the migraines (that I hope I didn't cause), through the tears and the wonderful ideas you proposed and those we wrestled over. *Quest* would not be what it is today without you, Susan. You are a master, and I thank God for our friendship. And to your dearly departed son-in-law, Grayson Wells, whom you so often spoke of, this book, and especially your work, is dedicated to him. I bet you were a great mother-in-law!

Lastly, to Joan Shoup, Penney Carlton and Cary Johnson. Thank you for your vision, your editing expertise, and for your determination to bring *Quest for the Nail Prints* to fruition.

And if I have left anyone out, I am deeply sorry. It certainly wasn't intentional. Thirteen years is a long time.

Don Furr is a teacher, soloist, author, and CEO of Exhibit-A, Inc., a trade show exhibit company located in Arlington, Tennessee. Married for twenty-five years to his wife, Karen, Don is the proud father of three children and grandfather to three beautiful grandchildren. He is also an avid fixed-wing and helicopter pilot. But by far his true love lies with all facets of movies, play writing, and his novels.

Don has written several screenplays and produced many live productions of Judgment House through his church, First Baptist Church of Lakeland, Tennessee. Don continually searches for new ways to utilize his talents for Christ. His latest endeavor, *Quest for the Nail Prints*, is a culmination of thirteen years of writing, editing, rewriting, more editing (well, you get the picture), and it has been the most rewarding and emotional journey he has taken to date.

Please visit us at:
www.questforthenailprints.com

Feedback? We'd love to hear from you!

questforthenailprints@gmail.com

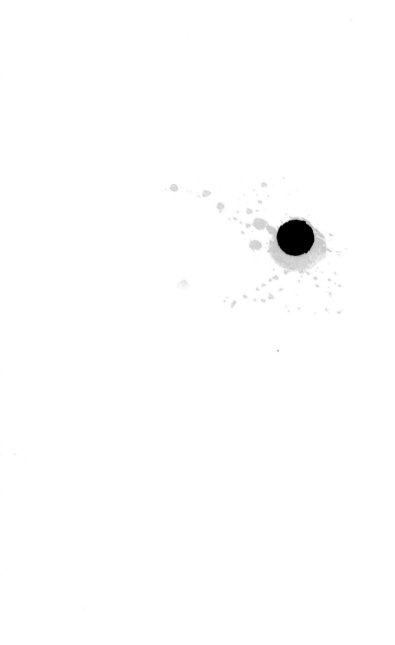